I0760421

WOLF CAPTIVE

LONE WOLF SERIES
BOOK TWO

HEATHER HILDENBRAND

WOLF CAPTIVE

Wolf Captive

Lone Wolf Series, book 2

By Heather Hildenbrand © 2021

Cover Design by Danielle Fine

Character art by Samaiya

www.heatherhildenbrand.com

My head pounded so hard that my eyes watered from the pain. Lying flat on my back, my body jostled, and even without opening my eyes, I sensed I was moving. Fast. In a car maybe? But the softness underneath me felt more like a bed than a seat.

"Slow down. You're going to miss it."

The harsh female voice drifted in through the cracks in my awareness. Unfamiliar. And with an edge I didn't like.

With another bump, my body was thrown hard to the right. Hands wrapped around my arms and legs to steady me.

Someone groaned, and it took me a long moment to realize the sound came from my own mouth. But the noise only made the headache worse, so I choked back the rest of it and tried very hard to remain perfectly still. Anything to help calm the drum beat going on inside my skull. Could you die from a headache? Because that's exactly what this—

"She's coming to," said an unfamiliar voice.

This one male.

Not cruel, exactly, but definitely not concerned.

I'm not sure how I knew that, but something inside me —some instinct—recognized he wasn't my friend.

A growl escaped me, and before I knew it, my wolf was rising to the surface, pressing against my skin like it was a cage to escape. If it would help me get rid of this damned migraine, I was more than willing to let her out.

"She's going to shift," the male said. Urgent now. Worried.

I already didn't like him.

My wolf wanted to shut him up. For good.

I cracked my eyes open, squinting against the single overhead light that sent sharp lances of pain through my skull. Rubbing my hands down my hips and thighs brought small relief. My clothes were still on, though that fact didn't mean their intentions were pure. We were in a van. Or maybe a bus? It was small but large enough to fit me on a stretcher inside.

What the hell was happening to me?

My memory felt just out of reach.

I blinked.

A man loomed over me, frowning in earnest as another figure moved in close beside him.

A woman.

Harsh features. Worn. Like she hadn't aged well.

Something about her eyes felt familiar, but it was there and gone so fast before my headache eclipsed everything else.

She held a syringe up, and I immediately bucked against whatever she intended to do with it. But leather straps held my arms and legs firmly in place. Another had been fastened across my torso just over my ribs. I couldn't sit up, and I couldn't get away.

"No," I gasped. "Don't."

"Hurry up," the man insisted.

The woman complied. My skin pricked as the needle slid into the crook of my arm.

I hissed then snarled at them both, my human teeth bared as my wolf imagined their blood coating her mouth.

Enemies, she screamed inside my mind.

But then my veins turn cold with whatever the needle contained, and the headache receded—right along with my grip on reality.

When I woke again, I found myself on a hard cement floor. The stretcher and straps were gone. Nothing bound me, and I sat up slowly, relieved the headache had mostly gone away. Now, the dull ache was concentrated on the back of my head. I pressed my fingers to the spot and found it swollen and tender.

I dropped my hand and looked around as my eyes adjusted to the near-darkness of the space.

Whoever had brought me here had left me unbound. Maybe I could find a way to get out again. To get home. Wherever that was. Last I remembered, I'd been driving out of Ridley Falls in an attempt to flee from a pack I'd just been accepted into right before they found out I was the "chosen one." In other words, the curse breaker capable of freeing them from a twenty-year-old curse that kept their wolves from recognizing true mates or an alpha. As a result, the Lone Wolf pack ran around like, well, lone wolves. Causing chaos and mayhem and just generally being a bunch of hellions.

Sure, I could stop that.

But I'd learned enough about the pack members to know not everyone wanted their wild streak to be tamed.

That made me a target.

Literally.

Because instead of driving to another town to hide out, our car had been hit, and I'd been kidnapped by... whoever was holding me now.

As it all came crashing back, my hand drifted to my throat. To the tender spot Kai had bitten when we'd claimed one another as mates. I still couldn't believe I was mated.

My hand slipped lower, and my fingers brushed over my collarbone.

My necklace!

I ran my hand over my throat.

It was gone.

Dismay sent my shoulders sagging. The one thing my father had left behind before he died was a pendant my mother had passed to me before she'd abandoned us years ago. I hated that necklace for years—more like hated *her*—but Dad had made me promise to never take it off.

And I hadn't.

Even if I hated Mom's choice to leave us, I loved my father, and I intended to honor my last promise to him. But the necklace was gone.

I couldn't even remember the last time I'd felt it against my body.

As I tried to make my memory work, the shadowy shapes of my surroundings finally clicked into focus. I'd been left in some sort of windowless space. It felt big, but the cage they'd locked me inside was not. Iron bars on all sides. A hard cement floor underneath. And not a single soul in sight, friend or enemy.

Awareness slammed into me then.

Whatever drugs they'd given me must have worn off now because, along with the pain in my head worsening, the memories came flooding back.

Vorack's dead body on Kai's living room floor. Kai driving us out of town in Vorack's car. Drake sending Vorack after me. Silas finding Drake's stalker wall dedicated to me. Both of them—and who knew who else—knowing the truth about me. About my mark.

I remembered the van that had crashed into us. On purpose. The man with the tattoo wrenching me out of the car. Me fighting back and ultimately getting myself knocked out in the process.

The man's tattoo had been unmistakable. Three letters scrawled in black ink against his skin: HEX. I hadn't been taken by one of the pack members after all. I'd been taken by witches.

My father had tried to tell me, and I hadn't understood. Kai's last words, a perfect match to what my father had warned me about before he'd died: Don't let them put you in a cage.

That's exactly what these people had done.

But why?

Somewhere above me, a door creaked open. I jerked toward the sound, straining to see movement through the shadows.

My heart thudded in time with my aching head as footsteps approached.

I slid back into the furthest corner of my cage, wary and terrified.

Enemy, my wolf called. Rather than resist, I reached for her, perfectly willing to let her rip throats out if it got me out of this. But she was faint now, and try as I might, I couldn't call her any closer. Whatever they'd done to me, it had trapped my wolf. Made it impossible to shift.

What could possibly do that?

Magic.

I knew the answer even before the man strode into view. A small light clicked on, casting a dim glow that only reached as far as he stood. He met my eyes, and when he saw that I was awake, his mouth curved upward into a smile, though it held no humor. No goodwill.

"Hello, Ash."

His voice was smooth and polished but with edges sharp enough to cut should he decide. His blue eyes were the same sharp weapons. And his body language spoke of someone always calculating. Right down to the way he clasped his hands together in front of his button-down shirt. He reminded me of a used car salesman. Or someone trying to reach you about your extended car warranty.

The only thing that contradicted his whole polished act was the tattoo inked into the side of his neck. A star with a circle drawn around it.

Also, the fact that he'd used my name was next-level creeper status.

"How do you know my name?" I demanded.

"My sources have informed me of many things about you, Ash Langford. Not the least of which is your name."

"What the hell does that even mean?" I asked.

Sources? What sources?

"It means I've been looking for you for a long time."

"Well, considering you knew my name and apparently exactly where I'd be and when for that car crash, I'd say you kind of suck at looking."

His expression tightened. A quick twitch that smoothed quickly.

"I see now you were hidden from us on purpose. Your lupin side is a disgrace to our bloodline."

"What do you mean *our bloodline?*" I asked, really not a fan of the weird possessiveness of his words. "And where the hell am I? This is beyond illegal."

"You're where you belong as far as I'm concerned. Your parents should have never been allowed to create something like you," he said, his expression twisting with disgust.

I glared. "Back at ya, asshole."

Another eye twitch.

"Look, stop lecturing me about shit I can't control, and let me out of here immediately," I demanded in a voice that sounded like it had smoked a pack a day for the last twenty years.

My words ended in a dry cough that seemed to snap him out of whatever holier-than-thou monologue he'd seemed intent on carrying out. He blinked, looking almost contrite.

"Of course. Apologies," he said in a voice that was anything but sorry. "The cage was for your own protection."

He snapped a finger, and another man materialized from the shadows behind him. My eyes narrowed even further as I recognized him. The man who'd grabbed me. The one who'd ordered the syringe to keep me from shifting. The one who'd taken me away from Kai.

The man didn't bother to acknowledge me directly as he came forward and unlocked my cage door. When the lock sprang free, he stepped back, holding the door wide.

I gritted my teeth as I crawled out and climbed to my feet. The humiliation of crawling wasn't something I'd forget. And something told me these men used humiliation as a tool. For now, I filed it away and faced the man in the suit.

"Let me go now," I said. "And I won't call the cops."

He merely smiled.

I couldn't blame him. It wasn't like I had any leverage for a demand like that one. Still, I had to try.

"I apologize for our … methods," he said as if that excused everything they'd just done to me. And Kai.

Even now, I felt a strange tugging in my stomach. The mate bond. I had no idea how close he was or how far of a range the feeling stretched, but I could feel Kai now. And he felt like he was losing his shit.

I swallowed hard against the fear that rose. Was he okay? Would the twins find him? He'd been hurt and basically unconscious when they'd taken me.

"If anything happens to my friend," I said to the suit, "the cops will be the least of your worries."

Something flashed in the man's eyes, and I realized he'd taken my words seriously. Interesting.

"Your friend," he said, glancing at the man with the keys.

"He's fine," my kidnapper grunted.

I turned to glare at him, noting the swollen eye from where I'd punched him.

Good.

It was the least he deserved.

"You better hope so," I said. "Or I'll kill you first."

The man looked away.

Wow.

Was I really that scary?

"As I was saying," the suit began, "our methods were necessary to ensure everyone's safety."

I stared at him incredulously. "Are you fucking kidding me? Safety would have been not crashing into us in the first place. Or maybe not kidnapping me. Or maybe not injecting me with whatever drug that was. Or locking me in a damned cage—"

He raised a hand. "Yes, you've made your point."

"What the hell do you want from me, anyway?" I asked.

"That's not a simple question, but let me start by saying it's an honor to meet you, Ash Langford."

An *honor*? Was this guy for real?

"You'll understand why I can't say the same."

He smiled, and from the recesses of my mind, my wolf promised to kill him simply for that look.

I had a feeling when the time came, I wouldn't stand in her way.

"I've waited a long time for this moment," he went on. "We've been looking for you."

"Why is that exactly?" I asked.

"You're the curse breaker," he said as if that explained it all.

The casualness of it all sent off alarm bells in my already pounding head. How could he possibly know this? I had to play it cool. I wasn't beyond fighting in human form, but with no weapons and two against one, my odds weren't great.

"Maybe I am," I said, shrugging noncommittally. "So what?"

"So, you are the one the magic created to restore us. We're very excited you're here."

I blinked.

Restore them?

I was definitely missing something.

"I thought the curse was about the wolves."

"The lupin's problems are their own," he said, his eyes flashing with obvious hatred at the mention of them.

"Okay, I'm confused. Is there some other curse I'm not aware of?"

I mean, how many curses did they expect me to break anyway?

The suit nodded. "The wolves may have told you their side, but the curse they're under isn't the only consequence of the magic cast that night twenty years ago."

Interesting. The hexerei had felt the effects too then.

"What were the other consequences?" I asked.

The suit hesitated. But the other man nodded, urging him on. "We've come this far," he said. "Can't stop now."

"Right." The suit cleared his throat and looked at me. "The fact is our kind were stripped of our magic as a result of that spell cast twenty years ago."

"Seriously?"

Was he telling me the all-powerful witch coven whom the wolves deemed enemy number one were magicless? That was news to me. And I had a feeling it was news to the wolves too. Otherwise, something told me the wolves would have come calling for their revenge a long time ago.

"We've been looking for the chosen one ever since," he added.

"Why?"

"Because when our magic was removed, it didn't just disappear," he explained. "It was funneled somewhere else. For safekeeping as it were."

The man behind me snorted. "Safe, my ass." He looked at me with disappointment.

My eyes widened as I read between the lines of what they were saying. "Wait. You think *I'm* the one with all your magic?"

"You have the mark," he said.

My face heated as I realized he wasn't asking. That meant they'd seen it. Just helped themselves to a perusal of my body. Rage rose within me at that violation.

"You're going to pay for that," I said.

"Apologies," the suit said without a shred of regret in his eyes, "But we had to be sure. There've been so many misses over the years. Mistakes. We couldn't afford another."

I hated to think what he meant by "mistakes" considering everything they'd done to me already.

"We need your help, Ash. You're the only one who can give us back what was taken."

I shook my head. This guy had some balls, that was for sure.

"Let me get this straight. You knocked me out, shot me up, and put me in a cage. And now you're asking for a favor? Why in the hell would I help you?"

"Because if you don't offer it up, we'll just take it anyway," the goon behind me said.

Uh, nope. Didn't like the sound of that.

"You can try," I said, packing as much bravado into my voice as my circumstances would allow.

The suit didn't look nearly so inclined to force, though. He cocked his head thoughtfully.

"The stories are true then. You have no idea what you are or how to access what's been given to you."

"That's where you're wrong, asshole." I lifted my chin, refusing to accept this jackwagon knew more about me than I did. "I'm Ash *Lawson*." I used my true last name on purpose since he'd used the alias my parents gave me at birth. "I'm a werewolf. Uh, I mean, wolf shifter. Daughter of the once-alpha of the Lone Wolf pack. And my wolf will promptly rip your throats out just as soon as she's done sleeping off her little hangover."

The goon behind me snorted. "That beast of yours is down for the count, darlin', so good luck with all that."

The suit's eyes gleamed.

"Ah, but you're so much more than that, Ash. Didn't your mother tell you anything?"

I frowned.

"What the hell do you know about my mother?"

"I know she made a grave mistake," he said. "Though she was smarter than I gave her credit for in hiding you so well for so long."

"Whatever," I said, unwilling to let him bait me. He clearly wanted me to keep playing his little game of cryptic comments and smug certainties. I wasn't having any of it. "Your turn. Who the hell are you?"

"I'm Cohen Roth," he said. "Coven leader."

"Cohen." My eyes widened. I knew that name. "You're the one sending the witches to spy on us."

It wasn't lost on me I'd just said "us." Since when had I become "us" with the wolves who'd treated me like shit up until literally yesterday?

"I've done what was necessary to ensure our enemies did not learn our secret," he said. "And I've made sacrifices that were required in our search for you."

"You let your people get captured," I said, stomach twisting in disgust at his detachment from it all. "Tortured," I added. "Killed. And for what?"

His expression darkened. "Like I said, you are what matters, Ash. Or, the magic inside you. We will have what belongs to us one way or another."

"And what will you do with it?" I asked.

"Excuse me?"

"The magic," I said. "If I give it back to you, what will you do then?"

He didn't answer, and my gut churned at the obvious answer. The cage behind me. Their blatant hatred for the wolves. Whatever they did with that magic, it would be very, very bad for the pack who'd just accepted me as one of their own. And for my mate.

I decided I didn't need to hear his answer after all.

"I'm not helping you," I said. "I don't have your magic nor do I know where it is, but even if I did, I wouldn't give it to you if my life depended on it."

Cohen's eyes flashed.

"Put her back inside," he snapped.

The asshole beside me grabbed my arm and flung me back into the cage. My foot caught on his boot, and I fell, landing hard on my ass. The door swung shut with a crash, and the asshole turned the key, locking me once again inside.

"Your unwillingness to work with us is unfortunate," Cohen said, coming forward to peer in through the metal bars at me. He'd let the neutral mask slip, and now unbridled murder shone in his sharp eyes. "Because without that magic, you're just another lupin, girl. And lupin only belong in one place."

I braced myself for him to say this cage.

"Six feet under," he finished, and my snappy reply caught in my throat.

He turned and walked back the way he'd come, the asshole who'd manhandled me hurrying to follow as the shadows swallowed them both. Alone, I listened to the retreating footsteps then the open and close of some faraway door.

Then, silence took over, and the only sound I heard was the hammering of my own heart. I had no idea what came next, but I had a feeling it was going to make everything the wolves had put me through feel like a walk in the park.

2

The air hung heavy with the smell of meat. I opened my eyes, inhaling the full aroma, and my stomach growled. Loudly. I sat up, wiping the sleep from my eyelids, and found a woman standing just outside my cage staring back at me, a tray of food in her hands. The darkness was brightened by a single glowing light from somewhere behind her, and I couldn't tell if the glow emanating from around her was because she was pure angel or pure evil. Depended on what happened next.

Then I noticed that, halfway between us, my cage's door hung wide open.

"Are you hungry?" the woman asked.

Her voice was vaguely familiar. I hesitated, trying to place it. Then I remembered. The van. She'd been the one to inject me with whatever drugs had trapped my wolf inside me.

Part of me wanted to reject the food she'd brought. But survival demanded that I swallow my pride—and swallow that meal.

Reluctantly, I crawled through the cage's opening and climbed to my feet, slightly woozy and seriously starving.

The woman watched me. Not like Cohen had. More, curious. Expectant. Up close, I could see the lines worn against her cheeks were just as pronounced as I remembered. Her skin looked wrinkled and papery thin, but her eyes… they suggested a mind that was still much more agile than her body.

"Hello," I said warily.

"You're Ash."

It wasn't a question, but since I didn't know what else to do, I nodded.

Her hair was long and straight and midnight black, like mine. Her smile was kind. But I'd met the devil in this exact spot earlier, so I wasn't in the mood to give the benefit of the doubt.

Before I could say a word, she handed me the tray. I took it and sat down on the floor, digging into the turkey and potatoes with zero shame. The food was still warm, and the flavor had my mouth watering even as I swallowed entire chunks whole. My stomach demanded to be filled.

"You'll throw it all up if you eat it too fast," she warned.

Hating that she was right, I forced myself to slow down. After a few more bites, I felt full enough to focus on more than just my plate. Glancing up, I found the woman watching me with interest. Wow. Was every hexerei as creepy as her and Cohen?

"What?" I demanded between bites of butter-smothered potatoes.

"You look better than the last time I checked on you," she said.

The last time? How long had I been out for?

"What day is it?" I asked.

"Tuesday."

I gaped at her. The crash had been Sunday.

"I've been here two days already?"

"Cohen thought you might feel more reasonable about things if he gave you time to recover from the accident."

I didn't bother pointing out that nothing about the crash had been an accident. She was there; she knew.

"Who are you?" I asked.

"I'm Arnell. You can call me Arnie." No fear or wariness shone in her face. In fact, she looked about one social cue away from hugging me. Her eyes sparkled with the sort of intimacy reserved for friends.

"Okay, Arnie," I said. "Are you here to let me go?"

"Well," she said, "I did notice your cage door had a bad spring and popped open. And then I did notice how you let yourself out just now. And I will have to report that to Cohen, of course. But I'm notoriously slow up the stairs, and I'm also known to become distracted when there's a coven dinner going on. So, I'm not sure how long it'll take me to find him."

She was here to help then. But why? Especially after everything she'd done to help bring me here.

"What do you want in return?" I asked.

Arnie frowned—like my question had somehow offended her. "Nothing. I just had to meet you," she said. "To see for myself. You look… you look so much like her."

Her chin wobbled, and she blinked back tears.

I tensed at her words, a strange sort of anticipation ribboning through me. "Like who?"

"Claudia," she said as if the answer were the most obvious thing in the world. "My sister."

I blinked, and just like that, everything I knew about the entire concept of being Ash Lawson changed forever.

"Your sister is Claudia?" I asked.

She nodded.

"That's my mother's name," I said, feeling stupid but also like this had to be a coincidence. It had to be.

Except Cohen had brought her up too. And he'd spoken like he knew her personally.

"Yes, it is," she said simply.

I eyed her suspiciously. A full-body scan that made me feel stupid because what was I hoping for? A flashing neon sign to tell me whether this was some sort of trick? A full DNA report pinned to her chest?

"You're my aunt?" I asked. Like if I framed it differently, the answer would change. But it had to change because what the hell? My mom was related to a hexerei?

Though, when I thought about it, weirder things *had* happened. Like, my dad being a werewolf, specifically an alpha, and therefore making me a werewolf by genetics. Or my dad leaving his pack behind and raising me in secret without bothering to tell me the strange tattoo on my hip was the mark of a magical curse. Still, Mom as a witch? What in the actual fuckery?

"I am," Arnie said. Still patient. Still waiting for me to get it.

"Are you telling me … my mother was a hexerei?"

Arnie nodded again, earnestly now. "She was the best of us all. Do you know where she is?"

"My mother?" I gaped at her. "Um, no. Not since she ran out and abandoned me and my father years ago. Sorry."

"Oh." Her expression fell, and I felt my impatience bubbling up and over. Any semblance of politeness vanished as this new version of my identity settled in around me.

I shoved the tray aside and stood up, dusting my hands off on my dirty, stained pants.

"Look, I don't know what you expected from me, but I can't help you. In the last few weeks, I've learned I'm a werewolf—an alpha's daughter at that—and a curse breaker, and now you're telling me I'm half witch. And you want me to help you find a woman who made it so clear she doesn't want to be found that she abandoned her own daughter? If this is the deal, I'll just get back in the cage and save us both the trouble. You can tell Cohen his little bribe or trick isn't going to work."

Her eyes widened with the first real hint of panic. She spoke in a hushed voice. "Cohen doesn't know I'm here. Listen, I just had to ask. I've always wondered what happened and—it's okay. Just go."

She motioned behind her, toward the darkness and, beyond that, the door.

I didn't move. "You were in the van," I said. "When they took me."

"I'm a medic for the coven," she said, regret transforming her wrinkled features. "The drugs we used to sedate you are sensitive and must be dosed just right, which is why I was there to oversee it."

"Is that supposed to make me feel better?" I asked.

"No, of course not. I'm so sorry. In the old days, we never would have resorted to kidnapping."

"Are you sure about that because my father's the one who warned me about a cage?"

Her forehead creased, and she looked both thoughtful and guilty. Her shoulders sagged as she sighed heavily. "Cohen's line has always preferred this method. It's why your mother— You have to understand, it wasn't supposed to be like this anymore. It was supposed to be different. Better. Cohen—he's lost himself. Without magic all these years—we don't know who we are anymore."

She looked desperate. Like she was pleading for me to understand. What was she hoping for? My forgiveness?

"If you're asking me to feel sorry for you, my kidnappers, you're going to be disappointed."

She shook her head. "I don't want sympathy. I just want to warn you."

"I think it's a little late for that," I said.

She shook her head. "He's just getting started, believe me. And you don't deserve what he'll do. But Cohen, he won't be easily stopped. You have to leave. It's the only way. And even then, you're not safe. Now, go," she said again, more forcefully this time.

I stared at her, suspicious and undecided. If Cohen was trying to use this woman to break down my defenses or make me want to help him, it wasn't going to work. But something urgent tugged at my gut, and I glanced past Arnie toward the stairwell.

The tugging came again.

Kai.

I didn't bother with a goodbye as I took off at a run. Without my wolf senses to help me adjust, I stumbled more than once through the darkened space. Finally, I found a set of stairs and raced upward. At the top, I shoved the door open and stumbled into a large kitchen. A woman stood at the stove, stirring something in a pot that made my stomach cramp with hunger. The scent of meat was stronger up here. As was the tugging in my gut.

The woman looked up at me, her mouth frozen in an "o" shape.

"Where's the door?" I snapped.

She didn't answer, clearly too shocked.

I snarled and shoved past her and out of the kitchen. The feeling in my gut was growing stronger and much more urgent. Something was wrong.

Kai was close—and really, really pissed.

The kitchen led into a short hall, and I ran to the end, flinging open the door. Outside, the sky was dark but cloudless. A moonlit sky was more than enough to see the shadowy shapes looming in the sprawling front yard before me.

"Get her," one of them ordered.

It sounded a lot like Cohen's little minion, my kidnapper, but it was impossible to tell for sure.

In the next moment, a group of men broke off from the others and ran toward me.

I made it down the porch steps before strong hands grabbed me, holding me still. Twisting and kicking, I fought back, but just like earlier, my wolf was still still out of reach. Without her, the assholes had me pinned. They wrapped rope around my wrists and ankles, lifting me by the arms as they carried me out into the yard.

The noise brought more hexerei. The front doors of the nearby houses opened, and people began to emerge, slowly at first then faster when they recognized what was happening.

Several onlookers yelled when they saw me. Some just stared in silent awe. Sort of like Arnie had. Like I was some sort of celebrity. Or shiny, expensive jewelry. I didn't understand it, but right now, none of it mattered.

Only the rage howling through the mate bond did.

I looked right past them all until I found what I was looking for.

My eyes landed on the suit standing amid a casually dressed dozen men. Cohen.

He smiled at me, not a shred of friendliness reflected in his sharp gaze. "Ash, my wife sent you out right on time."

My stomach sank to my knees like lead.

Arnie.

She'd meant to let me out. To lead me here. Into whatever the hell this was. Because she was married to the enemy.

Cohen's smile widened as he watched me think it through.

"What the hell is this?" I demanded.

On my left, I noticed a group of hexerei with guns aimed at something past where Cohen stood. I craned my neck to see what the threat was. Something sinister tugged at the mate bond.

"It appears this is a reunion," Cohen said way too calmly. The fucker had something up his sleeve.

"What's going on?" I asked.

Cohen stepped aside.

And beyond him, surrounded by hexerei, was Kai.

My heart leaped into my throat as my eyes quickly scanned Kai to check for injuries. Blood covered one side of his face, and the sight of it broke the last of my control. I struggled against the ropes and the hands holding me back, screaming things I couldn't even make sense of.

"Relax," Cohen called.

I ignored him and kept fighting. One of my elbows landed, and I heard a grunt as the man beside me went down. Another stepped up to take his place, handling me roughly.

Across the lawn, Kai snarled and fought his own captors the same way I was doing. He managed to knock three of them to the ground before they recovered their grip on him.

Chains, I realized as the sounds reached me.

They didn't just have him tied with rope, like me. They'd chained him. Like a worthless prisoner.

We had to find a way out of this. But fighting through chains and rope wasn't the answer. Not without the strength of our wolves to aid us. Beaten and broken-hearted, I stopped fighting and stared at Kai.

"Did they hurt you?" he asked in a voice raked raw by emotion.

I shook my head. "You?"

He grunted, which I knew meant he would be okay. Despite the blood. It was more than I could say for the man who'd done this to us.

I rounded on Cohen, rage boiling in my veins. "I'll kill you for hurting him," I said.

"He was found inside our borders, which goes against our agreement," Cohen began.

"You gave up your right to enforce that agreement when you took my mate," Kai said.

"Ash is here as a guest," Cohen said.

I didn't even bother to roll my eyes at that ludicrous statement.

"She's one of us," Kai told him. "You'll have the entire pack on your doorstep for this."

A flash of worry crossed Cohen's careful features before his neutral mask returned. "Ash is more than just lupin," he said. "It was time she knew this part of her heritage too."

Kai looked from Cohen to me and back again.

His eyes narrowed. Through the mate bond, I could feel his distrust. It stung, making me wonder if that distrust was aimed at me. If he saw me as an enemy now. But I couldn't stop to care about that. Not until he was safe.

"Let him go," I told Cohen.

"Or what?" One of the men holding Kai snorted.

The others around him muttered their agreement.

"What are you gonna do?" called another. "Lecture us to death?"

I reached for my wolf but found only emptiness.

The men laughed.

"Tell you what, Ash," Cohen said, "You agree to help us out, and we'll let your friend go. No harm, no foul."

"Don't give them shit, Ash," Kai warned.

One of the men yanked on his chain, and he stumbled back then fell to one knee.

Desperate to stop this, I strained forward, unable to move more than an inch or two. Cohen watched me with interest and not a shred of regret for the way he was using us.

"I told you I don't have what you want, and even if I did, I wouldn't give it to you," I said.

Cohen started to respond, but another voice interrupted.

"Cohen, stop this."

A woman's voice rang out, clear and loud. The others around me straightened as a woman strode into their midst. She looked a few years older than me, and her body was fit and muscled in a way that suggested she could probably take out every one of these losers if she wanted to. Her dark brown hair hung in a braid down her back. Everything about her suggested "no-nonsense."

The crowd parted easily for her to pass. She marched up to Cohen and pinned him with a look.

"What in the hell is going on here?" she demanded.

"I'm restoring us, Kel. What do you think?" he snapped.

"You're using these two innocents against each other."

"I'm doing what's necessary."

"You're being an asshole."

I snorted.

The woman glanced over at me. Our gazes held for a

long moment, and then she did a quick sweep of the length of me.

"I'm Kel," she said. "Kel Archer."

"Charmed," I said dryly.

Kel cut her gaze back to Cohen, and I noticed she didn't have a neck tattoo like most of the others. "Did you even offer her any food? Drink? A shower?" she asked.

"Well, we had to make sure we didn't give anything away if she decided not to go along."

"Oh, for goddess' sake. Cohen, this is the chosen one we're talking about. And you have her out here in the front yard like you're going to do some cowboy duel bullshit for her honor. It's beneath us."

A few of the other hexerei mumbled what sounded like an agreement.

Interesting.

Cohen held the woman's gaze. He didn't back down, but he didn't tell her to get lost either. For a moment, I thought the woman, Kel, would win out as the voice of reason, and all of this would end in a peaceful parting of ways. But then Cohen's eye twitched, and I knew he wasn't going down that easy.

"Take the boyfriend to the altar," Cohen said. "If she won't restore us, maybe his blood will renew our connection to the elements at least."

My eyes widened as the men holding Kai began dragging him away.

"No," I screamed.

But Cohen ignored me.

And while the woman, Kel, looked pained, she didn't press it.

Kai roared and shoved hard at the hexerei who held his chains. One of them rose up and plowed his fist into Kai's jaw. Kai went down on one knee before he was hauled back up again. I could feel the tugging between us, the desperation Kai felt at not being able to call his wolf.

My own panic rose with it, straining and pulling taut against the shared bond between us. The adrenaline in my blood was like a jumpstart to my system. Whatever drug they'd given me was finally beginning to recede, and my wolf stirred, angry as she woke.

Hot rage sang in my veins as my wolf rose to the surface. She was pissed—and ready to let the world feel her wrath.

I felt the pop and snap of bone as she not only stirred but took me over. Giving in to her wrath, I shifted faster than I thought possible.

Some of the hexerei screamed as I changed. The men holding me scrambled to get clear.

The rope fell away, broken easily now that my wolf strength had returned.

Cohen yelled something, but I couldn't hear it over the roaring of my own blood.

No one was going to hurt my mate.

The moment my paws touched the ground, I pushed off again and leaped at the man who'd just struck Kai. He screamed. My teeth closed around his throat, and I didn't bother to fight my wolf's desire as we ripped his throat out.

The man's scream died abruptly, and in the silence, a single shot rang out close enough to make my wolf startle.

I looked over to see Cohen holding a gun. It was pointed toward the air, but as our eyes met, he lowered it until it was leveled straight at me. I glanced at the men flanking him. Every single one of them had a gun aimed at me or Kai.

We were trapped then.

They'd have to kill us because I couldn't and wouldn't give them what they wanted.

A second later, I nearly screamed when I felt a hand slip into mine. I looked over and found Kai beside me. I hadn't even realized I'd shifted back, but when I looked down, I found my human body had returned.

My clothes, however, had not.

Kai slid in front of me and faced Cohen.

"Let her go," he called out. "I'll take her place. You can do whatever you want. Just let her go."

"Kai, no," I said, but Cohen wasn't having it.

"The girl stays," Cohen said. "At least until she returns what belongs to us. You, on the other hand," he said, glaring at Kai, "are completely disposable."

The men with guns repositioned themselves, ready to fire on command, and my stomach clenched in terror as I realized Cohen would absolutely tell them to kill Kai without a single hesitation.

"Wait!"

I stepped out from behind Kai, which wasn't easy considering he was relentless about trying to keep himself between me and Cohen's army. I tried not to think about how naked I was and met Cohen's hard stare with one of my own.

"I'll do it," I said.

Kai looked over at me sharply. "Don't help them," he hissed.

"I will do whatever it takes to keep you alive," I whispered back. And then to Cohen, "I'll find a way to return your magic. But only if you let us walk out of here right now."

"Right." Cohen snorted. "You think I'm stupid."

"You found me once," I said, sick with the truth in my words. "You can do it again. If I don't return to restore your magic, you're free to do what you feel is necessary. Hell, I'm sure you don't need my permission to come after me again, but there it is."

Kai's heavy breathing made it clear what he thought of my offer, but he didn't argue again. I had a feeling his mind was too busy trying to put the pieces together of what I'd just said about the hexerei's magic.

Cohen seemed to notice it too because he looked from me to Kai and back again.

"You will tell no one," he snapped.

I nodded. "You have my word."

Cohen laughed humorlessly. "Forgive me if your word isn't something I can count on just yet."

"Likewise, asshole," I snapped.

He looked ready to argue again, but then Kel stepped up beside him and whispered something in his ear. He listened, considered, and finally nodded at her. She started walking, making her way over to where Kai and I stood.

"That's far enough," Kai snapped.

She stopped and lifted her hands, palms out. "I'm unarmed. I just want to talk."

"So talk," Kai said.

Her gaze flicked to me. "Ash can go," she said. "Both of you can. But we need assurances that she'll hold up her end of the deal."

"I gave you my word," I said. "What more do you want? My firstborn?"

She flinched, which confused me, considering the severity of what they were willing to do so far.

"A blood oath is more appropriate for the situation."

I stared at her. "You're serious."

"Blood oaths are common to seal a bond, especially where distrust runs high," Kai explained quietly to me. He hadn't taken his eyes off Kel, and I knew her close proximity bothered him. I could feel the tension radiating from his body, but he seemed to be letting me take the lead on this.

"Fine."

Kel produced a short blade from her back pocket. She flicked it open and sliced the blade across her palm. When the incision welled with crimson, she held the blade out to Kai.

"Swear you'll tell no one what you learned about us tonight," she said.

Kai took the knife and slashed his palm open. When the cut welled with crimson, he said, "I swear an oath on my own blood to tell no one what I've learned here tonight."

Kel held up her hand and they pressed their palms together, joining their blood. Then Kel dropped her hand and looked at me.

"She's next."

Kai handed me the knife.

Gripping it with white knuckles, I slashed the tip of the knife across my own palm. Biting back the wince of pain, I watched as blood pooled on my skin.

Kel approached slowly, her hand outstretched.

I stepped around Kai and took her hand. It was warm and slick already.

"I swear on my blood to tell no one what I've learned here," I said. "And to find a way to return your magic."

But instead of a quick release like she'd done with Kai, Kel wrapped her fingers around my hand and held tight.

"We'd like you to swear the oath on your mother's namesake," she explained. "To anchor your promise to return our magic."

"What the hell does my mother have to do with this?" I asked. "She's gone. Abandoned you just as much as me."

"Her name still carries weight in this coven."

Those close enough to hear her words murmured an agreement or bowed their heads.

Kel noted my confusion and cocked her head. "Has no one told you?"

I pressed my lips together, fighting the urge to yank my bloody hand out of hers and use it on her face instead. I was getting seriously tired of people knowing more than I did about my own life.

"Told me what?" I asked through clenched teeth.

"Your mother was next in line to lead our coven," she said softly. Her eyes filled with understanding as shock rippled through me. "Cohen was her betrothed," Kel added gently.

My gaze snapped to Cohen. He watched me with interest, but judging from the neutral mask he wore, he hadn't heard Kel's soft words just now. I squeezed Kai's hand, completely done with all the bombs these people were dropping on me.

"You're lying."

"I'm not. Listen, I can see this is all new for you, and I'm sorry." She looked like she meant it. "No one handled this right, and that's messed up. But the majority of the coven really is on your side."

"Yeah, I can feel the support dripping out of the gun barrels aimed at my head," I said.

"Guys, weapons," she snapped loudly.

As one, the men holding the guns lowered them.

I studied Kel with renewed interest. How much power did this woman really have here? And why hadn't she used it to remove Cohen as head?

"Look, once you swear the oath—"

"I swear on the life of Claudia Lawson, Langford—Whoever the hell she is—that I will return to restore your magic once I figure out how to do it." Satisfied?"

"So mote it be." She released my hand. "Thank you."

"We're leaving," I snapped, ignoring her attempt at kindness. Too little, too late at this point.

"Safe travels," Kel said, stepping back and making it clear she would do nothing to stop us.

"Come on." Kai tugged on my hand and led me away from the group of hexerei. Together, we hurried toward the woods, both careful not to turn our backs on Cohen and his men.

Cohen's voice rang out like a knife in my back as I left. "See you soon, Ash. Hopefully, very, very soon indeed."

4

The moment we were clear of the hexerei and their guns, Kai pulled me into a fierce hug. His arms squeezed tight, his body pressing against mine until I was hyper-aware of our skin-to-skin contact. Sure, layers of blood and sweat coated that skin, but this was Kai. And me. And my wolf wanted her mate in all the ways that counted.

"I was so terrified something had happened," he whispered, finally pulling back to look at me. His dark eyes were stormy; a promise of unfulfilled violence. And I had no doubt he'd come to hexerei territory, ready to do whatever it took to get me back. Even to kill for me.

Instead, I'd been the one to kill for him.

"Are you okay?" he asked, searching intently as I struggled to accept we were safe now.

"I'm…"

What was I?

"I don't know," I admitted.

He pressed a kiss to my forehead, his hands soothing against my bare back.

"Come on. Let's find some shelter. Then we can talk."

He grabbed my hand and led me deeper into the forest. While we walked, I used my wolf senses to check for pursuers. But the woods were clear. The hexerei hadn't come after us.

My fear faded slowly, replaced by worry for Kai's injuries. The cut on his forehead still bled. And the bruise on his cheek was swelling by the minute. He was silent, but through our bond, I could feel the exhaustion beginning to affect him.

"How long was I gone?" I asked.

Kai looked over at me, his expression grim. "Two days," he said. "Tomorrow morning will make three."

"Did you sleep at all during that time?"

He frowned. "Not really."

"What about the others? Idrissa, Isaac, Oscar…" I trailed off as his expression registered. "You did tell them what happened, right?"

His jaw tightened. "I destroyed our phones."

I stopped walking. "You what?"

"I didn't think it was wise to leave any more evidence than we already had at the scene of the crash."

Shit. Vorack's rental car. I'd forgotten it being smashed to pieces by Cohen's guys.

"Right." I started walking again, slower this time as my thoughts raced. "Do you think the police will trace the car back to us?" I asked, worried now as I remembered Vorack's dead body on Kai's floor.

"No," he said, and the look in his eye had me tensing.

"What did you do?"

"I burned it," he said as if he did that sort of thing every day. Hell, in a pack like this one, maybe he had. "No evidence to find if the whole thing's a pile of char."

I nodded. "Okay." I squeezed his hand, reassuring the

desperation that still clung to him. Through the bond, so many emotions churned.

Fear. Relief. Regret. Guilt.

I knew the fear. Understood it. But the guilt made no sense. I wanted to ask what it meant, but I was already walking naked through the woods with my bloodied boyfriend. That was enough vulnerability for the moment.

After what felt like forever, Kai motioned for me to follow him into a small cave.

I hesitated. My wolf did not like the look of it, and the idea of being trapped or cornered in some way agitated her.

"They're not following us," Kai said, making me wonder if he could read my thoughts now too. He brushed a hand absently against my hair, and I noted the dark circles ringing his eyes. "We crossed back into pack territory a couple of miles back. It's okay."

Reluctantly, I followed him inside the cave. A few steps in, I took the lead, using my wolf sight to find my way through the darkness. After a short passage, the rock walls dead-ended in a larger room. I was surprised to find a pile of wool blankets against one wall and the remnants of a fire in the center.

"We use this place during scouting trips to check the hexerei aren't pushing the boundary line," Kai explained. "Do you see matches?"

Spotting a pack, I picked them up from where someone had chucked them near the firewood and pressed them into Kai's hand. Bending down, he lit a match and used it to light the remaining log. "I'm going to get more firewood." He pinned me with a look. "Stay here."

"Me? You're the one who's bleeding and asleep on his feet. Let me go."

"Ash, please don't fight me on this. For two and a half days, I've had to wonder if you were even alive. I can't let you go out there alone. I can't worry about whether you're safe right now."

"But your senses are only human," I argued.

"My wolf senses are coming around."

I rolled my eyes, and he chuckled.

"Saw that."

I scowled.

"See?" he pressed. "I'll be fine. Five minutes. We just need enough wood to get us through the night."

He moved past me, but I grabbed his wrist.

"Kai. Wait."

Now that we were safe and sheltered, all of the feelings from earlier returned. The fear of losing him, the relief at seeing him alive.

"Thank you for coming to find me."

"How did you know I was out there?" he asked in a gravelly voice that sent a shiver down my spine. "The way you ran out of that house, it was like you knew."

"I felt you," I said. "Through the bond."

He stepped closer, his eyes wandering the full length of my naked body. A thousand different things swirled in the depths of his gaze. But I only felt one of them through the bond now.

Need.

I wasn't even sure if it was his or mine.

"Kai," I said, breathless. My body ached, but not from injury. I ached to be touched. To reassure myself as much as him that we were both alive and okay. "I want to feel you now. Not through the bond. Please."

My words broke the dam of control, and Kai closed the distance with a kiss hotter than the fire he'd just lit.

His tongue swept into my mouth, reclaiming me as if I'd been gone for weeks instead of days. My muscles turned liquidy, and I wrapped my arms around his neck, clinging to him like a lifeline. His hands tightened around me, and for a moment, I thought we'd lose ourselves right here, but Kai pulled away, panting and looking just as dazed as I felt.

Although he hadn't let me go, I could see the reproach in his dark gaze.

"That was cheating," he said.

I smiled, smug.

"No rules in our pack, remember?" I shot back, citing the Lone Wolf pack motto.

He scowled and set me back on my feet, stepping back and purposely averting his eyes from my naked body.

"Five minutes. I'll be back with more wood, okay?"

"Fine," I grumbled. "Five minutes. Any longer, and I'm going to make a very Isaac-like joke about the exact kind of 'wood' you're bringing back for me."

Kai blinked at me, shook his head, and walked out.

I smiled to myself; a moment that faded quickly in the isolating silence that followed. Using my senses and the mate bond, I tracked Kai's progress. I felt no sense of danger coming through, but still, I paced impatiently.

Minutes ticked by. I had no idea how many, but I didn't care. Kai wasn't somehow more expendable than me. If anything, we should be doing this together. Risking ourselves as a team seemed much smarter than agreeing to stay behind like some damsel.

I'd just started for the door when Kai returned. The sound of quiet footfalls might have alarmed me if I hadn't felt him so strongly through our bond. He emerged into the cave's back room, arms full of firewood.

I exhaled as I watched him go to work stacking the wood and stoking the fire until it crackled hungrily. The firelight danced off Kai's back, and I stared, lost in the smoothness of his skin until he stood and turned to face me.

His eyes flicked over me and away again. The gash on his forehead was still wet with fresh blood, the shine glinting in the fire's light. Worry tugged at me. His cheek was still swollen and already bruising. He had to be exhausted. Probably in pain too.

"Come here," I said, taking a step toward him.

But he backed up, and I halted, suddenly unsure.

"What's wrong?" I asked.

"We should talk," he said. "I need to hear what happened to you."

He still wasn't quite meeting my eyes. In fact, he seemed to be looking everywhere except me.

"Is it not okay?" I asked, "Me being naked, I mean."

"What?"

"You aren't looking at me," I said. "It's awkward. And kinda giving me a complex about body confidence."

His eyes widened then darkened with desire that was very evident even through his shorts. "Ash, I want you. I want to look at you, and when I do, I want to touch you. Everywhere."

My body warmed at the words, tingling in all the right places.

"But what matters most is your safety. So, before we do any of that, we need to talk."

"Right. Talking then looking then touching," I said.

He winced. "Maybe don't say the word touching."

I bit back a laugh. "What happened to no rules?"

His glare turned molten before he looked away again with a groan. "Ash, you're killing me."

He walked over and grabbed one of the wool blankets discarded on the floor. Shaking it out, he wrapped it around me and pulled it closed across my shoulders.

This time, I couldn't hold back the laugh. "Sorry." But my laughter died at the sight of the blood drying on his forehead.

"You're hurt," I said.

"I'll heal." He waved me off.

"Your wolf..."

"It's starting to wake up," he assured me. "I can already feel it. And look, the bleeding has stopped now."

He was right. The blood coating him was drying in patches. Hopefully, soon, the wound would begin to close.

"I thought they were going to ..." I swallowed hard, unable to say the words. But I hadn't stopped imagining it yet. The image of the guns aimed at Kai. Of Cohen's dismissal of Kai's life. Of all lupin, as he put it.

Kai reached forward and cupped my cheek. I blinked, refocusing on his warm eyes.

"Are you okay?" he asked. And the full force of his concern hit me square in the gut. The worry, the panic—it all flooded into the bond held between us. "I mean, really," he said. "Did they do anything to hurt you at all?"

"No," I said. "I'm really okay. They just wanted to talk to me."

He snorted. "Right. Kidnapping is a pretty dick way of starting a conversation."

"That's what I told them," I said, my voice growing stronger at the memory of my conversation with Cohen.

His lips twitched. "Did you now?"

"Well, actually, I told them they were assholes, and if they'd hurt you, I'd kill every last one of them." I sobered, remembering it. "They looked afraid of me, Kai. It was weird."

"They should be. You're a badass."

"No." I shook my head. "This was more. It was … I don't know. Reverent or something." I shook my head. "That sounds crazy."

Kai's brow rose. "Crazier than your mom being hexerei?"

I winced. "You caught that, huh?"

"Ash."

I backed away, trying to block out all of the emotions coming through the bond. If Kai was upset or disgusted or angry at what I was, I couldn't bring myself to feel it.

But he grabbed my hand and led me over to the remaining blankets. "Come here."

He pulled me down next to him, and I waited for him to speak. To put me out of my misery.

"I'm sorry about your mom."

I whipped my gaze back to his, unsure. He looked at me with concern and caring. Not pity, which I appreciated.

"It's nothing I hadn't already begun to suspect, I guess."

"Doesn't matter," he said. "She left you and now you have to hear it from those assholes that she's one of them. It can't be easy."

My eyes filled with tears that I refused to shed for her.

"She wanted nothing to do with me, so the feeling's mutual," I said with a shrug that felt forced.

"Do you think she might have had a good reason for leaving?" he asked.

I frowned. "What does that mean?"

"I don't know. I'm not saying it's right, but given what you just learned…I mean, she's a hex, Ash. And your dad was lupin. That was forbidden. I mean, the peace treaty would have helped but still." He shook his head. "They might as well have been Romeo and Juliet."

My brows shot up. "Shakespeare?"

"What, I read it in school," he insisted, and I shook my head. "My point is she might have had reasons that have nothing to do with you."

"Reasons like Cohen being a dick."

"For one, yeah." He shrugged.

"Maybe you're right." I sighed. "Apparently, she was supposed to marry him."

"Damn. That would be enough to make me cast a curse," Kai joked.

"I guess. None of that excuses her decision to abandon us, though."

"True. But at least, now you know the truth about where you come from."

I frowned, picking at a corner of the blanket. "I met my aunt while I was there. Arnie. My mother's sister."

"What was that like?"

"Weird," I admitted. "She's married to Cohen. I mean, who marries their sister's betrothed?"

"Whoa. Does that make Cohen your uncle?"

"Cohen is nothing to me," I said.

His brow lifted. "You're not claiming Cohen then?"

"Hell, no," I said firmly.

His mouth lifted at one corner. "I can't blame you there. Some of the others seemed friendly."

"You mean the ones who stood by and did nothing to intervene while Cohen tried to have you shot?" I snorted. "Right. Super friendly."

"Kel did what she could. She seems to have the support of quite a few of them."

I shook my head.

"It's just messed up. I mean, I went my whole life

thinking I only had my dad. Him and me against the world, you know. And now, I have Oscar and you. And witches? It's a lot."

"Come here." He pulled me into a hug that helped ease some of the tension I felt when I thought of all the family bombs being dropped.

Finally, I eased back, needing to say the words out loud that I'd been thinking since the moment I learned of my mom's connection to the hexerei.

"I'm starting to think my mom is the reason for all of this," I said.

"What do you mean?"

"My mom was a hexerei so powerful she was going to lead the coven. Then a curse went into effect right around the time my parents took off in order to be together. And the minute my mother sees I'm the curse breaker, she ghosts me. What does that tell you?"

"You really think your mother cast the curse?"

"I know, crazy. But…crazy is the new theme of my life. All I know is the witches lost their magic, and the wolves lost, well, their sanity, and now both sides want me to fix them so they can destroy the other."

"And what do you want?" Kai asked quietly.

"I want…" Emotion welled, and I trailed off, overwhelmed with the question. I shook my head. "I don't even know. No one's ever asked me before."

"I'm asking."

"I just want you," I whispered, looking at him with eyes full of tears threatening to spill over. "And Oscar. And the twins. And maybe even the pack. Hell, I don't know. I just want a place. A people. I want to belong, Kai. I've never belonged anywhere."

His smile was somehow both sexy and the sweetest

thing I'd ever seen. "You belong with me, Ash Lawson. Always and forever."

The tears spilled over then.

I ignored them, reaching for Kai and pulling his mouth to mine in a searing, salty kiss. He made a sound that had my body aching for more, and I tightened my arms around his neck, refusing to let go this time.

"Kai," I whined against his mouth, and he growled, pushing me onto my back against the blankets.

The blanket fell away, and in the firelight, Kai's eyes slid the length of my exposed skin with undisguised need. I stared in appreciation at Kai's hard chest and ripped abs. He was mine. All of this was mine.

"You're really beautiful, you know," I said.

He grinned down at me.

"Is that weird?" I asked.

"Being told I'm beautiful? Nah, I can take it." He leaned down and swiped a kiss across my already swollen lips. "Feel free to hit me with the weirdest compliments you got, Ashes."

I grinned. "Same to you."

"In that case, you have a really sexy tongue."

A laugh escaped me, cut short by Kai's tongue invading my mouth until we were once again reduced to grunts and moans and sighs. Kai took his time, exploring my body with his tongue in a way I'd never experienced before. By the time he lowered himself over me again and slid inside me, his words about belonging to him felt truer than ever.

Kai was home for me now. My heart and body were his.

I woke in a tangle of limbs and blankets that left me cozy and warm against the chill of the space. It took my sleepy brain a few moments to recognize my surroundings—a space now illuminated by filtered sunlight coming in through the cave's opening.

I shifted, and Kai's hands came around me, pulling me close against his chest.

"Cold?" he asked.

"Cozy," I replied.

He pressed a kiss to the top of my head. "We should head out. Find a way to call home."

"Shit." I sat up abruptly, the blanket pooling at my waist. "Oscar will be panicked. We need to get home."

Kai grabbed my waist.

"I think we should start with finding a convenience store and getting a prepaid cell so we can check in with Idrissa. We need to know what the pack knows about what happened."

I bit my lip.

"She can get word to Oscar that you're safe," he added. "And then you and I can do what we originally set out to do and lie low for a while."

I sighed. "Kai, the hexerei aren't going to forget about my promise to them. I can't just hide out in another town somewhere. I have to find a way to break this curse. I mean, what happens if I break my oath?"

He shook his head. "I'm not letting anything happen to you, okay? We'll figure it out."

I didn't like the look of worry he was wearing now. But he took a deep breath and added, "You're right about not hiding, though. We can't look for ways to break this curse and keep you hidden."

He fell silent, and I knew he was thinking through all possible strategies. I'd done the same while I'd been locked in that cage. But now, with the oath to the hexerei hanging over me, it felt bigger than just me. Bigger than just surviving.

"Kai, I think the wolves need to know about the hexerei."

"You mean about their magic being gone? Ash, you understand that could spark an all-out war, right? Not to mention the oath we just took that will literally prevent us from saying the words."

"Both sides lost something in that curse. Not just the wolves. Maybe if they knew that, they wouldn't be so quick to blame the hexerei for the curse."

Kai shook his head. "You don't know those guys like I do. They aren't reasonable like you. They're hotheaded, and the only thing that stops them from attacking the hexerei is the threat of magic. Take that away and I can't predict what they'll do."

"I don't want to keep more secrets," I said.

"I know that. But first, we make sure you're safe. Then we can think about the greater truth and all that."

I studied him. "You'd make a great alpha, you know."

His eyes snapped to mine. "What makes you say that?"

"You're diplomatic. Always thinking about the big picture but also making me feel like my personal safety matters."

"That's a little biased considering you're my mate," he reminded me.

"True but you know how crazy the pack can be and you somehow manage to balance the order the elders want with the chaos the younger wolves crave. Something tells me the pack would have spiraled into a lot worse behavior than this if you weren't keeping that balance up."

He gave me a look I couldn't decipher.

"You can't tell me you don't want it," I said when he didn't answer.

"I think—"

A rustling noise outside silenced us both.

My nerves pulled taut as my wolf rose up, listening and sensing for what had made the sound. Somewhere nearby, a branch cracked.

"Something's out there," I whispered.

Kai stood up, still naked, but with the noise outside as a possible threat, I couldn't quite lose myself to the distraction of his body. My breaths came in short bursts.

"I'm going to check it out," he said quietly.

"I'll go with you," I said, scrambling to my feet.

Kai shook his head, already pulling on the shorts he'd discarded last night. He opened his mouth to argue, but I didn't let him get the chance.

"You can either let me come willingly or I'll just follow you once you're gone," I said. "Don't tell me it's too dangerous. That shit goes both ways, and in case you haven't learned this about me yet, I am not the damsel type. We're in this together or we're not in it at all, Kai Stone."

Kai straightened and his expression softened. "Okay," he said.

"Okay," I echoed.

He picked up the blanket we'd curled up with last night and draped it over my shoulders. Then he threaded his fingers through mine, and together, we made our way outside.

The sun had risen over the treetops, glinting down through the canopy in cheery rays. Shade from the branches overhead left the air cool, and I tugged the blanket closer around my body as I scanned the woods.

Another branch snapped.

Farther out than before. Moving away from us.

That was good. It meant whoever lurked out there wasn't moving in to attack.

Kai held a finger to his lips, and we both made our way

quietly uphill toward the sounds. We rounded a large tree and stopped at the top of a small ridge. Without a word, Kai pointed at something moving through the woods down below us.

I glimpsed a patch of brown fur as a wolf hurried past, its paws making small rustling sounds against the ground. A small backpack dangled from its teeth.

Familiarity hit me. I'd seen this wolf before.

Then its scent hit me, and I froze, zeroing in on the sight of the still-healing wound along its shoulder.

Drake.

What was he doing out here?

For a moment, I felt a rush of panic that he'd tracked us down to challenge us for revenge. I was the one who'd bitten half his shoulder off after all. But then I watched as he kept right on walking past where we'd hidden—luckily too high above him for the wind to bring him our scent. Instead, he was headed in the same direction Kai and I had come from last night.

The only things that waited for him down that path were hexerei.

I looked at Kai, who noted my expression and nodded silently.

Dropping the blanket, I stepped back as Kai peeled off his shorts and left them in a heap beside the tree. We both shifted and made our way down the hill, trailing Drake from a safe distance.

After a few minutes, we stopped, watching up ahead as Drake stepped over the hexerei's borders, which I saw now was marked with an orange "x" painted on the trees, and shifted back to two legs. He rifled through the bag he'd carried and pulled out a set of clothes. Once he was dressed, he slung the backpack over his shoulder and headed straight for Cohen's.

5

My wolf whined, straining with impatience at being left alone.

Kai and I had run to Franklin where he'd made me promise to stay in the woods and wait while he went for a phone. I hated the idea of him going without me, but he was the only one of us with a set of clothes currently. Like it or not, it wouldn't go over well to walk into a convenience store naked. We had to stay under the radar for now.

I shifted my weight, trying to get comfortable inside the brush I'd crawled through to find a hiding spot as close to the store as possible. Kai had been in there at least five minutes, and as far as I was concerned, it was five minutes too long.

I was nearly headed to find him when he re-emerged. I scanned his face and posture for any sign of trouble. But his expression was clear, and the bond between us was calm.

I exhaled and crawled out of my hiding spot to shift back to my human form. I'd carried one of the wool blankets from the cave in my teeth, and now I grabbed it and wrapped myself in it as Kai approached.

"Did you get it?" I asked.

He planted a quick kiss on my cheek and then held up a prepaid phone. "Yep."

"Everything go okay?"

"No problems," he assured me as he tore into the packaging.

He dialed a number, muttering about a low battery, and then we waited.

Idrissa answered after what felt like forever.

"Hello?"

"Dris, it's me," Kai said.

"Finally. Where's Ash?"

The worry in her voice spiked my own fear.

"Right here with me," Kai said.

"Thank goodness." She sighed audibly. "I found the crash site. The rental car was totaled. When you two weren't there, I thought—"

"We're fine," Kai assured her.

"What the hell happened? It's been three damn days."

Kai's eyes flicked to mine, and I nodded for him to go ahead.

"We had a run-in with some hexerei," he said.

"What?!"

I winced as Idrissa's voice came screeching through the phone.

"Relax, we're fine," Kai said again. "We need to know what's happening there."

She snorted with zero humor as she said, "What's not happening here."

Kai frowned. "What does that mean?"

"Is that Ash?" Isaac's voice came through, drowning out Idrissa's answer. "Ash, sweetie, I miss your face. Are you okay? Do you have room service? Is there complimentary turndown or does Kai do it for you?"

"Isaac, shut up," Idrissa hissed.

"I told you they were fine," Isaac shot back at her. "You worry too damn much."

"I do not."

"Ash, let me live vicariously. What's the weirdest position you've done it in so far?"

"Isaac," Idrissa shrieked. "Give me the phone back, asshole."

Scuffling and muffled curses came through the line. Kai's face looked pinched like he was trying very hard not to scream.

"Guys, focus," I called.

The sound of my voice seemed to snap them out of it. Their end of the line quieted, and Idrissa said, "I'm here. Listen, Silas and Presley and a few others cornered Isaac and me a couple of days ago."

"How much do they know?" Kai asked.

"After a thorough look at Drake's wall of crazy? Everything."

Kai cursed, and I remembered Idrissa mentioning Drake's hidden obsession with me right before we'd left the other day.

"But how did Drake know?" I asked.

"Apparently, he's been doing a bit of old-fashioned stalking," Idrissa said.

My blood ran cold. "What do you mean?"

"There are a lot of pictures of you from a distance. Grocery shopping. Training with me and Isaac. Making out with Kai against a tree." Idrissa hesitated and then said, "That last one shows your curse breaker mark. It's blurry, but it's there. And there's another one of the two of you, naked, sleeping in the woods. Ash's curse breaker mark is clearly visible and circled in red ink."

I looked at Kai, mortified. "When the hell did we sleep naked in the woods?"

"The night we fought Drake," Kai said. "We spent the night as wolves and then fell asleep at the overlook."

"Shit," I breathed, the memory coming back to me. And with it, the knowledge that Drake had been right there, close enough to kill us both if he'd wanted to, but instead he'd been snapping pictures so he'd have proof of my secret.

Somehow, that was worse.

"But if he didn't have confirmation of my mark until that night … that's not enough time to get Vorack there so fast, is it?" I didn't even know why it mattered that I understand all of this, but it did.

Idrissa didn't answer.

Kai's jaw ticked, and he shook his head, his eyes conveying how much he hated to say, "I don't know, Ash, but we'll figure it out. Drake will be dealt with for what he did to you."

"That's one thing we definitely agree on," Idrissa said.

"Samesies, biotches," Isaac called out.

I exhaled, trying to let the promise of answers soothe me for now. The violation of privacy wasn't something I'd be able to let go of easily. Kai was right. Drake had to be dealt with.

"Silas and Presley. Where do they stand in all this?" Kai asked quietly.

I knew him well enough by now to know the softness in his voice was a direct contrast to the anger boiling inside him.

"There were a few questions raised about Ash's trustworthiness," she said. Kai growled, but Idrissa went on.

"Mostly because they feel she kept it from us while pretending not to be one of us, but they all agreed to give Ash the chance to come back and explain."

"Will it be safe for her?" Kai asked.

"Silas and Presley are with us," she said. "And for now, that'll be enough for the others who know. They think we should at least discuss it as a pack."

"Discuss what?" I asked warily.

Letting me live?

"How to protect you," she said, and I blinked in absolute surprise.

"Oh."

I looked at Kai and felt a wave of varying emotions pass through the mate bond we shared. Worry. Fear. Hope. Determination.

I didn't ask what he thought. The answer came through the bond. Not to mention the two hours we'd talked about it on our way here to Franklin. If Drake was secretly working with the hexerei, that couldn't be good for the pack. If we didn't go back and help fix things, who would?

"We're coming home," Kai said. "Let the elders know we want a meeting immediately. If they're not going to accept Ash as she is, we need to know upfront so we can get the hell out before it becomes a problem."

"Okay, let me know when and I'll set it up."

"I'll text you the details. And Idrissa?"

"Yeah?"

"Stay away from Drake."

"You don't have to tell me twice."

"Drake's a dicknugget," Isaac chimed in from the background.

In spite of the bleak homecoming that awaited us, I smiled. Only a few days had passed, and already, I missed the twins. And Oscar. In our short time together, my uncle had become an important part of my life. Despite the uncertainty that awaited me, I was glad to be going back to Ridley Falls.

"And the mess we left behind?" Kai asked pointedly. "How did that go?"

"Taken care of," Idrissa said confidently.

The "mess" in question was Vorack and his right-hand guy, Frank. They'd been after me for a debt my father had owed them and planned to take it out in sexual favors or who knew what else. But then Kai had ripped their throats out and left their bodies in his entryway. Idrissa had promised to clean it up so the Ridley Falls police wouldn't come looking to charge Kai with human murder —apparently, that was the one crime they drew the line on in a town full of criminal werewolves.

"Okay, we're going to get moving," Kai said. "We've got some ground to cover, and I don't trust the roads right now."

"We'll put the meeting together," Idrissa said. "Don't worry about a thing."

"Tell Oscar I'll explain everything," I said, hoping he wouldn't be too pissed that I'd run off and not come home for three days. Who knew what the twins had told him about what happened. Or the real reason I'd left.

"See you soon, lovers," Isaac called just before we disconnected.

Kai looked at me. "Are you sure you're okay with this?" he asked.

I nodded. "We can't let Drake get away with this," I said. "He's working with the hexerei and for what? Cohen wouldn't bother associating with a wolf unless there was something in it for him. And there's only one thing Cohen wants."

"I know," he said, rage flashing in his dark gaze. "But your safety comes first even if that means leaving the Falls behind."

Just the magnitude of power that rolled off him was enough to make me shiver. It also turned me on, but that was a whole other issue.

I tightened the blanket around me even as Kai gave me a knowing look. Stupid bond giving away all my feelings.

"I can't leave," I said, forcing myself to focus on the conversation and not on what it would be like to just "whoops" and let this blanket fall to the ground right here behind this seedy convenience store. "Oscar's my family, and I won't desert him or give that up. It means too much."

"I get it. He's my family too," Kai said.

"How about this: The minute it gets unsafe for either of us, we bail."

He nodded. "Deal."

I stuck out my hand, but instead of shaking it to seal our agreement, he grabbed the blanket and yanked it off my body. It fell, leaving me standing before him, completely naked.

"I'd rather seal the deal another way," he said, his eyes glittering as he reached for me and pulled me close against his chest.

"I'm not going to argue, but I have to ask." I batted my lashes innocently, letting my hands slide up his chest. "How many deals have you made with Silas and the guys? And were they all sealed this way too?"

"Oh, you're going to get it now." His hands reached along my waist, tickling, and I shrieked, prying myself out of his grip and taking off at a run. I shifted mid-stride, knowing full well Kai would do the same, and the chase began.

I let him chase me halfway to Ridley Falls before his wolf caught mine. Or maybe my wolf let him. All I knew was my wolf felt free. She'd been caged and cornered and threatened. We needed this.

I also reveled in how easy it was to shift. Nineteen years of thinking I was nothing but human, and only days into triggering my wolf, it already felt natural. She was part of me. And she loved Kai just as much as I did.

By the time we both shifted back again, I was on top of him, clothes-free. Exactly where I'd hoped to be all along.

Kai grinned up at me, his dark, stormy eyes swirling with a desire that made my skin tingle.

"Time to seal the deal," he said.

I smiled down at him, pressing a kiss to his mouth as I ground my hips against his. "With pleasure."

Kai's hands gripped my hips, guiding me as I moved against him. The sensation of his body against mine sent me soaring, and I let myself forget all about the complications that awaited us. A pack who couldn't trust anyone. A coven who wanted us dead. None of it mattered in this moment. All I knew was my mate, our joined bodies, and the ecstasy it gave as Kai filled me.

As my release built, my wolf surged. And when I found my orgasm, my wolf tipped her head back and howled into the afternoon sun.

I'd face the wrath of the entire pack for the chance at a life with my mate. Destiny be damned.

"You kids planning on charging for this show, or is the first one a freebie?"

My eyes popped open at the unexpected voice. At the sight of Kai's friend, Presley, standing several yards away, I screamed. Not because he was threatening to harm me but because I was still very much sitting on top of Kai's naked body without a single shred of clothes on myself. I used my hands to cover my breasts as my blood pumped full of adrenaline.

Presley's slow perusal made my cheeks heat with temper.

"Turn around, asshole." Kai's wolf surged to the surface, thickening the air between us with a crackly energy.

"Damn. Relax, Stone." Presley turned around, shaking his head like we were the ones being unreasonable. "Since when is nudity such a big deal? I've seen you naked plenty of times, bro. It's not that impressive anymore."

Ignoring Presley, Kai looked at me. "Shift," he said, and with no other way to cover myself, I scrambled backward and did just that.

When I was back in wolf form, Kai stood up. He clearly wasn't as worried about being naked. "All good."

Presley whirled. When he saw me on four legs, he winked.

Kai let out a growl and took a step forward.

Presley's smile vanished, and he stared at Kai. "Dude, sorry. Damn, I thought you'd be happier to see me. It's not like I planned on finding you while you were indisposed. Happy accident, ya know."

He started to smile at his own joke, but when he saw Kai's stony expression, it vanished.

"Fuck. Tough crowd." He ran a hand through his blond hair, but it simply fell right back into perfect placement. The guy was like a movie star. If movie stars were werewolves who went around trying to attack females to force them to fight.

"I'm happy to see you, Pres," Kai said warily. "I just need you to stop eyeing my girl so my wolf doesn't try to rip your throat out."

Presley's brows lifted at that. "Your girl, huh?" He

glanced at me then back to Kai quickly. "This sounds serious. Hey, where you been anyway? You took off, and no one's heard from you in days."

Kai and I both kept silent. We'd already decided mentioning the hexerei would only bring questions we weren't ready to answer.

"What are you doing here, Pres?"

"Silas and I agreed adding some more security around town was a good idea." His gaze flicked to me. "You know, until things calm down around here."

"So you just happened to be guarding this part of the woods?" Kai asked.

"That and Idrissa called an hour ago and said to be on the lookout." He made a face. "Damn, the whole area smells like sex. Well, sex and the two of you. Wait—"

His expression tightened in concentration. Then, very deliberately, he sniffed the air.

His eyes widened.

"Holy shit, dude. You're mated."

I tensed. Out of all the things I knew we'd face coming back to the Falls, I hadn't even considered the pack finding out Kai and I were mated. Or that they would figure it out as easily as noticing our joined scents. Considering I'd just triggered my wolf for the first time a couple of days ago, there was still a lot about being a wolf I didn't understand.

"We are," Kai said simply.

Something about the way he said it told me he'd already expected this—and welcomed it.

Presley just stared at him. "*We are*? That's all you're going to give me? Dude, it's a fucking miracle." He looked at me, awe shining in his baby blues. "It's true then. You're the curse breaker."

"She's also my mate," Kai said pointedly, stepping

between us. "And that makes her protected no matter what you think of the curse."

"Relax, bro." Presley sighed. "Look, I know I was a dick before, but after Drake— Everything's different now." He gestured to me. "She's one of us now. And that means she's my pack sister. I'm not going to hurt her."

Kai didn't look convinced. I couldn't blame him. Presley had been the Vice President of the "Fight or Die, Ash" club since the moment I arrived. (Silas, Kai's other best friend, had been president.) And now, he was completely accepting me? Pardon me if I needed a bigger glass of water to swallow that sudden change.

"It's a bit more complicated than just being one of the pack," Kai said.

"No shit. She's the curse-breaker." Presley looked at me. "You can change back, you know. Nudity isn't that weird for wolves, and I'm not interested in Kai ripping my throat out, so you don't have to worry about wandering eyes."

I hesitated.

Public nudity might have been normal for them, but it wasn't for me. Not yet, anyway. Still, I had to know some things before we just blindly went home with him, and I couldn't ask any of my questions in wolf form.

I stepped behind Kai and shifted back to two legs, using his body for cover. Presley shook his head but didn't comment.

"Kai's right about complicated," I said. "You might have to choose between pack members before it's all over. If that's not something you want to do, you should walk away now."

"If you're talking about Drake, fuck that guy."

Well. Okay then.

"Where do Silas and the others stand?" Kai asked.

Presley shrugged. "With you."

My heart swelled at that. Kai had built so much loyalty here. And we needed it more than ever.

"We're calling a meeting," Kai told him. "With the elders."

"Idrissa told me," Presley said. "She also told me if I ran into you, I should protect you with my life or she'd rip my dick off."

I grinned. Yep, that sounded like my bestie.

"What she doesn't know is her offer isn't the first I've had today."

"I guess your winning personality has begun to catch up with you," I told him.

He snorted. "Trust me, compared to the rest, I'm the nicest guy you'll run into in this town."

"Pres," Kai said, his tone somehow both a warning and a question.

"Dude." Presley stuffed his hands into the pockets of his leather jacket and shook his head. "There have been four pack members hospitalized in the last day. And that's not counting the sixteen bar fights last night."

"Sixteen?" I screeched.

Ridley Falls was definitely a bit of a wild card. More specifically, the pack itself was wild. Without an alpha or mates, their wolves were a bit unhinged. Bar fights were a normal day. But not sixteen of them.

I looked from Presley to Kai. "Are there even sixteen bars in this town?"

Presley snickered, but his smile died when he saw Kai's expression.

"What the hell?" Kai demanded.

"Everyone's fine," Presley said, scowling as he rubbed his shoulder. I smirked, realizing he'd been one of the brawlers. Good. Asshole deserved a little pain and suffering. "But," his eyes flicked back to Kai now. "Two of those bar fights were alpha challenges."

"You're shitting me," Kai said.

"Alpha challenges?" I echoed. "What does that even mean?"

"It means our pack is beginning to feel a call to leadership," Presley said. "Something that should be impossible."

"It means the curse is breaking down," Kai said, disbelief coating his words.

I wasn't sure whether to be happy or terrified. That many fights meant everyone was already on edge, and that didn't take into account the bomb I was about to drop about being the curse breaker.

"So … it's done?" I asked.

"I don't think so," Presley said with a shake of his head. "No one else has mated, and the alpha challenges aren't coming from anyone considered worthy of winning the role."

He gave Kai a look.

"I'm not challenging for alpha," Kai said.

Instead of responding, Presley's gaze swung to me. "Prophecy says the curse breaker will be alpha. That true?"

"I don't know," I said, suddenly unsure what to say.

If the rest of the pack thought Kai would be alpha, where did that leave us?

"Right. Well, I'm sure you two will figure it out," Presley said, clapping his hands together. "In the meantime, apparently there's a meeting to get to. You two ready or what?"

"We'll need to stop for clothes," Kai said.

"No need." Presley took a couple of steps back and grabbed a bag I hadn't noticed earlier. He tossed it at Kai's feet. "Idrissa sent a few things."

My eyes narrowed. “You had clothes with you this entire time?”

Presley grinned again. “Oops,” he said. “Forgot.”

“Kai,” I said solemnly, “I’m sorry in advance for kicking your best friend’s ass.”

Kai laughed. “I forgive you, mate. Do what you gotta do.”

6

Kai and I got dressed, and then the three of us trekked out of the woods where Presley had a car waiting at the road. Idrissa had sent me a pair of tight jeans and a tank but no bra. I just hoped this meeting wasn't supposed to be formal because braless nipples were never going to be anything but very, very casual.

Presley and Kai talked while we drove. Mostly about people I didn't know and events I'd never been part of. But every once in a while, Presley's eyes would find mine in the rearview. Something about the way he looked at me had changed. I wasn't quite sure what it meant yet. For now, I kept my guard up and my game face on.

At least, he wasn't trying to get me killed anymore.

Well, so far. The day wasn't over yet.

When we arrived in the Falls, Presley drove by the Twisted Throttle, the motorcycle repair shop my uncle Oscar owned—and above it, the apartment I now lived in. The sense of home I felt at seeing it startled me. I'd never felt that for any of the houses I'd lived in with my father.

My father.

A pang of grief seized my heart. He hadn't been gone that long yet. And the heartbreak still crept up on me, but bittersweetness lay underneath the pain. My dad had sacrificed everything for me. The irony of it all was that his death had led me to the one thing I'd always wanted.

A home.

We passed the crystal shop where I'd had to run from Silas and Presley in their attempt to corner me and force me to fight before I was ready. And the grocery store where I'd first met the twins. It was surprising the number of memories I'd already created in this town. And I realized, more than ever, I didn't want to run away or leave. I wanted to find a way to stay.

Hopefully, that's what this meeting would provide.

Otherwise, I would do what I'd always done. I'd run. Start over.

It wouldn't be so hard for me. I'd already reinvented myself dozens of times. But Kai? He'd lived his whole life in this town. I hated to think he'd have to leave it just to be with me. Mated or not, I didn't want to make him choose between the things he loved.

Eventually, Presley turned onto a side street and parked in front of a building that looked a lot like a church without the steeple. The sign out front read "Ridley Falls City Council," though I could barely make out the words through the graffiti someone had painted over it that looked suspiciously like a penis.

"You two ready?" Presley asked, cutting the engine. "They're going to smell that mate bond the minute you walk in, you know."

Kai turned to look at me. "You up for this? Because we can turn around right now and keep on driving. Anywhere you want to go."

Considering his words carefully, I thought about the oath I'd made to the hexerei about breaking their part of the curse. And about Oscar and the twins and every "root" I'd begun to put down since coming here. My dad had died, leaving me completely alone, but moving here had already taught me I had more than just a past full of secrets and solitude. I could have a future too. One with a family, and maybe, just maybe, if I was lucky, happiness. But only if I fought for it.

"I'm ready," I said with a hell of a lot more confidence than I felt. "Let's go."

We got out of the car, and Kai took my hand.

Before Presley could get far, I grabbed his wrist and tightened my grip hard enough to get his attention.

"What the hell," he said, looking offended more than pained.

"I hope you meant what you said about being on our side," I told him. "Because if you walk us into a trap and Kai gets hurt, Idrissa's not the only one who'll rip your dick off."

He looked at Kai, wide-eyed. "What is up with these females ripping off dicks?"

Kai shrugged. "Power move, I guess."

Presley looked back at me. "Relax, Ashes. There's no trap."

"You'll have to forgive me if I don't believe you," I said. "What with you trying to kill me before."

"Whoa, hey, no killing happened."

"Oh? So you didn't attack me behind the crystal shop when you knew I couldn't shift?"

"Is that what this is about? Look, we did what we thought we needed to bring your wolf out, okay? Besides, you weren't one of us before. You are now."

"Like Drake is one of you?" I shot back, still squeezing.

"Ash," Kai said gently.

"What?" I demanded, not tearing my eyes off Presley.

"Do this later."

His words sank in, and I became aware of the eyes on us. Several people had stopped on their way into the council building and were fixated on us in a way that didn't quite feel friendly.

Still glaring at Presley, I released his wrist. With a pained expression, he gently rubbed his wrist, which made me feel slightly better about the whole trying-to-attack-me thing from before.

"Even if I can trust you, I don't like you," I told him icily.

"Get in line," he said with an eye roll that made me wish I'd squeezed harder.

"Let's go," Kai said, and Presley led the way inside.

We passed through the double front doors, crossing the foyer into a large meeting room. I hesitated, noting not a single chair remained empty. The space was packed full with a few people even standing against the wall on each side.

"Is it always this crowded?" I whispered.

Presley glanced back and shrugged. "How should I know? Never been to one of these before. Hell, most of these people haven't either."

I watched as Presley sauntered off, leaving us alone in the center aisle. Uncertainty rippled through me.

Kai's hand tightened on mine. Through our bond, I could feel his nerves and mine mixing to create a slow climb toward panic.

At the front of the room, someone stood and motioned to us.

Idrissa.

Her fiery red hair was unmistakable. Like a siren's light. The sight of her helped to calm me.

Beside her stood Isaac and then Oscar. All of them watched me expectantly. Oscar's expression held more than just anticipation, though. Uncertainty for sure and, coating it all, anger.

I took a deep breath, shoving the panic down, and then let Kai lead me down the center aisle.

A hush fell over the room as we made our way toward the front. It wasn't the first time my presence had shut down conversation or that I'd felt the entire place stop to stare at me. A small town like this didn't bother hiding their nosiness. But I'd never been good at pretending anyway. So, this time, I stared right back.

"Hey, Ashes," someone called as we passed. Devon maybe.

I kept moving.

In the front row, I spotted Mick, one of the other mechanics who worked at the Throttle. I'd heard Oscar mention him as one of the last few pack elders left. And beside him, another guy around my dad's age watched us. Amberly, the twins' mother, sat on his other side, and I realized this must be their dad, the other remaining elder. Amberly waved at me, smiling encouragingly, and I waved back.

Then Oscar pushed his way over to me, pulling me into a hug that surprised me. He wasn't exactly the affectionate type. When he pulled back, I saw worry in his eyes and a flash of temper.

"Kid, I've been worried sick."

"I'm sorry. I..." I had no idea what to say. This wasn't exactly the place to get into the details. Not with so many listening ears.

But Oscar ignored my lack of details and grabbed my

arm. His dark eyes bored into my own. "You can't just run off like that, do you hear me?"

"Yes, sir," I said, and he exhaled, though something told me he wasn't done with me yet. Then he glared at Kai. "We're going to talk later. You might be like a son to me, but that doesn't mean you can run off with my niece and not give a guy a call to let him know."

Oscar's nostrils flared as he drew in a deep breath, clearly not done blasting Kai yet.

"Yes, sir," Kai began. "Totally my fault. We—"

"No way." Oscar's jaw fell open. Recovering, he inhaled again. "Impossible," he breathed. "The curse…."

I didn't have time to formulate a response.

"Well, hello. This must be Ash."

The man who'd been seated beside Amberly walked up beside Oscar, nudging his way into our exchange. He flashed a tight smile at me.

"I'm Warren Close, pack elder."

"Nice to meet you," I said.

I shook his hand, noting the way he squeezed mine extra tight then immediately let go and turned his complete attention to Kai as if I'd already been forgotten. Ugh. Patriarchy power moves annoyed the hell out of me.

"Kai, I understand you called this meeting," Warren said. "Care to fill us in?"

"Actually, Ash and I both called it," Kai said, and even though I was grateful for the point he was making, I wasn't sure I liked the way all eyes fastened on me.

"Yes, I've heard some interesting details about Ash," Warren said. He turned to me. "Care to share with us what all this is about?"

"Um, should I address everyone at once or…?"

"No need," Warren said. "That's our job as the council.

Now, I have to ask—is this business about curse-breaking true?"

"Warren, stop being a politician," Amberly said, smacking his arm as she pressed in closer. "Can't you smell it?"

"Smell what?" Warren asked, frowning.

Idrissa and Isaac appeared beside Oscar, shoving in close until we were in some sort of seven-person huddle. Hands grabbed me from behind, and I nearly swung on them until I realized it was only Isaac trying to hug me.

"You smell like sex and pine cones," he said in a voice absolutely everyone could hear.

"Isaac," I hissed.

"What?"

"Not appropriate," I said through clenched teeth.

"Fine. Such a buzzkill. But we need to debrief later about all the *debriefing* you've done already." He winked at me and let me go without waiting for an answer.

I looked back at Warren, who seemed to be the leader here, to find him staring at me with a look of concentration. Then, his expression transformed to one of understanding.

"You two have...mated."

I couldn't tell whether he approved underneath the shock in his voice.

"We have," Kai said calmly. His hand still held mine. "Now, if we could call this meeting to order, there are a few things I'd like to say."

I'd never seen him so in charge before. It was kind of a turn-on.

As soon as I had the thought, Kai glanced over at me, a small smirk forming on his lips. My cheeks heated as I realized he'd felt my lust through the bond. Not to mention whatever smell I was putting off right about now.

Idrissa and Isaac smirked knowingly.

Ugh.

"Yes, of course." Warren waved us toward the small stage. "You have the floor."

Amberly offered me a warm smile and then urged us both forward.

I must have looked as unsure—okay, terrified—as I felt because Idrissa gave me a small shove and grinned.

"Break a leg," she said as I passed her.

Kai climbed the steps, and I followed. Then, we both turned to face the roomful of wolf shifters waiting to hear why in the hell we'd called them here.

I looked out at the faces. Some looked friendly. Some confused. Several were obviously annoyed. I spotted Silas, who gave me this weird sort of chin-nod that I assumed was supposed to be encouraging. Beside him, Presley watched us with mild interest. His arms were crossed, and I told myself it was to hide his throbbing wrist. In the next row sat Devon, who'd hit on me when I'd first come to town—and been nearly maimed by Kai in the process. Behind them, I recognized a few other pack members. Tiffany and Luke. Vinny. Even Gordon was here; a little glassy-eyed but upright nonetheless.

What would they think when they learned what I was?

"Welcome," Kai said in a loud voice.

A few more murmurs went up, but then the crowd fell silent.

"Thanks for coming," Kai went on. "We've called you here to discuss a few things, but before we get into that, I'd like to formally introduce our newest pack member." He gestured to me. "This is Ash. She's Oscar's niece.

Daughter of our former alpha, Caleb Lawson. She's one of us now."

Kai paused.

No one said a word.

After an awkward beat of silence, someone began clapping.

I cringed, glancing down at where Isaac had begun applauding enthusiastically. Idrissa joined in and then Amberly and Oscar until reluctant applause rang out across the crowd.

Embarrassment heated my face. I resisted the urge to jump off the stage and haul ass out of here.

"Ash is a Lone Wolf now," Kai said when the applause had died off. "And as such, everything we discuss today, every decision we make as a pack, should be done bearing that in mind."

"We have a lot to bear in mind, son," Warren chimed in. "Why don't you start by telling us what else Ash is? She's not just a pack member or a wolf shifter, is she?"

I tensed.

"She's much more than that," Kai said, nodding in agreement. "But I want to remind you all she's one of us. And that means she's entitled to our protection."

"What the hell does she need protection from?" someone in the crowd called. "I heard she whooped Drake's ass the other day."

A few others laughed.

"She fought and won her place here," Kai said.

"Then she's protected," someone said with a shrug. Teddy, the bartender from Bo's. I recognized him even with the bruises covering his face. What the hell had happened to him? One of the bar fights maybe?

"She smells different."

I looked down and saw Tiffany staring up at me, eyes

narrowed in concentration. She cocked her head, studying me then Kai. "Why is that?"

"We're mated," Kai said, and I watched the shock register on nearly every face in the crowd.

Some jaws fell open. I heard a few gasps and murmurs of disbelief. Several curses. No one argued it. Or looked angry. Well, okay, Tiffany looked slightly jealous. As did a few of the other girls. But otherwise, mostly they all looked intrigued.

A middle-aged woman near the back stood up. "How is that even possible?" she asked. Her eyes brimmed with tears, and I could see the emotion written across her face. "The curse..."

"Ash is immune to the curse," Kai said, "for reasons we will explain in a moment. Her immunity allowed our wolves to recognize one another as true mates. We've completed the bond successfully, and the connection is absolutely there."

Murmurs rose.

The woman wiped away a falling tear. My heart squeezed at her emotional display.

"What does this mean for the rest of us?" Tiffany demanded over the noise. "Will we find our mates now too?"

"I don't know," Kai said. "We hope so."

"The curse is broken?" Vinny asked hopefully.

"Unfortunately, it's not quite that simple. I'm going to let Ash tell you about that," Kai said.

Silence fell as all eyes turned to me expectantly. I took a deep breath, bracing myself against the onslaught of emotion. Between the mood of those in the room and Kai's nerves, my body felt full of adrenaline now.

I cleared my throat, determined to exude confidence.

"Hi," I began, my voice only slightly wobbly. "First, thank you all for coming."

At the far end of the aisle, the door opened, drawing my attention as someone else strode in.

My heart slammed against my chest.

Drake.

He stopped at the back of the room, and our eyes met. His lips curved in a slow, deliberate smile. "Hello, Ashes. I've been looking all over for you two."

My wolf growled, and it took all of my control to keep the sound from escaping my lips. All over. Did that include hexerei territory?

His showing up here could only mean he had something up his sleeve. Drake had made it clear he would do just about anything to stop me from breaking this curse. Otherwise, he wouldn't have sent a murderer after me to keep me from doing just that.

Traitor, I wanted to scream.

Instead, I didn't give the asshole time to somehow ruin this moment or delay it any longer.

I yanked the waist of my pants down to reveal the curse's mark on my hip. Then, I looked out over the crowd and said the words before I could change my mind.

"My name is Ash Lawson, and I'm the curse breaker."

This time, the response was a roar of noise.

Voices rose, calling out demands, questions, and accusations that had Kai snarling at the ones brazen enough to get up and approach the stage with their shouted interrogations. Idrissa and Isaac jumped up too, rushing up to act as security for anyone trying to shove their way up the stairs.

Kai tugged on my hand, yanking me farther back on the stage. But that only seemed to egg them on. Drake stood back, arms crossed as if satisfied with the chaos surrounding him. I purposely turned away from him.

"Who says she's the curse breaker?" someone yelled.

"Prove it," called another voice.

"Screw the curse. We don't need it broken."

"We like our chaos just the way it is."

"Why are you backing away? Are you scared?"

"What do you have to hide?"

The owners of the voices were indistinguishable, blending together into an angry clash—proof Kai and the others had been right all along. Plenty of pack members didn't have warm fuzzies at the idea of this curse going away.

A few others tried intervening, yelling about finally having their control back. I was relieved to see so many who seemed open to what I was offering. But the ones shouting demands were hard to ignore.

My stomach tightened as their energy seemed to climb, driving my wolf somewhere between panic and outrage. The need to defend grew stronger too, and it was all I could do to continue standing here and just taking it.

Warren appeared, shoving past the twins and marching up to us.

"You two might want to start talking," he said over the noise. "Either that or we'll reconvene at a later time. This is crazy."

"Don't let them leave, Warren." Amberly stood with the twins at the bottom of the stage. "Just talk fast," she added, looking at me. "They need to hear this."

I nodded, glancing up again at the faces who were paying attention instead of ranting.

"I was born with a mark I didn't understand." My voice was lost over the noise, but I kept going. Supernatural hearing had to count for something. "My parents never told me what the mark meant or what I was. I didn't even know shifters existed until I got here to Ridley Falls. So, I wasn't lying to you or keeping secrets like some may think."

Some of the noise died down, but not all of it.

I kept going.

"The mark was given as a counterbalance. A yin and yang."

No one responded to that.

Near the back, a fight broke out. Someone yelled for

Kai to look them in the eye. He ignored them all and urged me to keep going.

"This is insane," Idrissa yelled.

"Ash, do something," Isaac called.

"The curse is going to be broken, like it or not," I screamed. "And as a member of this pack, I demand your cooperation."

The people surging for the stage stopped.

For a split second, I thought it had been my words that had calmed them. But then Drake stepped forward, and I realized the angry group gathered in front were all looking at him, not me.

His eyes gleamed with the kind of smug confidence only an asshole like him could pull off.

"You're in over your head, Ashes. Leave now, and it won't come crashing down around you."

"You're one to talk," Kai growled. "Tell them what you're doing."

Drake's gaze swung to Kai, and his eyes narrowed shrewdly. They locked gazes, and for a long moment, they simply stared one another down. The rest of the room fell into a hushed silence as they began to notice whatever this was.

Then Drake smiled in a way that would put a serial killer to shame.

He knew that we knew.

I could feel it.

Instead of confirming or denying, he said something I never expected.

"Kai Stone, I challenge you for the position of alpha of this pack. A fight to the death. Do you accept?"

"Kai is not fighting you," I said, fury rising as my wolf threatened to take over and end this right here and now.

She'd had enough of Drake. And I couldn't say I disagreed.

But Kai squeezed my hand. "Ash, don't."

"What?" I gaped at him.

But he turned back to Drake, calm and cool. "I accept."

"Kai, you can't," I protested. "He's not worth it."

"It's him or you, sweetheart," Drake said. "But your mate here's already figured that out."

"You're not worthy of being alpha," I snarled.

"Look around you," Drake said. "Already, the curse is breaking down, and wolves are feeling called to secure their place."

"You don't want the curse broken," I said, glaring. "What does it matter to you who's alpha?"

"I would have preferred to keep things as they were," he agreed. "But you took that away when the two of you mated."

Anger flashed in his eyes. Raw hate that made my blood run cold. Drake's anger went a lot deeper than letting his wolf run wild. Whatever his problem was, it couldn't have started with me. But I was determined to be the one to end it. Or him.

"Your mating set things in motion, and there's only one way to stop you," Drake threatened.

"How do you know so much about this?" Idrissa demanded.

"Unlike the rest of you, I've done my homework on this curse rather than just waiting to be yanked around by whatever these two claim to have done for us."

"It's not a claim," I shot back. "Our mating has clearly unlocked the alpha call. The curse has already begun to fade."

"You're halfway right," he said snidely, clearly enjoying the fact that he knew more than I did.

I blinked, realizing Drake had known all along what I was still trying to figure out. The curse, how to break it, and how to stop what we'd already started.

"What's the other half?" I snapped. "If you know so much, enlighten us."

"The curse was created in three parts," he said. "That means it will unravel in threes. Your mating was stage one. You becoming alpha, stage two." He paused, his lips curving in a secretive smile. "Stage three's a little more complicated, but I hear you've recently been filled in on that particular situation."

I stilled.

The hexerei, their magic. Stage three was returning their magic to them?

I'd have to dissect that one later because, right now, the problem wasn't magic I didn't know how to find. It was stage two that was causing my heart to race.

Alpha.

The prophecy had been right.

I had to become alpha.

And Drake had known it all along.

It hit me then.

Why he'd challenged Kai in the first place.

"He's working with them," I declared, desperate to stop this fight from happening.

"Working with who?" Warren asked, clearly trying his best to keep up with things he knew nothing about.

"The hexerei."

At that, the entire room fell silent.

I looked at Warren and then Oscar, who'd positioned himself at the stairs to protect me from the people who'd tried rushing the stage. "Drake is working with the hexerei. That's how he knew what I was. And why he sent Vorack here to kill me. So I wouldn't break the curse."

"Vorack?" Warren blinked, frowning. "Who's that?"

"He was a bookie my dad owed a gambling debt to," I said, the words tumbling out faster now that I understood Drake's strategy. I would beat him at this. I had to. I couldn't lose Kai. Couldn't risk Drake pitting us against one another.

I looked at Warren, explaining as quickly as I could. "After Drake found out, he called Vorack and told him I was here in the Falls. A few days ago, Vorack came after me, but Kai stopped him. Then, the hexerei kidnapped me and held me at their compound. Kai showed up and helped get me out, but when we were leaving, we saw Drake going into their camp. He's working with them. He's a traitor to the pack."

"Oscar, are you hearing this?" Warren asked.

I exhaled, waiting for them to put it all together and turn on Drake.

"Yeah," Oscar said, "I heard it."

The dismay in his tone confused me.

"Can't you detain him?" I pressed. "Or lock him up or banish him or something? He's a danger to the pack," I said.

Drake simply stood and waited. Still smug, the asshole.

"Ash, stop," Kai whispered in a strained voice that sent a note of fear through me.

"What?" I asked, my voice dropping now that the room had gone utterly silent. "I'm just telling them what happened. It's why we came back."

"How exactly did you stop this bookie, son?" Warren asked, and it took me a long moment to realize he was talking to Kai. And not about Drake.

Kai squared his shoulders. "Ash is my mate, sir. I will always protect her with my life."

I stilled, the hot fury in my veins turning cold as I realized what I'd just done.

"Hell," Oscar said. "He was threatened, Warren. You heard him."

"Doesn't matter," Warren said.

Amberly met my eyes. Her expression was sad. Resigned.

"Kai, you know our rule about humans," Warren began.

Dread filled all of the empty parts inside me. "Wait. No. It was self-defense," I said. "They had guns."

"I understand," Warren said. "Unfortunately, the law is the law, and while we don't uphold much these days, this one is sacred. Kai, you'll need to remand yourself into police custody until we can get this sorted."

"I understand."

"Noah," Warren called out.

He motioned for someone at the back of the room.

There was some shuffling and then a man came forward from the crowd. He wore khaki slacks and a button-down. Not exactly a police uniform, but the cuffs in his hand were unmistakable.

"I know it's your day off, but we've got a bit of a situation here. Kai will need to be held until we can look into this story about a bookie named Vorack," Warren told him.

"Human?" Noah asked.

"Unfortunately," Warren said.

"Understood." Noah hopped onto the stage and headed right for us.

"No way," I said, stepping in front of Kai. I had no idea what my intentions were, but letting Kai be locked up wasn't one of them. "You can't do this."

"Ash, resisting will only make it worse," Kai said gently.

I didn't move.

"Ash." He tugged on my arm, and I turned to face him.

His expression was calm. Clear. The feelings coming through the bond were an attempt to comfort me. And dammit, it was kind of working. I didn't want to be comforted. I wanted to fix this.

"You're doing that on purpose," I said.

"I'm letting you know everything will be fine," he said, his hands on my shoulders.

But my eyes burned with hot tears.

"You were just protecting me," I whispered.

"They'll realize that once they investigate," he said. "It's okay."

Still, I didn't move. I couldn't. How could this happen? We'd come back to face this together, and now Kai was being torn away? Screw the curse. I'd rather have Kai than some magical undoing of my parents' crimes.

"Here, take this." He pressed something into my hand.

I looked down and recognized the prepaid cell we'd bought together in Franklin. My hand curled around it even as my heart constricted.

"I can't do this without you," I whispered.

"You can. And you will."

The calmness was a front. It had to be. There was no way Kai felt this okay about being arrested and led away from me. Especially considering how volatile the crowd had been just moments ago.

"Listen to your mate, Ashes."

Drake's sardonic voice raked across my every nerve.

I snarled at him. "Shut your mouth, traitor. All of this is your fault."

"About that. Do you have proof?" He lifted a brow in

challenge, and I made a silent vow to rip that eyebrow right off his disgusting face just as soon as the opportunity presented itself. "Because without proof, I'm afraid you don't have a case. And as you know, once you're a pack member, you're afforded certain rights and protections. One of those is protection against baseless claims."

I didn't answer.

There was nothing I *could* say.

Not right now with half the pack on Team Drake and the other half watching with silent condolences as my mate was led away in cuffs.

"It's going to be okay." Kai pressed a quick kiss to my cheek and stepped around me, holding his wrists out to Noah.

"Take care of Ash," Kai said to Oscar.

"Of course, son."

I watched, helpless and barely holding back my emotions, as Noah cuffed Kai and then led him out. In his wake, most of the crowd dispersed. Clearly, the meeting was over. All that remained were Drake and his supporters.

"You won't get away with this," I told Drake with a conviction I wasn't sure I believed.

He merely smiled and shrugged like he wasn't worried about anything. "Neither will you."

8

"If you'll all take a seat please, we'll discuss our final order of business," Warren said. His words startled me back to the present moment where my mind reeled. First, at the fact that Kai had just left in police custody, and second, that Warren was just casually moving on like this.

Everything I'd just said about Drake, and he was going to just ignore it?

I opened my mouth to interrupt, to demand he listen to me and investigate Drake, but Idrissa tugged my hand—hard.

"Come sit down," she whispered forcefully enough to make me reluctantly listen.

If Warren wasn't going to take me seriously, I'd just have to figure out how to handle Drake myself. First, I had to get through the rest of this meeting. Idrissa pulled me down to the front row where I sat between her and Oscar.

Warren waited another moment until everyone else was seated and then went on. "For the first time in nearly thirty years, the alpha challenges have officially begun. For those too young to remember our customs on this, that means anyone can submit their names as a challenger. The deadline for submission is ten days from today. Again, this is our custom, and no exceptions will be made. Please see me or Oscar to submit your name as a contender. Fights will be announced as soon as we have the submissions. In the meantime, thank you for coming."

"That's it?" someone demanded.

I turned to see a man in the back push to his feet.

"She just announced she's going to break the curse. No details on how she'll do it or when?"

Warren cleared his throat. "We'll need some time to gather the details surrounding what Ash has revealed to us—"

"You're not even asking what we want." The guy's expression tightened, and I faced front again, my cheeks hot with anger and discomfort.

This meeting had gone right to hell and was getting worse by the second. Part of me wanted to return to the stage and explain, but what would I say? I didn't have the answers they were looking for. Not yet.

Drake did, apparently.

My eyes flicked to where I'd watched him take a seat. Across the aisle, second row. Our eyes met, and he winked.

I turned away.

Asshole.

Warren tried again. "Once we know more, another meeting will be called—"

Another voice rang out.

"Yeah, what if we don't want the curse broken? Shouldn't we take a vote?"

"That's enough." Warren glanced at me then back at

the crowd. "We'll reconvene when some of these ... issues have been sorted. For now, we're dismissed."

Issues.

Right.

He meant me.

When *I'd* been sorted.

Ugh.

Drake left first, taking his little band of followers with him. After that, a few of the remaining pack members demanded to question me, but Warren declared the meeting officially over. Again.

When the crowd refused to leave, Warren lost his temper.

"The meeting is adjourned," he roared, sending a wave of power out with his words that had the people in the crowd bowing their heads in submission. The power washed over me too, but I didn't have the same strong urge to copy their body language. It was more of a suggestion than a command.

I stared at Warren, mostly curious at what he'd just done. And why I'd been immune. Maybe it was like the curse. I wasn't bound by its magic and rules like everyone else seemed to be.

"Go home," Warren ordered.

Finally, to the sound of grumblings, the remaining crowd turned and left.

When they were gone, Warren released whatever pressure he'd used, and the energy in the room returned to normal. Idrissa and Isaac both stood from where they'd each sunk to a chair during the whole exchange.

"Dad really needs to get control," Isaac said.

"You mean he's done that before?" I asked.

Idrissa glanced from Warren to me, her expression tight. "It's the closest thing we have left to alpha power.

And he's been using it more often lately. His temper's getting worse."

I started to ask what she meant when Amberly walked up to us. She looked ruffled. "We're headed out," she said. "See you two at home. And Ash, I'm glad you're back safe."

"Thanks," I said, noting that Warren didn't bother to walk over or say anything else to me.

With a quick goodbye to the twins, Warren and Amberly exited too.

Only Oscar and the twins remained.

Isaac said something about alpha energy on the rise. Oscar grunted back.

I barely heard them. All I cared about was Kai. He'd been arrested because of me. And now, I was on my own against Drake, who'd evidently made it his mission to take me down.

It might have been a fair fight if I knew what he knew about the curse. But his comments earlier had made it clear his knowledge of the curse outweighed mine.

"Ash?" Idrissa called in a small voice. "You okay?"

"I don't know what I am," I admitted. "Ever since the crash, nothing's gone right."

"Oh, shit, speaking of the crash, I almost forgot." Idrissa dug into her pocket, pulling out a chain. She held it up, letting the charm dangle, and my heart leaped at the sight.

"My necklace!"

"I found it at the crash site," Idrissa said, dropping it into my waiting palm. "The chain was busted, but I swapped it out for one of my old ones."

For some reason, this dumbass necklace had become important to me. Maybe because I'd sworn to my dad I wouldn't lose it—my last promise to him before he'd died.

Whatever the reason, I put it on and felt something inside me settle at the weight of it against my chest.

"Thanks," I told her, feeling a little less off balance.

Idrissa squeezed my hand as we turned back to the others.

Oscar had been overly quiet during Kai's arrest and the meeting leading up to it, but now he looked ready to hit something. His hands were fisted at his sides, and he shook with barely restrained temper.

"Oscar, I'm really sorry," I began, but he waved me off.

"I'm going to make a call," he said and marched out.

I watched him go, guilt tugging at me. It was my fault he was upset.

"I can't believe I screwed things up so badly today."

"Don't worry about it. There won't be a case," Idrissa said, and I blinked, surprised to find her standing in front of me. I hadn't even seen her move.

"What do you mean?" I asked. "They arrested him. Of course, there's a case."

"They won't be able to keep him. Not without evidence." She leaned in closer, her hands wrapped around my arms, and whispered fiercely, "They'll never find the bodies. No bodies, no crime."

I stared at her, not quite sure how to feel about what she'd just said.

It was like that cliché best friend situation people made jokes about. Except, this was real life, and my best friend had literally hidden dead bodies for me, no questions asked.

I didn't deserve Idrissa Close.

"Thank you," I said, hoping like hell she was right. "I mean, I owe you, but I don't know how to make it up—"

"Sleepover!"

Isaac bounded over and shoved his way into our little friendship circle—literally. But that was Isaac.

"Whoa, brotato, back up," Idrissa said.

"We need a sleepover," Isaac said, looking as serious as a war council. "I mean it. We need to hear all about Ash's little mini-getaway. And we need to chat about Kai's current Home Away From Home status. Plus, friendship bonding is in order. Ice cream. Facials. The whole thing. Trust me," he added, turning to me. "It's the best therapy."

"Maybe for you," Idrissa said, making a face.

"Fine. What do you do for stress relief, buzzkill?" Isaac said.

She shrugged. "Usually, I pick a fight with Vinny or Devon to take the edge off. Scuff some knuckles."

Isaac just stared at her. "You're not right in the head, you know that?"

"Who's fault is that?" She gave him a pointed look. "You stole half my brain cells when you split our DNA into two bodies."

"That's not even how it works," Isaac said.

"Guys," I said, losing steam fast now that the meeting had ended. Reality was beginning to set in. Not to mention hunger and exhaustion.

The twins fell silent just as Oscar returned from whatever phone call he'd stepped out to make.

"Can we just get out of here?" I asked. "A sleepover is fine, but I need to eat and shower or I might end up ripping someone's head off. And I don't think this town can handle any more murder right now."

"We'll go to the Throttle," Oscar said. He looked at the twins. "You two are welcome to join us, but until things calm down, Ash is safest at home."

"We'll swing home and grab some stuff," Idrissa said. "Come on, brain thief."

She turned for the door, and Isaac kissed my cheek before hurrying to catch up to her.

"And then the grocery store," Isaac told her as they walked out. "We need whipped cream. A bottle for each of us. Ooh. And Jell-O for shots."

"Dear God," Idrissa muttered as they disappeared outside.

"You good?" Oscar asked me when we were alone.

"I'm a lot of things. Good isn't one of them."

He studied me then said, "Come on. We shouldn't talk here."

I sighed. "Okay."

Outside, the street was empty, and I was grateful no one else was around. Having my guard up was a draining thing, especially around so many people my wolf had deemed threatening earlier.

Oscar opened the passenger door of his pickup, and I climbed inside.

Movement caught my eye just as Oscar slammed the door shut. I stared out the open window as Drake stepped out from the alley. He was alone, but that didn't stop the ripple of fear sliding up my spine.

Oscar stopped and whirled as if finally sensing the threat.

His eyes landed on Drake.

"Get the hell out of here," Oscar told him.

"Last I checked, I was free to go where I wished," Drake said. He cocked his head at me. "Unfortunately, the same cannot be said of your boyfriend."

I shoved the car door open, but Oscar was there, blocking me.

"What the hell do you want, Drake?" I demanded.

"Chaos, mostly," he said with a grin that belonged in a padded room.

"You challenged the wrong person," I said. "I'm right here."

"Oh, I want you gone, believe me," he said, drawing a growl from Oscar. "I'm just using a different strategy than before to make that happen. This one feels way more fun."

"I know you sent Vorack here for her," Oscar said.

"Knowing and proving are two different things." He waved a hand. "But that was before I knew what Ash really was. Back then, I only suspected. And I'll admit, I didn't give her enough credit for being such a survivor." His eyes raked me over. But it didn't feel like a compliment. "Now that I know who—or what—I'm dealing with, I'll be more careful."

His eyes sparkled with awareness, and I couldn't help but think he already knew about my hexerei blood.

"Try anything, and the sheriff will have you in a pair of cuffs all your own," Oscar warned.

Drake chuckled. "I'm not nearly as reckless as you and yours."

Oscar snarled, and I reached through the open window, grabbing him before he could do something stupid. "It's not worth it," I said.

"Yes, old man, listen to your magical niece. I'm not worth it." His lip curled in a self-deprecating sneer. "I never have been. That's the problem."

He turned and disappeared, leaving me and Oscar alone on the street.

"Kid needs an ass whooping," Oscar muttered as he marched around and got into the truck.

No argument from me.

Oscar was silent on the drive back to the Throttle. I tried reading his emotions by glancing at his expression or body language, but it was impossible to tell with Oscar. No one played it closer to the vest than my uncle.

"I met the hexerei," I said when I couldn't take it anymore.

His eyes snapped toward mine. "So you said earlier. Care to elaborate?"

"They crashed our car and took me," I said quietly. "That's where I've been the last few days."

"Shit, Ash," he said grimly. His hand on the wheel tightened until his knuckles turned white. "Did they hurt you?"

"No," I said. "I'm okay. Mostly, they kept me knocked out. I think to keep my wolf from ripping their heads off."

"They know what you are?"

"They do. But there's more to the curse than we think," I said. "The witches lost something too."

His eyes narrowed, and I could tell part of him couldn't care less what they'd been forced to give up. "What was it?" he asked, glancing at me.

I opened my mouth, fully expecting that oath to stop me from saying anything, but the words slipped out effortlessly. "Their magic."

Huh. Apparently, I was immune to that little gem just like I'd been immune to the wolves' inability to discuss the curse.

His eyes widened. "No shit."

He looked back at the road, and I waited while he processed it all.

Finally, he shook his head.

"I should have seen it," he said. "None of the spooks we've caught over the years ever produced so much as a spark. Never made sense to me why they wouldn't use their magic to level us. Or, at least, save their own hides."

He cut me a look. "You going to tell the pack about this?"

"Not likely, considering I'm spelled against it. And I'm expecting you won't either."

He snorted. "Not unless you wanted total anarchy and chaos."

"That's what Kai said.

"He's smart."

My chest panged. Kai *was* smart. I was the idiot, apparently, who ran her mouth and got her mate locked up.

"Sounds like you two had quite the adventure," Oscar said.

"There's something else. Kai didn't rescue me like I said. They had enough firepower aimed at us to start World War Three. No way were we getting out of there in one piece."

"How'd you get back?" he asked, suspicion knitting his brows together.

"I made a deal."

"Ash, goddammit."

"It was the only way to walk out of there," I said.

His mouth was a thin line as we pulled into the gravel lot behind the Throttle. "What deal?"

"They think I'm their chosen one. The curse breaker. Except, they don't give a shit about helping the wolves. They want me to get their magic back. So, I promised if they let me go, I'd find a way to do that."

He parked and cut the engine, turning to me with a fierce expression.

"If you tell me you sealed it in blood, I swear to—"

"I didn't have a choice. They would have shot Kai."

Oscar swore fiercely.

"I'm sorry," I said, shoulders sagging. The last thing I wanted was to be on Oscar's bad side. Especially now that Kai was a prisoner.

"Don't apologize, kid. You're doing the best you can with what you've got."

His words surprised me into silence.

He twisted so he could face me more fully and said, "I'm damn proud of your bravery and smarts in all this, Ash. But look, you can't do this alone. And I'm here, so don't be afraid to tell me things. I just found you, so I'm damn sure not going to lose you so soon, do you understand me?"

I nodded, my eyes welling with tears.

"Thank you, Uncle Oscar."

He looked away.

It was the first time I'd ever called him uncle. And Oscar always got weird about the affectionate stuff. But we'd have to both get used to it because we were family now.

"Let's get you inside," he said in a gruff voice.

He got out of the truck, and I followed, letting him lead the way into the back door of the shop. My steps felt a bit lighter. Not just because I'd needed to tell someone the whole truth but because Oscar felt safe. And I didn't take that for granted.

"You go on up and grab a shower," Oscar said. "I'll wait downstairs for the twins."

"Thanks."

I made my way up to the apartment and went straight to the shower, turning it up as hot as it would go. For the next few minutes, I did my best to let the grime and fear and craziness of the last twenty-four hours wash away. By the time I was done, I'd steamed up the entire room, and my stomach was growling.

I'd just finished dressing when the door opened, and I heard footsteps entering the apartment. I rounded the corner from my bedroom, unsurprised to see the twins shoving their way in, hands full of shopping bags. Behind them were two more additions whose faces were the last I'd ever expected to see here.

Silas. And, slouching beside him, Presley.

"What the hell are you doing here?" I snapped, glaring at them both.

"I told you she'd be pissed," Isaac said.

"Shut it," Idrissa told him. She looked at me, expression pleading. "Just hear them out, okay? Then you can kick my ass and throw them out."

I crossed my arms. "Where's Oscar?"

"Downstairs. On the phone again," Idrissa said.

I frowned. Who the hell was he calling?

"Ash," Idrissa prompted.

I rolled my eyes. "Fine. What do you two want?"

Presley merely smirked. Or maybe that was his resting expression.

Silas stepped forward, looking just as cool about getting thrown out as he did being invited inside. "Kai's being held alone," he said. "Thought you'd want to know I requested he stay that way. For his own protection."

"Protection from what?"

"Fights." He paused as if waiting for me to understand. When I didn't respond, he went on. "Drake isn't the only one who wants to challenge Kai. Or didn't you notice all the tension in that room earlier?"

"Of course I noticed," I snapped. "I just assumed they all wanted to kill me."

Silas snickered. "You're not entirely wrong."

Idrissa smacked him.

"But," he added, "Kai's the only one powerful enough to actually be a contender for alpha. Besides you."

Silas thought I was a contender?

"I don't want to be alpha," I said.

He shrugged. "Doesn't really matter what you want."

Idrissa smacked him again. "Ash, listen to me. You and Kai mating… it set things in motion. And it can't be stopped."

I bit my lip, resentful toward Silas for helping Kai when I couldn't. I didn't want to be his friend. Hell, I didn't even want to be his ally. But I wanted to be his enemy even less.

"You're wrong," I said, the edge in my voice gone. "There is one way to stop it."

"Drake thinks if he fights Kai for alpha, he'll keep you from taking the role."

Silas' matter-of-fact explanation grated on me. No, wait, it was just Silas himself.

"How do you know so much?" I demanded.

The others remained silent, clearly invested in how this exchange was going to end.

Silas cocked his head. "This curse might be new to you, but it's old news for the rest of us who've lived it our entire lives. Drake wasn't the only one doing research into it. He's just the only one who wants to murder your ass to stop it."

"Silas," Idrissa hissed. She tried smacking him again, but he moved faster this time and dodged her. She glared. "Do you want her to throw you out?"

Silas shrugged, amusement lighting his blue eyes as he stared back at me.

"I'm half hexerei," I said flatly. "Does that change your current policy on murdering me?"

Presley snorted.

Isaac's eyes bulged.

Idrissa looked irritated with both of us now.

Silas merely grinned. "Tell me something I don't know, Ashes."

I didn't know whether to be angry or relieved at his lack of surprise.

"How did you know?" I asked.

"The spook."

"From the cabin," I realized. The one he'd ordered killed when he found out I'd spoken to him. "I'm guessing he told you the same thing he told me."

"It took a hexerei to make the curse, and it will take a hexerei to break it," Silas said, repeating the hexerei's words verbatim.

Words that had been burned into my brain since the moment I'd heard them. And now, I understood.

"I can't believe you both knew this and didn't tell me," Idrissa broke in. She glared at me. "I hid bodies for you."

"I didn't really believe it myself," I said. "Not until I woke up in a cage to find a woman with my mother's eyes standing over me."

Idrissa's eyes widened. "That's why the hexerei took you, isn't it?" she asked.

"Wait. Hold the fuck up. The hexerei took you where?" Silas asked.

He sounded pissed, and I couldn't be sure at what. Hell, this was Silas. I couldn't be sure of anything with him.

"None of your business," I told him. "You've delivered your message. Thanks for helping Kai."

I looked pointedly at the door, fully expecting Silas to take the hint and march out. But he didn't move. Neither did Presley.

When I pinned Pres with a look, he shrugged. "This shit's just getting good."

I scowled and considered making good on my threat to rip his dick off.

"Ash," Idrissa began. "We could use the help."

I stared at her, wide-eyed. "Since when do you want help from the alphaholes?" I demanded.

"Alphaholes?" Presley echoed, brows lifting. "Really?"

"What? It's creative," Isaac said.

Presley snorted, looking way too pleased at the title we'd given him.

"They're the strongest in the pack," Idrissa said.

"Hey," Isaac protested.

Idrissa rolled her eyes. "Besides us, I mean."

"Hmph," Isaac said.

She looked at me. "Silas is an asshole, but he's not a monster like Drake. And he wants to help Kai. To help you."

"Okay, let's not overstate it," Silas put in.

Idrissa smacked him, and I wondered if this time, he let her. Hell, maybe we could make it a drinking game. "Be serious, Si. We have to work together if we're going to stop Drake."

Silas' eyes flashed with quiet rage.

"Do you want to see Drake become alpha?" Idrissa pressed.

"He'd never win against Kai," Presley said.

"I wouldn't put anything past him," I said. "He's not doing this alone. And I'm not talking about the pack members siding with him."

"What you said about Drake working with the spooks," Silas said. "You really saw him there?"

"Ask Kai if you don't believe me."

"I believe you," he said, and I blinked in surprise. "Look," he said, "I'm not going to sit here and braid your hair, okay? But maybe we agree the enemy of my enemy is my friend. At least for a while."

"You want to work together against Drake?" I asked warily.

"I want to see the pack come through this without destroying itself." He blew out a breath, glancing at Presley then back at me. "For what it's worth, it was never personal."

"Wow. Is that your idea of an apology? Because trying to get me killed and then telling me it wasn't personal almost makes it worse."

He shrugged. "I'm just being honest."

I glared at him. "I don't trust you."

"Noted."

We stood that way, in some kind of silent standoff, for a long moment. I could sense the others watching, waiting. Like this moment, the outcome, mattered—a lot.

Finally, Presley nudged Silas.

"Just give her the name," Presley muttered.

Silas' expression tightened. He didn't take his eyes off me.

"What name?" I asked, my gaze never wavering either.

It felt like some sort of childish staring contest. Except that my wolf was treating it like the precursor to war.

Silas's nostrils flared. Lines appeared across his forehead as if he were concentrating. Or straining. I could feel my wolf growing larger inside me like she was making herself big.

Dominant. Demanding ... what exactly? Submission?

It felt a little like what Warren had done at the meeting earlier.

And just like before, the others looked down, moving a step back even.

This was so weird.

Silas grunted. And just like that, he blinked and looked away.

Inside, my wolf smiled, satisfied.

"Holy shit, Ash," Isaac began. "You just—"

"Vinny," Silas said quietly.

"What?"

I couldn't even remember what we'd been talking about.

"The name," Silas said.

"The guy who bit you," Presley put in.

"It was Vinny?" Idrissa went from looking rattled to raging in less than a breath. "I'm going to murder that piece of—"

"No."

My voice was strong enough that Idrissa fell silent.

"We can't hurt him," I said. "It'll only fuel Drake's campaign against me if we commit violence."

"Okay, then what do you want us to do?" Presley asked.

The rest of them fell silent, clearly waiting for an answer.

I rolled my eyes. "Fine. You guys want to help take Drake down, then help. Follow him. Investigate. Find proof he's working with the hexerei."

"What are you going to do?" Presley asked.

I opened my mouth to answer, but Silas cut me off. "Don't say you're going to free Kai."

I glared at him. "Why not?"

"Because Kai can handle himself, and you don't know shit about how things work here. You'll only make it worse. Besides, he can't have a visitor right now. I already checked."

Before my temper could spill over, Isaac stepped between us.

"Ash, Silas is kinda right. Don't hit me," he added quickly as I turned my glare on him. "Kai being locked up means he can't fight Drake, which is a good thing."

"So we just let him stay in prison for the rest of his life?" I demanded.

"Of course not. It's a short-term solution. But it buys us time to figure this out." I huffed, unwilling to admit out loud that he had a point. "And, Silas, Presley, Ash is right too," Isaac went on. "We have no reason to trust you. So, if you want to help, go help. But we're not sharing state secrets until we have assurances. Capiche?"

When no one answered, he continued, obviously taking our silence as agreement. "Okay, great. Silas and Presley will get eyes on Drake. Keep tabs. See where he goes. Work on that proof. Ash, Dris, and I will work on breaking the last of the curse. And Kai will be safe where he is," he added, giving me a pointed look, "until his situation is all sorted out. Now. Blink twice if you agree."

Silas muttered something, but it didn't sound like a refusal.

Isaac turned to me. "Ash?"

"Whatever," I muttered.

"Idrissa?" Isaac said.

"What do I have to do with this?"

"You're going to stop managing everyone," Isaac said. Idrissa opened her mouth, but Isaac held up a hand. "No backroom deals. No under the table side promises. Nothing. Not unless they specifically ask for it."

Idrissa deflated. "Fine. But it's not my fault if this little alliance backfires."

"Aww." Isaac beamed at us. "Look at us all playing nice."

"Are we done?" Silas asked.

"Very," I said.

"I'll call you when I hear anything," he said, shoving past Isaac to the apartment door.

"Later, curse breaker," Presley said before following Silas out.

When the door shut behind them, Isaac whooped.

"Now, that was some sexual tension," he announced. "Did you feel that?"

Not bothering to respond, Idrissa pushed past him into the living room and sank onto the couch.

"Tell me you felt that?" Isaac said, looking at me.

"Uh, I felt tension. Not sure it was sexual."

"Are we going to talk about what happened to Ash or what?" Idrissa interrupted, looking back at us from the couch.

"Right." Isaac's eyes lit up. He grabbed me in a hug and squeezed so tightly I struggled for breath. "I can't believe you were kidnapped by the spooks."

"Relax," I told him. "I'm fine."

"Pssh. Of course you are." He stepped back and grabbed my hand, leading me to the couch where Idrissa waited. "Tell us everything, baby girl."

Glad to be off my feet, I sank onto the couch opposite Idrissa as Isaac lowered himself to the floor, reaching for the duffel he'd brought.

"Well," I began. "Kai and I were headed out of town like we discussed. We nearly made it too before the hexerei crashed into our car. It was a mess. Broken glass. Kai and I were pretty banged up. Then this hexerei got out of his van like it was nothing and dragged me out of the car."

"Kai didn't stop them?" Isaac asked, looking up from the box of nail polish he'd pulled out.

"No, he . . . was too injured to shift." My muscles tensed as I remembered what those moments had been like. Not knowing if Kai would be okay. "He passed out, and that was when they took me."

"Did they hurt you?" Idrissa asked, leaning forward. I could see the wrath written in her eyes. If I said yes, she'd burn them all to the ground. It was a comforting sentiment, although I still wasn't sure how to feel about the witches considering I was related to some of them.

"No," I said. "Not on purpose. I tried to fight back and hit my head, but otherwise, the only thing they did was inject me with something that knocked me out and made it impossible to shift."

"Nightshade," Idrissa said, looking ready to break something.

"What? How do you know?"

"It's an herb that mutes our wolf," she said. "Makes it impossible to shift. We don't allow it grown anywhere nearby for obvious reasons. Of course, the witches would know about it, though."

I frowned, thinking past my abduction to my life before Ridley Falls. "Would it mute someone's wolf so much that they never even knew they had one?"

"If given enough of it, why?" Idrissa's gaze searched mine knowingly. "You think that's why you never shifted before coming here?"

"I don't know. The more I learn about this curse, the more convinced I am that my parents had something to do with creating it."

Isaac looked up from where he'd spread bottles of nail polish across the coffee table.

"Ash, what are you saying right now?" he asked slowly.

Part of me didn't want to say it, but I couldn't ignore it any longer.

"I think the hexerei who cast the curse was my mother."

Quickly, I told them about everything that had happened with Cohen and the witches. Including Kel and

Arnie, my aunt, and the fact that I was, apparently, not just one of them but the daughter of the rightful coven leader.

"I think my parents created the curse," I finished, hating the pain that came with the words. But I had to face the truth. No more hiding or pretending. Ignorance was not going to make this go away.

"This shit is bananas," Isaac said in a soft voice.

"Isaac, are you really quoting Gwen Stefani right now?" Idrissa demanded.

"What better time is there?" he challenged. When she didn't answer, he huffed. "B-A-N-A-N-A-S."

Idrissa groaned.

"There's more," I said, and I couldn't be entirely sure about the decision I was about to make, but my gut said to trust them. Oscar was right. I couldn't do this alone. "The hexerei say I'm their chosen one too. They want me to help break the curse on them."

"Whoa, the spooks have a curse too?" Isaac looked interested, but it wasn't out of concern.

Still, I went with my intuition. "The hexerei lost their magic. And they want me to help them get it back."

There it was again. Definitely immune. Maybe the whole blood oath thing didn't work on me after all.

Idrissa's eyes widened. "Holy shit. No magic? Are you serious?"

"Wait." Isaac shook his head in confusion. "How did they mute your wolf without magic? Don't they need a spell or something to activate the nightshade?"

"Nope," Idrissa said, popping the "p" angrily. She shook her head. "They've been using nothing but natural herbs and remedies this whole time, and we never noticed the difference." She looked from Isaac to me. "That means they're completely vulnerable."

"I wouldn't go that far," I said. "They had enough guns to arm a small country."

"Guns are a threat, sure," Idrissa said, "But they're more useful as a defense. What they want is an offense, isn't it?"

I nodded. "Cohen hates the wolves. I don't know why because Kel and some of the others seemed neutral or at least unwilling to be cruel about it."

Idrissa's eyes glittered with a violence that easily matched Cohen's. That girl scared me. Good thing she was on our side.

"I don't get it," Isaac said into the silence that followed. "What could Drake have possibly been doing in a camp full of magicless witches? I mean, they might as well be human at this point."

"Drake must have a deal with them," I said. "Maybe it was about me, but something tells me it's bigger than that."

"Silas and Presley will find out what it is," Isaac said.

I wasn't sure I shared his confidence in those two, but Drake would never let his guard down if I was around. Maybe with those two, he would.

"In the meantime, we need to figure out this curse," Idrissa said. "All three stages, if Drake was telling the truth."

I bit my lip. "I think he was, about that part at least."

"Stage one, mating. Stage two, alpha," Idrissa said, and I winced at that part. "Stage three…magic?"

I nodded.

"Where do we start?" Isaac asked.

"That part's simple. We approach this one at a time," Idrissa said. "Sort of like our curse and theirs. Obviously, we focus on our problems first."

"I don't think it's that easy," I said. "Cohen wants to

destroy the wolves. I can't let him do that, but I also swore an oath to get their magic back."

"Wait. You swore an oath to the spooks?" Isaac said, looking at me like I was insane.

"It was the only way to leave without dodging bullets," I said.

"She did what she had to do," Idrissa told her brother. Then she turned to me. "An oath is not a small thing, but right now, we have to think about the most pressing problem: the pack's unrest," Idrissa said. "Some of them are one road rage away from losing it entirely."

"Dris is right, Ash. We're running out of time. In fact, I think shit might have gotten crazier since you and Kai mated."

"Dammit," I muttered.

"Stage two," Isaac added with a pointed look aimed at me. "You have to become alpha."

"How do we know that's safe, though?" I asked. "What if undoing it for us undoes it for them too?"

"You mean, what if you becoming alpha is the thing that gives them their magic?" Isaac asked.

"Yes. Exactly. How do we know that won't happen?"

Idrissa didn't answer.

Neither did Isaac.

I tried not to let that frustrate me. It wasn't their fault. We'd all been saddled with a problem created two decades before us. A problem my own parents had likely created. For the first time since my mother had left me, I wished she were here. Not in a warm fuzzy way. Mostly so I could demand answers.

Why had she done this? If it had been her at all.

And why had she spent her life covering it up?

If I had the mark, I would find out what it meant eventually. Especially without her there to keep me in the dark about everything.

It didn't make sense. All it did was raise more questions.

And if I was sick of one thing, it was questions.

I stood, frustrated and tired and aching at the idea of Kai locked away somewhere.

"I can't sit here anymore," I said, heading for the door.

Idrissa jumped up. "Where are you going?"

"To get answers."

Oscar wasn't in the shop when I got downstairs. In fact, no one was. The emptiness felt eerie after everything else. It took me a moment to remember it was Sunday. We were closed on Sundays. Still, it was a strange feeling, having the place so still and quiet. No air compressors running. No wrenches being turned. At least, Drake wasn't here. I shuddered to think about the kind of toxic work environment that awaited me tomorrow when we were all back together again.

At the far end of the garage, I glanced out the window and spotted Oscar pacing the gravel lot out back, still on the phone. Behind me, Idrissa and Isaac were hurrying to catch up, but I didn't wait for them before flinging the back door open and marching out into the late afternoon sun.

Oscar whirled, and when his eyes landed on mine, he seemed to understand something was up.

"I'll call you back," he said to whoever was on the other end.

Then he hung up.

"What is it?" he asked.

"I need to go back to the witch's camp," I said.

"Are you crazy?" Without waiting for an answer, he shook his head, "No way, it's too dangerous."

"I met someone there," I said. "She was kind to me."

He grunted at that.

"Okay, kind considering the circumstances," I amended. "She didn't condone Cohen's methods."

"Ash," he began. "These people held you against your will."

"And Kel made sure they let me go," I insisted. "Oscar, she knows things about the curse. I need to find out what if I'm going to end this. You said yourself that I can't do it alone."

"Not what I meant," he said dryly. "I can't let you put yourself at risk."

"Then come with me."

He scowled, glancing from me to the twins who'd come up behind me. When his expression became more of an amused appraisal, I glanced back to find them striking contrasting poses on either side of me. Idrissa stood, feet planted, hands fisted, eyes gleaming with the yearning for a fight. Isaac had angled himself away so his back was toward me, his hand on his hip and leg bent just enough to make him look sassy.

"You guys look like Charlie's Angels," Oscar said on a half-laugh.

"Who?" I asked.

"Never mind." He looked back at me with scrutiny. "What exactly do you think this Kel can do for you anyway?"

"Drake said the curse breaks down in stages," I said.

Oscar growled, and I nodded.

"I don't want to take his word for it any more than you

do. We need a second opinion, and since no one in the pack seems to know anything, we have to look outside for answers."

"You think this Kel has those answers?" Oscar asked.

"I don't know, but she was helpful once already. And we don't have any other options."

He ran his hand over his head.

"Fine. We go tonight. After dark. And if anything looks shady, we haul ass, am I clear?"

"Crystal."

He looked at the twins.

"Absolutely," Idrissa said.

"Ten-four," Isaac chirped.

Both of them looked thrilled at the idea of what we'd just planned.

"Good." Oscar stalked back toward the shop. "Now let's order pizza. I'm starving."

Three hours later, I'd eaten pizza and tried everything I knew to use the mate bond to contact Kai. My first choice had been to see him in person. I'd even called the police station to ask but was told in no uncertain terms that Kai Stone would not be permitted visitors until further notice.

"I don't know why you're straining yourself for this if you've never done it before. Telepathy isn't common among bonded mates," Idrissa said.

"I know. But I have to do something."

"How do you even know about it?" Isaac asked.

"I overheard someone at the council meeting asking about whether we'd fully bonded," I said. "They mentioned being able to communicate in our minds."

"It's very rare, so stop beating yourself up." Idrissa uncapped a bottle of water and took a long drink.

"You can feel him, though, right?" Isaac asked. "When you're together?"

He sat beside me on the couch, both of us with our feet propped on the coffee table so our toenails could dry. Isaac had painted ours to match so both of us now had black polish with hot pink stripes. A compromise since Isaac wanted pink and I wanted something to match my mood. Or maybe my soul.

"Yes, I can," I said on a sigh. "But we're too far away for me to feel him now. My wolf doesn't like the distance. Or the not knowing."

Neither of us did.

"He's safe," Isaac said. "That's what matters."

I didn't answer. Safe and absent was not good enough for me. Not when I already had a mother living that life.

"Wheels up in ten," Oscar announced as he strode from his bedroom to the door. He'd gone in to change a moment ago and now wore dark jeans, heavy-looking boots that clicked when they hit the floor, and a black leather vest with the wolf pack logo on the back.

With his salt and pepper hair and hard-as-granite gaze, he looked like a badass motorcycle thug. Except that he was so much more than that.

I grabbed the bag I planned to use for my own clothes, and the three of us followed him downstairs and met in the back lot of the Throttle.

Oscar stopped in front of a giant red and brown motorcycle with the word "Indian" painted across the gas tank.

"Okay, look," he said, "We're driving out so we have a way of getting back that doesn't include our wolves."

"Our wolves are just as fast as this," Isaac pointed out.

"Not if our wolves are injured," he said pointedly.

"I see your point." Isaac frowned.

"Here." Oscar handed me a set of keys.

"What's this?" I asked.

"One of my customers traded his truck for payment last month. No one who sees it will trace it back to us."

"You're not riding with us?" I asked.

"Having more than one vehicle will help if something goes wrong. And my bike is faster than the truck."

"Okay."

I didn't want to ask what could go wrong. It was better not to know.

"Take the truck to the county limits," he said. "Park at the edge of the tree line near Rainer Farm. It's the closest access point from our borders to theirs." He looked at Idrissa. "You two help her find it." They nodded. "Park there and wait for me. I'll hang back and be sure we're not followed. Any questions?"

"No, I'm good," I said.

He grabbed his helmet. "See you there."

The twins and I piled into Oscar's truck. Idrissa directed me to take back roads, avoiding driving through the middle of downtown. Oscar gave us a head start, and despite constantly checking my rearview, I never saw him or anyone else behind us.

The twins were noticeably silent as we drove.

"You both think I'm crazy, don't you?" I said.

Beside me, Idrissa snorted. "Have you forgotten what kind of pack we come from? Crazy is normal around here."

"True," I said. "Must be why I fit in."

She shot me a sideways smirk. "Besides," she added, "I want to meet a hexerei I don't intend to kill. Well, unless she tries to kill us first."

"No one is killing anyone tonight," I said firmly. "Isaac?"

He looked up from where he sat staring out the window.

"You good?" I asked.

"I don't know," he said with none of his characteristic snark. "I don't have a great feeling about this."

"We're sneaking into enemy territory to ask for help from the one group of people who'd dance on our graves," Idrissa said with a snort. "No one feels great."

Isaac didn't answer and turned back to the window. My stomach tightened as I tried to remember when, if ever, Isaac Close had tried talking us out of something crazy. But that had happened exactly never before. So, the weight of it now felt like lead against my bones.

Finally, we reached the pull-off and parked.

Climbing out of the truck, I shook off Isaac's words, refusing to let it get into my head. We were doing this. I couldn't afford to doubt my decision now that we were here.

Underneath a sliver of moon, we all stripped. I shoved my clothes into the bag I'd brought and then shifted while we waited for Oscar.

The twins' wolves were gorgeous. Matching dark brown fur with a streak of auburn across their noses. The only discerning detail between them was the red tip on Idrissa's tail.

Incredible.

The moment we were all on four paws, Isaac sauntered over and nudged his shoulder to mine in hello.

Idrissa stood back, scanning the woods and road in turn.

I tried to do the same, using my newly heightened senses to detect any movement or danger lurking nearby.

But everything was still.

It wasn't long before I heard the sound of Oscar's

engine. A moment later, he pulled off the road and parked. Instead of joining us and shifting into his wolf, he reached into a side compartment and pulled out a couple of pieces of black metal. I watched while he clicked them together then pulled out a few more smaller pieces, screwing it all together to assemble whatever he'd had stashed.

Finally, he turned and joined us, a rifle propped against his shoulder.

Wow.

He'd had that thing tucked into his bike's storage?

"Okay, I'm staying back and out sight," he said. "If anything goes wrong, you all get the hell out and meet back here."

I stared at the gun he carried, unsure how to feel about it.

"Relax, kid." Oscar caught my eye. "We have one compared to their hundred. I'm just evening the odds a bit. And I won't use it unless they attack first."

One look at his expression, and I knew there would be no talking him out of bringing it.

He had promised not to fire unless they did first. It would have to be good enough.

With a weird sort of nod from Idrissa, we all turned for the woods and headed in. I carried my bag of clothes in my teeth like I'd seen Drake do before. It felt strange at first, and I drooled a bit until I got used to it.

Darkness quickly closed in around us with only Oscar's footfalls making a sound, and even that was muted compared to a human. But my wolf's eyesight adjusted easily, and I marveled at how clearly I could make out, well, everything.

It was amazing.

Everything was sharper.

And not just my eyesight.

Sounds, smells, and more than that—a knowing. The farther we walked, the more my instincts seemed to lead me rather than deferring to Idrissa, who walked just ahead—a slight curve to the right here, a slant to the left there.

By the time Idrissa came to a silent halt, I knew we'd arrived at the border between our lands and the hexerei's.

Something inside me simply *felt* the change.

Somewhere behind us, Oscar's footsteps stopped too, and I knew exactly which tree he decided to climb in order to wait and watch. My wolf instincts were getting sharper every time I shifted. It was kind of cool.

Idrissa and Isaac both waited as I darted around a tree to shift, slipping into the clothes that were stashed in the bag I'd carried in my teeth.

When I was dressed again, I stepped out.

Isaac grumbled, which I suspected was a laugh at my attempt at continued modesty.

"Not all of us grew up seeing each other's parts," I defended.

Isaac flashed his teeth, his fur shaking in laughter.

Idrissa just looked focused.

"Okay, you two stay here," I said.

They both growled in protest.

"You knew this was coming," I said, impatient to get moving now that I was so close. "If you get spotted on the other side, they'll shoot first and ask questions never."

Idrissa still looked pissed.

Instead of growling again, she simply shifted.

Back on two legs, she breezed past me to the bag I'd left behind the tree.

"Idrissa," I began.

I heard a shuffling of fabric, and then she stepped into view again, wearing a familiar dress.

"That's mine," I said in surprise. "I bought it at the thrift store."

"I know." She gave me a smug look and then rejoined us. "Looks nice, doesn't it?" She did a quick flourish that had my mouth dropping open. "Ash, you can't go in alone. It's bad strategy."

I started to interrupt, but she cut me off. "Isaac will stay here as a go-between for Oscar." Isaac pouted at that, but she ignored him. "I'll come with you as a liaison between you and Isaac. Think about it. What if you run into Cohen instead of Kel? Or worse, an armed guard who doesn't recognize you as the chosen one? You'll be shot. Or, at the very least, recaptured. If I'm there, I can get word to Isaac, and he can get word to Oscar." She paused to let her words sink in before adding, "You both knew this was coming."

I glared at her. "Hilarious."

She smirked, a hand on her hip. In the moonlight, her red hair nearly glowed.

"Fine," I said. "Let's go."

The forest seemed to get darker as we went. Or thicker. My senses made seeing easy enough, but the feeling of being watched only grew stronger until goosebumps rose along my arms and neck.

Idrissa grabbed my hand, stopping me abruptly.

"Someone's here," she said so quietly I almost missed it.

I inhaled, catching an unfamiliar scent and the unmistakable presence of a body just ahead.

They hadn't announced themselves.

But they hadn't shot us yet either.

I tried to take the latter as a good sign.

"I need to speak with Kel," I said into the quiet.

I kept my voice low. Who knew how many hexerei were out here guarding the perimeter, but we had one thing they didn't: supernatural hearing. As long as I kept my voice low, hopefully, it wouldn't bring the entire army running.

For a long moment, no one answered. The presence just ahead didn't move either.

I hesitated.

Attacking whoever stood ahead was probably a bad idea considering their weapons. But we couldn't afford to give them time to call reinforcements.

My mouth went dry as I considered all possible scenarios.

Any longer, and we risked more of them finding us.

Or maybe they were already on their way now that they'd found us on their land.

"Ash?" came a low voice.

Beside me, Idrissa didn't move a muscle. I tried to determine who the voice belonged to, but it was too soft to know for sure.

"I need to speak with Kel," I said again with way more confidence than I felt.

Footsteps sounded as the body lurking ahead moved toward us. A face came into view.

Narrow cheekbones. A braid. And piercing green eyes.

Kel.

"It's me," she said. "What are you doing here?"

I frowned, trying to figure out what was happening. It felt too easy, Kel being out here to meet us. My senses went on immediate alert.

"How did you know I was coming?" I asked.

Had this all been a trap?

Idrissa scanned the trees around us, and I was

suddenly glad I'd brought her. She was right. I couldn't talk to Kel and watch my own back.

"It's complicated," Kel said.

An answer that did zero good against my suspicions.

"This is way too easy," Idrissa hissed. "We should go."

"Easy?" Kel snorted. "Hardly. I nearly got myself shot sneaking up on the sentries so that I could dose them with valerian. We have a ten-minute window before the next patrol comes by. Whatever you came to say, do it fast."

"You knew I was coming," I said again.

Kel sighed. "I recently came into the ability to see things."

"Clairvoyance," Idrissa said.

"Yes."

She gave Idrissa a look that dared her to try and insult the ability. But my heart raced with what this meant.

"How long ago?" I asked.

"I woke up at three this morning with, well, let's just say clarity about a number of things."

Supernatural clarity from the sound of it. In other words, her magic had returned. Or, at least, parts of it.

So the wolves weren't the only ones regaining what they'd lost, which meant I'd been right. The two were intertwined, not separate issues like Idrissa had suggested.

"Does Cohen know?" I asked.

"Hell, no. And I intend to keep it that way."

Her tone was sardonic. But there was so much complexity to the way she spoke about him.

"If you hate him so much, why don't you just take his place?" Idrissa asked.

Kel gave her a hard look. "Is stealing leadership that easy with your kind? Because it's a bit more complicated here."

"He acted scared of me," I said. "So did his little lapdog. The one with the Hex tattoo."

"Cohen and the others revere you," she said. "Or they did before they knew the curse breaker was the daughter of their greatest traitor." She eyed me with a look that seemed almost sympathetic. "If you'd been anyone else, they would have rolled out the red carpet and treated you like a queen."

"Anyone but Claudia's daughter?" I asked.

"Anyone but a lupin. Nine minutes," she added pointedly.

Whatever she'd done to distract the guards, it had a specific expiration.

Idrissa nudged me. "Hurry up."

"I need to know what you know about the curse," I said.

"Can you be more specific? I've been hearing about the curse my whole life. Not exactly a short answer."

"What do you know about how it will be broken?" Idrissa asked.

"Well, Cohen thinks it's as simple as a transfer of power," Kel said, derision lacing her words.

"What do *you* think?" I asked.

"Considering my magic's returned but not the others, I think it's going to break in stages."

Stages. Exactly like Drake had said.

Ugh. I did not want him to be right about this.

"How do you know the others don't have their magic too?" Idrissa challenged.

Kel gave her a look. "If Cohen or any of his supporters had magic, trust me, we'd know."

"The wolves are gaining theirs in stages too," I said. "Alpha callings so far." Idrissa shushed me, but I ignored her. "We're trying to figure out what triggered it and what I can do to trigger the rest."

Or not do.

I didn't say that part.

"What have you done out of the ordinary?" Kel asked.

I snorted. That was a long fucking list starting with coming to live with an uncle I never knew I had and ending with this conversation I was currently having with both a witch and a werewolf while risking our lives to men with guns. "I wouldn't know where to start."

"I meant anything that might remotely relate to the curse," Kel said.

Idrissa looked at me. "Kai."

Right. Kai.

"The guy who came here to get you," Kel said.

I nodded. "We … mated," I said, my cheeks heating as I stumbled over the words that basically meant I'd had deeply satisfying sex with a guy who was sometimes more predator than human.

Idrissa bit back a laugh.

"Anyway, we think that's what started the, uh, gifts returning," I said. "But what we don't understand is what to do next. How to break the curse completely."

Kel nodded. Even in the darkness, her expression seemed only focused. No judgment or disgust at what I'd just told her. If anything, she seemed encouraging.

"Hmm. I did hear a theory once," she said.

"What theory?" I asked.

"Well, most magic is pretty straightforward. If you want something done, you cast for it using your power of intention and clear language. But if that's true, any witch should be able to break this curse by simply casting for it."

"Please tell me someone has at least tried that," Idrissa said.

"Believe me, Cohen has spared no expense in bringing in supposed experts. Wizards, witches, even a sorceress. Nothing worked. That's when he started researching the counterbalance. Every bit of magic has one, and Ash is ours."

"What does this have to do with the theory?" I asked.

"According to my mother, the magic your mom used in those days had a certain flair to it. A distinct style." She smiled fondly. "It's what made her such a great witch. She didn't do things by the book, you know?"

Idrissa huffed. "You can say that again."

"What's the theory?" I asked.

"She thinks your mom built in the answer to the actual spell she used to cast the curse," Kel said.

"What was the spell?" I asked, unable to hold back my excitement. We were already closer than we'd ever gotten before.

"The only part that was recovered was this: Death over a life. Life over a death. In the end, a wolf and a demon must choose each other."

Idrissa and I exchanged a look.

"What?" Kel asked.

"We may have come across that language somewhere," I said. "But what does it mean?"

Kel shrugged. "Hell if I know. But it has three parts."

My shoulders sagged.

"How do you know that's the actual spell?" Idrissa asked.

She hesitated, and I could tell she was holding something back.

"Whatever you know, holding it back will only prolong this whole process," I told her. "If you want your magic back, you have to tell me what you know."

"All right. Claudia's ritual instruments were found at a

campsite near the border the morning the curse began. Along with remnants of a fire. She tried to burn the paper she'd written the spell on, but I guess she left in a hurry, and those words were recovered."

"Found by who?" I asked. No one else had mentioned this kind of proof before. It was damning, for sure. The final evidence that my mom had truly been the one to do this.

"My mother," she said quietly.

"The one with the theory," Idrissa said.

Kel nodded. "They were friends. And, of course, family. She knew Claudia better than anyone." Her eyes flashed as she added, "Well, besides your dad, I guess."

"Wait. Did you say your mother and mine are related?"

Kel cocked her head at me. "You met her when you were here," she said. "She didn't tell you?"

Finally, it clicked into place. "Arnie."

I couldn't believe I hadn't seen the resemblance before.

"Let me get this straight," Idrissa said. "You two are…cousins?"

Kel and I studied each other.

"Cohen's not my father," she added. "Does that win me any points?" Kel asked, arching a brow.

I snorted. "What do you need points for when you have a blood oath and an army of gunpower?"

Kel's expression darkened. "Cohen's methods are not a reflection of the entire coven."

"Your mom sure seemed to be playing for his side when she pretended to let me escape and instead sent me running right into Cohen's trap."

Kel's mouth tightened. "My mom walks a fine line," she said quietly. "She's not a warrior, like us. And she does what she must to survive."

To survive? I wanted to ask what that meant, exactly.

But Kel's expression slackened as if she'd suddenly fallen asleep.

"Kel," I whispered uncertainly.

She swayed.

"Kel," I hissed again.

I reached over and grabbed her arm, and her entire body jolted with shock. The shadows of the forest were swept away, and I sucked in a sharp breath as I was transported to...well, somewhere not here. Colors, vibrant as the sun, lit every angle, but mostly it was white light radiating outward from the exact place where I stood. I looked up and met Kel's eyes, knowing instinctively, wherever we'd gone, we were here but not.

Somewhere in between reality and immortality.

Kel's skin glowed with the light surrounding us.

"What is this place?" I heard myself say.

Had my lips moved? I wasn't entirely sure they had.

Kel's eyes filled with tears, and she leaned in, breathing one word at me. "Magic."

Something slithered in from the outside.

Maybe it was only my sense of awareness—this couldn't possibly be real life. Maybe I'd hit my head. Maybe security had found us and killed us after all. Maybe this was the afterlife.

Whatever it was, it snapped me back to where I stood. In the dark forest beside Idrissa. Asking Kel for answers that made sense.

I blinked, coming back to myself.

Immediately, I dropped my hand from Kel's arm, severing our physical connection.

"What the hell was that?" Idrissa demanded, but she sounded a bit awed underneath her wariness.

"That," Kel said, shaking herself and then straightening again, "was magic."

She looked right at me.

"Was that your clairvoyance?" I asked. "Showing us something?"

She shook her head. "That wasn't anything like what I have."

The way she looked at me felt unsettling. I wanted to ask what she meant, but something held me back.

The silence was broken by a soft buzzing. Kel checked her phone.

"Our time is up. I have to get back," she said. "I'm sorry I wasn't more help."

"You have been," I said. "And I appreciate you meeting us like this."

"It's the least I can do. You've already given me more than I gave you."

"I'll come back," I said. "When I figure all this out."

"I know you will."

"You trust me? Just like that, huh?"

She gave me a strange look. "I can feel you in my blood, Ash. Don't you?"

I didn't answer.

The knowing I'd felt about the border. About someone being out here. Was there more to the blood oath than a simple promise?

Somewhere in the forest, a branch cracked.

A footstep.

"We need to go," Idrissa said.

"I'll be in touch." I started backing away.

"Hey. Ash," Kel called.

I looked up. "Yeah?"

"Be careful," she said. "I see a line being drawn by your kind. Take care to notice who's on which side of it.

I nodded, and then Idrissa and I turned and hurried back the way we'd come. With our meeting behind us, I focused on getting the hell back to pack lands.

The sound of footsteps became louder. Closer.

My heart pounded.

Idrissa signaled me, and we broke into a run.

Up ahead, I spotted Isaac where we'd left him, pacing back and forth. When he saw us, he stopped, hackles rising as the footsteps reached his sensitive ears.

The moment we reached the border, we both stripped and shifted.

This time, I didn't waste time ducking behind a tree. And I damn sure didn't stop to see who was looking at what. All I cared about was getting out. Hopefully, Oscar would stay hidden until the danger had passed.

The footsteps came closer.

We were still near the boundary line; too exposed.

Signaling the twins, I took off at a run for the truck.

10

I ran faster than I ever had before. Considering I'd only been a wolf a handful of times so far, that might not have been saying much. But to a girl who'd never thought she was anything but human—and a terrible runner to boot—I felt like a bullet being shot from a gun.

Pure speed.

Adrenaline. Instinct. Raw animal power.

My paws hit the ground and pushed off again until the ground barely registered beneath my feet.

It was amazing; like nothing I'd experienced before.

Somewhere along the way, I gave over completely to the moment and just let my wolf have the reins.

My instincts flared brighter and stronger than ever.

Smells filled my nose, new scents with every inhale.

The dirt beneath me; the difference between dry ground and wet earth. I knew exactly where to place my feet to keep from getting bogged down in mud.

Sounds. Sensations.

A heartbeat.

I sniffed, never breaking stride. Oscar.

He'd gone ahead to wait for us at the truck.

I had no idea how I knew that, I just did.

Behind me, the twins had fallen back some. Or I'd gained. I wasn't even sure, but I couldn't make myself slow. My wolf needed this too damn much. Through the bond, I felt Kai's yearning for this kind of freedom right now.

And then the sound of a snarl.

A thud.

No one had to explain it. I knew the exact moment Isaac was knocked to the ground somewhere behind me. The way his flesh was torn open by another set of teeth.

Even before I heard his sharp animalistic cry of pain and rage, I knew.

Wolves.

Dammit, this wasn't the hexerei at our backs.

We were being hunted by our own kind.

And that meant we weren't any safer here in pack lands than we had been with Kel.

In fact, it made it all the more dangerous.

I didn't even have to rein my wolf in. She was already swinging around and speeding toward where Isaac had gone down. Nearby, I could hear Idrissa. Her wolf had sighted its prey and was already preparing to feint and counter its attack.

Not a moment's hesitation.

A blur of fur caught my eye, approaching fast, but my wolf was more than ready. I sidestepped my attacker and watched as a large grey wolf went sailing past me, missing me by more than a length.

Dumbass.

My wolf felt satisfied and smug—but out for blood.

Isaac had gotten to his feet and was going head to head

with a large brown wolf when I finally spotted him. Leaves coated his shoulder as if stuck there. Around their edges, I noted the blood.

He was injured but still well enough to stand his own.

Relief rippled through me, followed by a thirst for vengeance.

When Isaac leaped at the wolf's throat, I came at it from behind.

We took it down together, not even pausing to appreciate our kill before we were both forced to turn and fight the next one.

They came at us one at a time then two.

None of them was the wolf I wanted, though. None of them were Drake. These wolves smelled like him, though, which meant they had to be here on his orders. But the coward hadn't come himself.

Idrissa took the left, Isaac, the right, and I went straight down the middle.

Finally, my mouth and throat were so coated in blood, I wondered how I'd ever taste anything else again, a gunshot rang out.

The wolves surrounding us jumped. Shock then fear registered, and they backed away, still baring their teeth. Another shot.

This one had them turning and vanishing into the darkness.

Even their wounded managed to drag their furry asses off into the shadows.

Until only the three of us remained.

From the direction of the shot, a figure emerged. Marching like a general to war, Oscar appeared, his rifle raised and ready, scanning the area with the barrel of the gun just as much as his own eyes.

"They all gone?" he asked gruffly.

I shifted, no longer worried about modesty or decorum. Besides, with the amount of blood coating my body, nothing crucial remained visible anyway.

"They're gone," I said, drawing in a breath that tasted of wet copper.

Beside me, Idrissa shifted back too. "Should have never been here, to begin with," she ground out, still catching her breath.

Beside us, Isaac remained in wolf form, and I knew he was better off healing that way. My heart squeezed at the blood covering his fur, mostly because I knew, unlike me and Idrissa, some of it was actually his.

"You three okay?" Oscar asked.

"We're okay," I said. "Isaac—"

"He'll be okay too," Idrissa assured me, glancing up from where she'd leaned down to inspect his wound more closely. With the leaves and twigs peeled away, I saw that it wasn't as deep as I'd first suspected.

I breathed a sigh of relief.

"Thank God. Let's get to the truck before they bring round two," Oscar said.

We made it all the way out of the woods; far enough that I'd stopped looking over my shoulder for a second attack. Stupid of me. Of course, they wouldn't bother chasing after us when they knew exactly where we were going.

The moment I saw them crowded around the truck, a physical barricade between us and it, I realized what had happened earlier had only been the distraction. At least twenty wolves had formed a line, cutting us off from the truck and Oscar's bike.

I didn't care so much about the vehicles. I could easily get home without them. What I cared most about was the fact that Isaac was already injured. He didn't have the stamina to run all the way home. Not faster than they could chase. The only thing that could do that was the truck they were holding hostage. And they knew it.

Fear worked its way up my spine, and I fisted my hands to keep them from shaking.

"Get the hell out of our way," Idrissa demanded.

She'd realized the problem too.

At her words, not a single wolf budged.

Oscar leveled his rifle at the wolf standing in the very center of their ranks. Not Drake. He was nowhere in sight; still being a coward.

"Get the hell out of here, or you won't be going home with a heartbeat," Oscar warned them.

"Is that…?" I squinted.

"Vinny?" Idrissa glared daggers of rage at the brown wolf in the center of it all. "Don't worry, he's mine."

Oscar racked the gun.

"If you think I won't shoot a fellow wolf, you're dead wrong," Oscar told them in a voice that I could only hope they knew to take seriously. "You're threatening my family now. Forcing me to choose. And that ain't right, but make no mistake, I'm choosing my niece. Now git."

The wolf in the center bared its teeth and growled at us.

Fucking Vinny.

Idrissa had been right all along. He needed a good knocking out. And after what he'd done to me—biting me, triggering my wolf—I wanted to be the one to do it.

"Our move," I muttered.

"We can't run," Idrissa said.

"Don't plan on it," Oscar said.

"We shift," Idrissa said under her breath. "In three . . . two . . . one."

We shifted in unison. Oscar too. He dropped the gun

and chose to shred his clothes instead of wasting time peeling them off. I knew he could do more damage as a wolf anyway.

The wolves didn't back down.

If anything, our shifting only egged them on.

Vinny growled, which was, apparently, the signal.

They attacked as one, and the moments that followed were a blur of blood and fur, but my wolf didn't falter for a single second of it all.

If anything, their threat to Isaac had snapped what little control I had left.

There wasn't much left of *me* in what was happening now.

Only her. My wolf.

But the fight was too big. Twenty against four was batshit, and I realized very quickly that we weren't getting out of this. Not with Isaac's injury. And I'd die before leaving him behind.

Unfortunately, that's exactly what would happen if we didn't figure out how to end this.

My wolf took over then.

Like switching drivers, one second, I still had a say, and the next, she was running the show. I saw it all happening at once.

Idrissa baring her teeth at three wolves all stalking toward her. Oscar pinning one wolf while two more crept toward him from behind. Isaac, bleeding and clearly slowing in his counter-movements.

A pressure built deep in my chest, and then a strange buzzing filled my body. My fur stood on end, and my wolf stopped in her tracks. Instead of fighting, she tipped her head back to the moonlit sky and let out a howl.

Drake's army stilled.

In unison, all eyes swung to me. My wolf raised her

chin high, meeting their gaze with an authority I didn't know I possessed. One by one, all of the wolves dropped their heads, their eyes dipping toward the ground in silent submission. A couple of them whined, but not a single one lifted their heads or tried to move.

My heart raced as I tried to figure out what the hell I'd just managed to do to them all. Whatever it was, at least, they'd stopped trying to kill us.

The problem was, I had no idea what to do next. Or how to make it last long enough to get us the hell out of here.

"Tell them to go home."

A deep voice snapped me out of my anxiety.

I looked up to see Silas and Presley in human form, standing in the bed of the truck.

"Tell them," Silas repeated.

I hesitated.

Telling them to go home seemed awfully simplified and kind of lame, honestly. Besides, it would require me to shift back to two legs, and what if my weird freezing power wore off if I did that?

"Tell them with your mind," Silas added.

I looked over at him questioningly.

What the…?

Could I do that?

Refocusing, I concentrated on the buzzing sensation still humming along inside me. Glaring at where Vinny lay nearby, head bowed, I thought as hard as I could, *go the hell home, asshole.*

A second later, every single one of Drake's minions stood up and raced away from us.

Holy shit.

I'd just done that.

I looked back at Silas.

His lips curved in what might have been called a smile if actual smiles didn't exist yet.

"That was so fucking unbelievable," Presley exclaimed, shattering whatever weird little moment Silas and I were having.

He jumped to the ground, and I looked away, searching out the others. Oscar stood over Isaac, who'd dropped to his belly in the grass. Idrissa whined and rushed to her brother, licking at the wound he'd gotten earlier. Isaac didn't stop her.

Oscar backed away, shifting from four legs to two. "You hurt anywhere else?" he asked Isaac.

Isaac shook his head.

"Good enough." Oscar looked back at Silas and Presley. "Help me get him in the truck."

"You got it, boss," Presley said.

He and Silas came forward, gently lifting Isaac and carrying him to the truck bed. Idrissa stayed close, and as soon as Isaac was lying in the bed, she jumped up and lay down next to him.

Oscar looked at me and, thankfully, in my wolf form, it was easy to ignore the fact that he was naked.

Otherwise, I might have been scarred for life.

"You need to shift so you can drive them home," he said. "You have clothes in there?"

I whined, meaning, *no*. I'd lost my bag somewhere in the woods.

"I'll drive them," Silas said, wiping his hands off as he hopped out of the truck bed.

Presley secured the tailgate with a loud bang.

I winced as the sound echoed through the woods.

Oscar seemed to consider.

"Keys are in the visor," he said finally. Silas started for

the truck, but Oscar grabbed his arm. "You get them home in one piece or it's your ass."

"You have my word, sir," Silas said. "I'll drop them at their place. Amberly will fix Isaac right up. And then I'll bring the truck back to you when we're finished."

Oscar grunted in satisfaction. Then he looked at me knowingly.

"I'm guessing you're going to run no matter what I tell you," he said.

I snorted in answer.

Oscar shook his head and started for his motorcycle then stopped. "Ah, fuck it. I don't plan to burn my ass on a hot tank." He tossed Presley a key.

Startled, Presley barely managed to snatch it out of the air.

"Boss?" Presley said.

"Take my bike home," Oscar said. "We'll meet you there."

He didn't wait for an answer before he shifted again, and, together, we ran for home.

11

Oscar and I ran full speed all the way back to the Throttle. He surprised the hell out of me by nearly keeping up with my wolf. Even when I let her go like I'd done earlier, he was right there at my heels.

It felt good, letting my wolf stretch her legs like this. The adrenaline burned through my blood, so by the time we reached the Throttle, I felt somewhat steady again.

Isaac would be okay. He had to be.

Oscar shifted at the back door and punched in the code to disarm the alarm before pushing the door open for me.

"Get upstairs and find some clothes," he said. "I'll be up in a bit."

He turned away and grabbed his phone, but I no longer cared who he was calling. Not with everything else I had to think about.

Upstairs, I went straight for the shower, my thoughts racing at what it all meant. Kel's story about my mother's spell. Her magic returning. And then the attack. Drake had sent those assholes to rattle us. If he'd thought they stood a chance, he would have come himself. Or maybe not. Maybe he'd hoped they would kill me, and since he was nowhere in the vicinity, it couldn't be connected back to him.

But most importantly, what the hell had I done to make them all just stop fighting like that?

The whole night felt insane.

Surreal, even.

I'd fought other wolves. Drawn blood. A couple, I was pretty sure I had killed. And if not me, then Idrissa for sure. I wondered how she felt about that. If she'd known who they were.

I stared at the bottom of the tub, a sick feeling in my stomach as I watched all the blood and dirt slide off my skin and swirl down the drain. It wasn't okay. Defending myself was one thing, but this?

This felt like a war.

I hated the idea of the pack splitting because of me. We needed to stick together at a time like this.

I thought of Kai alone somewhere in a cell.

My heart ached for him. For someone to help me figure this all out. And mostly, for the idea that he might be punished or hurt because of my mess. It wasn't fair.

Finally, the shower water ran cold, and I had no choice but to climb out and get dressed.

Oscar was in the kitchen, a beer in his hands. An open can already sat on the counter in front of him. Empty if I had to guess. For once, it didn't bother me. Hell, if I wasn't so turned off from watching my dad lose himself to alcohol all those years, I'd have one too. I mean, if there were ever a night deserving of a drink, this had to be it.

"Hey, kid. You okay?" Oscar asked when he saw me.

"I just need some sleep," I said.

Another figure moved in the living room, startling me.

I sucked in a sharp breath then blew it out again when I recognized Silas standing near the window. He held a beer too, but he wasn't draining it with gusto like Oscar seemed to be. If anything, he seemed to be holding it more for something to do than anything else.

His eyes met mine.

The thing with Silas was that he didn't speak simply for the sake of filling silences. It might have been the single thing I liked about him.

"How's Isaac?" I asked him.

"Healing," he said. "Idrissa stayed with him. Said he'd heal faster with her there. Some sort of twin thing, I guess."

I nodded.

He'd be okay. He had to be.

If I repeated the words enough, maybe I'd fully believe them. And stop feeling guilty for getting him injured in the first place.

"Where's Presley?" I asked, glancing around.

"We got word Drake was on the move," Silas said. "Pres went to get eyes on him. See if we can connect him to Vinny's bullshit tonight."

Bullshit. Yeah, that was one way to sum it up.

"The wolves who attacked us…" I began, "were any of them hurt?"

"Not sure yet." His forehead wrinkled like I'd said something confusing.

"I've got a call in to Warren," Oscar put in as he set his second empty can on the counter.

Silas groaned. "Why the hell'd you have to go and call him?"

"He needs to know what's going on, Si."

"So he can stick his nose in it? C'mon, Oz. You know as well as I do Warren's just a politician in fur."

"Putting down one of our own isn't something we can just pretend didn't happen. The pack's losing their damn minds," Oscar said, eyes flashing with temper. "If they're going to run around attacking their own, this council's the only line of defense—or justice—we have against that kind of bullshit." He huffed, adding, "I don't want Ash ending up in a cell too."

Silas sighed. "Yeah. Okay."

"Should I be worried?" I asked, startled at Oscar's words. I hadn't thought about legal trouble for what I'd done tonight, but I should've considering Kai's situation.

"No," Oscar said firmly. "You were defending yourself."

I swallowed, nodding absently before glancing at Silas again.

"Have you…talked to Kai?" I asked.

Silas gave me a dubious look. "No. Do you want me to?"

"He'll want to know what happened tonight," I said, not sure why I felt defensive all of a sudden. Silas had a way of doing that.

"Sure, but he'll ask how you were able to end it peacefully," Silas pointed out.

Oh.

I bit my lip.

What was I supposed to say? Even I didn't know what had happened back there.

"It's the alpha call," Oscar said, reading my expression. His voice was weary, whether from physical exhaustion or mental, I wasn't sure. But either way, I could relate.

"The alpha call?" I asked.

Oscar's phone rang. He checked the screen.

"Shit, I better take this," he muttered then stalked out

the door and down the stairs. He was gone before I could figure out who was on the other end.

Leaving me alone with Silas.

Cue all the awkward tension.

When I finally got the nerve to look up, Silas was watching me. The hostility I expected was absent, though. If anything, he looked curious.

"Do you really not know what you did back there?" he asked.

"No," I admitted. "Should I?" And then I realized something. "Wait. Do you?"

"You made them submit," he said.

"What do you mean? Like forced them?"

"Yeah. Forced them. Forced me."

"You?"

"Earlier? When Presley and I came by?"

My eyes widened. "That was alpha power? But…how? I'm like a week old in wolf years."

"It has nothing to do with age." He cocked his head. "You really don't know this? There's only one kind of wolf that can do that."

I wasn't sure I wanted to know what kind of wolf he meant. Honestly, part of me *did* know, and I almost told him to stop before he said it out loud.

"An alpha," he finished before I could cut him off, and I groaned.

"That's not what I am."

"Sure as hell seemed like it back there."

"Well, I'll just turn it off then." For some reason, this whole thing was pissing me off. Was it logical to be pissed about saving myself and my friends from certain death? No. But here we were.

"You can't just turn it off, Ashes."

"Don't call me that," I insisted.

He ignored that. "What's your aversion to alpha, anyway? Isn't that part of breaking the curse?"

I sighed.

I was beginning to suspect it was the only thing left for me to do. And that made it all so much worse.

"If you're worried about Kai, he'd understand—"

"It's not about Kai," I said.

Okay, maybe it was a little bit.

"Then I'd say whatever the hell it is, get over it fast," he said. "Because you're fighting against a ticking clock. The pack is losing their damn minds, and it's like it's all been sped up."

"You think I haven't noticed that? Drake's drawn a line, made them all choose sides." My eyes burned with tears, and I turned away, refusing to let Silas see. "I don't want us to fight each other."

"If you just became the alpha, you could make them all submit like you did tonight. Even Drake. Boom. Problem solved.

I huffed, exasperated by this. "That's exactly why I don't want it."

He shook his head. "I don't get you."

"Look, if I force everyone to do what I say, I take away their free will. That's not an alpha anyone wants. This pack deserves an alpha they *want* to follow. Of their own volition. Not because they're being forced."

Instead of answering, he simply studied me.

It was the same look he'd given me earlier. Like I'd said something confusing. Or maybe he was still trying to figure me out.

Back at ya, buddy.

"How did you find me tonight, anyway?" I asked when he remained silent. "Kind of weird how you and Presley showed up at exactly the moment we needed help."

Silas shrugged, but his expression flickered with an uncertainty he worked to cover up quickly. "I don't know. We just knew."

"That doesn't make any sense."

"No shit," he said, and this time I could tell he was the one irritated by the questions.

Ha.

Too bad.

"You just knew," I repeated.

Silas scowled. "Look, Pres and I both had this feeling, and we just sort of followed it. I don't understand it, but that's the truth. What were you doing out there, anyway? You made it too easy on them being vulnerable like that."

"None of your business," I shot back.

He strode to the counter and set his beer down. "Tell Oz I'll see him at the fight tomorrow."

He pushed past me, heading for the door.

"Wait. Fight?" I called, startled. "Has someone new come to town?"

He stopped, not looking back at me as he spoke. "Not this time," he said in a tight voice.

"Then what—?"

"Drake challenged Devon Gruber for alpha."

"Can he do that? I mean, he already challenged Kai."

"Kai's a non-issue until he's released. So, yes, he can do that."

Heat rose as my temper flared. "And you're just going to let it happen?"

He whirled, eyes blazing with accusation. "You really don't get it, do you? There's no way to stop this. There *will* be an alpha. Our wolves might be untethered and chaotic, but their instinct for dominance isn't something we can just wish away. And we shouldn't. This is what we need now."

"But Drake," I argued, knowing he was right. About every damn word. "You can't let him hurt anyone else."

"I don't want to see him as alpha any more than you do. I'm going to see if we can find a way to get through this shitshow without more dead bodies than necessary. But by the end of that fight, either Devon or Drake will be left standing. And then, he'll be the one to beat for alpha—if anyone challenges him at all." He looked me up and down. "Until you decide whether that's you or not, I'd lay low."

He didn't wait for me to answer before he walked out.

12

By the time Oscar returned, I'd worked myself up into a seriously bad mood. He walked in and took one look at my face and said, "I need another beer for this."

He walked to the fridge, but I stopped him. "Silas left his out."

Oscar grunted and redirected, grabbing Silas' open can. He didn't even bother to take a swig. Apparently, holding it offered the stability he was after. It might have been funny if I wasn't on the brink of falling apart.

"Devon and Drake are fighting tomorrow," I announced.

"I know."

"For alpha."

"I know."

"That means one of them is going to kill the other."

"At the risk of sounding redundant, I—"

"We have to stop them."

Oscar's brows rose. "How do you propose we do that?"

"I don't know, but it's not right. No one needs to die."

His expression softened. "You don't really get a say in that, kid. This is a rite of passage for wolves. And frankly, one long overdue for this pack. It's not a bad thing, considering the alternative."

"How can you say that?"

"Ash, this pack has survived by the skin of our teeth for two decades. No other pack in history has stuck together this long without an alpha to bind them. Or mates to settle them. The fact that we haven't all killed each other before now is a damned miracle."

"So, we just have to sit by and keep letting the pack attack each other?"

Oscar sighed. "Tell you what, if you don't want to take my word for it, ask your wolf."

"What does that mean?"

"Tune in to your wolf, Ash. She can show you better than I can."

"How do I do that?" I asked.

"For starters, let her out. Go for a run. Give her space in your head. She'll do the rest."

A run. Like that would just solve everything.

"I don't think a run is going to solve my problems," I said.

He shrugged. "Suit yourself."

"Where are you going?" I asked when he turned away.

"To bed," he said, glancing back at me pointedly. "You should do the same."

"What about Isaac?"

How could I just sleep knowing my friend was hurt?

"He's going to be fine," Oscar said. "Idrissa will call when there's news."

I almost argued.

Insisted I stay awake to wait for her call. Or try to see

how Kai was doing. But I knew none of that would do a single bit of good. Not tonight.

For now, Oscar was right. Like it or not, my body was exhausted, and I wouldn't solve anything until I'd had some sleep.

I woke the next morning to find Oscar already gone and the unmistakable sounds of machinery coming from downstairs.

Monday.

That meant the shop was open.

It felt strange, getting dressed and going downstairs to report to work. How could everyone just be going back to business as usual when the world was falling apart?

Kai was in jail.

Isaac was injured.

And Drake was trying to kill me by proxy.

Not to mention everything I'd learned from Kel.

No version of this existed where I could just return to my normal life like nothing had happened. But that was apparently exactly what I was expected to do, according to Oscar's note I found on the counter.

See you downstairs.

-Oz

I hated to disappoint, but I couldn't just go to work. Not until I made sure Isaac was okay. I shot off a text to Idrissa, telling her I was on my way.

Dressing quickly, I grabbed a bottled water and left the apartment. Hopefully, Oscar would lend me his keys. If not, I'd have to be careful about the route I took to the twins' house. We had way too many enemies to count anymore.

My phone dinged as I left the apartment. I glanced down and then stopped to read the incoming message.

Been in wolf form all night. Isaac's finally starting to heal. Needs more time, but he'll be okay. Mom says no visitors.

-Idrissa

I exhaled the breath I'd been holding and slid the phone away. No visitors. That sucked. But at least he was healing. I tried to focus on that as I made my way down into the shop.

Oscar was at the front desk when I stepped into the lobby.

He looked up from the computer, deep lines etched across his forehead. His brows were crinkled, and I could tell whatever he'd been looking at onscreen had him frustrated.

"Uh-oh," I said. "What happened?"

"Nothing." He hesitated and then added, "This invoicing system you put together looks thorough," he said.

I resisted a smile as I read between the lines. "Would you like some help with it?"

"I know how to read my own damn computer system," he muttered.

"Okay then. I was just going to take an hour and—"

"Fine, yes. I would like some help."

He scowled.

I walked over and patted his shoulder. "I made some changes," I said. "Look, see this line? Accounts receivable. And this part here? Accounts payable."

"I just had charge and payment before."

"I know."

"And most of it was on paper."

"I know."

We shared a look.

"This way, you can easily access whether a customer

has an outstanding balance before you give them their keys."

"Huh." He grunted. "You're pretty good at this stuff."

"Thanks."

He eyed my shirt. "Where's your shop uniform?"

"Upstairs."

He frowned. "Something wrong?"

"Oscar, you can't expect me to just work today like everything's fine."

"Of course everything's not fine," he said. "But we work because we like to eat. You like to eat?" I nodded. "Yeah, me too. Bills don't stop coming because life gets crazy."

"I know that."

I shot a glance toward the garage where an air compressor had just shut off. When I looked back at Oscar, he was studying me.

"He's not in there."

"Who?" I asked.

"Drake. I fired him last week. Right after he challenged you in that asinine fight."

I softened. "I didn't know."

"Yeah, because you went and got yourself kidnapped right after." He shook his head. "After the week you had, I'd think you want to just sit here on this stool and click buttons on this damn machine."

"It's called a computer," I said wryly. "And I do more than click buttons."

"Yeah, but do you almost die?"

My lips twitched. "It's slightly more boring than that."

"Exactly. Boring might do you some good."

I looked away.

He was right. About all of it.

"I already called and checked on Kai," he added, and my eyes snapped up to his. "Still no visitors. Investigation's ongoing. That's all they told me, and it's all they'll tell you."

I sighed, doing my best to ignore the heartache that had become a constant since the moment they'd led Kai away from me.

"Idrissa texted me," I told him. "Isaac's beginning to heal, but his mom doesn't want visitors yet either."

Oscar nodded solemnly. "Told you, kid. He'll pull through just fine."

"What about Vinny?" I demanded. "And Drake? Shouldn't we go to the police? File a report or something? We can't just sit here."

I still had no idea what I wanted to do about Vinny. Especially knowing he was the one who'd bitten me in the first place, triggering my wolf. I was still pissed about that, but I kind of had my hands full with more pressing matters—like not dying. Besides, that bite had kind of saved my life. Not that I'd ever tell him that.

"The sheriff is looking into it, kid. I promise you that. And he'll want to talk to you soon, but in the meantime, we wait."

I scowled. That's exactly what I didn't want to do.

"Hey." He put a hand on my shoulder. "Take the quiet when you can get it. Storm's coming, kid. I hope you know that."

"I think it's already here."

"Exactly. You gotta play this smart. Conserve your strength. You run out there, all hellfire and determination now, you'll burn yourself right on out before the main event even arrives."

I tilted my head. "How'd you get so smart about this stuff?"

He clapped my shoulder. "This ain't my first rodeo, kid. Stick with me. You'll be all right."

I watched as he sauntered back into the garage, and when he was gone, I slid onto my stool and did the boring work of logging invoices.

Morning slid into afternoon.

Every time I popped into the garage for something, I noticed, with a sharp pang, the empty station that belonged to Kai. The one farther back that had belonged to Drake was empty too, but seeing that one abandoned felt good. It felt safe.

It also meant we were short-handed. With just Oscar and Mitch in the shop, everything fell behind. The afternoon picked up steam with customer drop-offs, and before I knew it, we were closing up.

I turned the sign to 'Closed' and locked the door, relieved to note none of Drake's little army had come looking for me. I wondered if that had more to do with what I'd done to them last night with my whole *alpha powers* or if the sheriff had knocked some sense into them. Either way, I had to admit boring felt good.

Mitch left without much more than a few mumbled words and a grunt. I didn't take it personally. Besides Oscar and Kai, I'd never seen him say more than three words at a time to anyone.

But now that it was just Oscar and me, with no work to keep me busy, my brain kicked into overdrive. It didn't take long to work myself into anxious overthinking.

"Sheriff called," Oscar said.

I looked over from where I'd been pacing by the window. Oscar stood in the doorway from the garage. He pushed off the doorframe and headed for the minifridge behind the counter.

"What did he say?" I asked.

"They're putting some extra patrols on the roads for the next few days. Make sure Vinny and Drake and the rest don't get any more ideas."

I nodded. "Does he need to talk to me?"

"Told him I'd send you over tomorrow."

My heart thudded. "Can I see Kai?"

He frowned. "Not likely but doesn't hurt to ask."

I nodded, afraid to hope, but afraid not to.

My wolf stirred at that, tense and straining against the confines of my human body.

"You did good today," he said. "I know you're under a lot of stress."

"Thanks."

His silence became awkward until, finally, he said, "Er, you want to talk?"

If the situation weren't so dire, I might have laughed. Oscar looked like he'd rather have a tooth pulled than have me take him up on his offer.

I shook my head. "No, my wolf wants my attention. I think she's feeling confined."

He blew out a breath in obvious relief. "Go for a run."

Last night, I'd turned down the idea in favor of sleep. But now, yeah, this pent-up energy wasn't going anywhere. A run sounded perfect right now.

"Do you think it's safe? I mean with Drake and his little army out there?"

"Drake doesn't want to fight you directly," he said.

"Yeah, I'm getting that," I said dryly, thinking of his alpha challenge to Kai. "He has no problem getting others to attempt it, though."

Oscar scratched his beard thoughtfully. "According to the sheriff, Vinny and the others aren't going to try anything again. At least, not until they figure out how you made them run away." He gave a short laugh. "Did you see their faces when you ordered them to go home? Priceless, kid."

"Do you think…" I bit my lip, trying to decide if I wanted to know the answer. "Do you think I should be alpha?"

"I think you should listen to your wolf, kid." He waved me toward the door. "Go get her opinion, and then we'll talk."

I blew out a breath and then gave in, heading for the back door since it was closer to the woods. Oscar reminded me to strip outside so my clothes would be there for me when I got home.

Then he shut the door behind me, and I breathed in the fresh smell of the forest. Just like it had that first night in town, the scent of this place called to me. Peeling off my clothes, I shifted and felt an immediate sense of release.

The moment my feet hit the grass, I felt my wolf pulling me toward the trees. Oscar had been right. She needed this. We both did.

All of the other times I'd shifted had been about survival. For the first time since I'd triggered my ability to shift, I was doing it for pure enjoyment. This wasn't about defending myself or others. It was about connecting with a side of me I'd neglected—maybe for my whole life.

The trees closed in around me, and I inhaled the scent of the forest, letting my instincts fill in the sounds and smells my human side couldn't.

Scents: something small foraged nearby. A fox maybe. It stilled as it sensed me getting closer. My wolf thought it smelled like a great dinner, but I couldn't quite let her be that much in charge.

Sounds: a light wind rustling the trees. The scraping of the fox's paw against loose dirt. If I strained enough, I could just make out the small animal's heartbeat. It was crazy how heightened my senses had become in only a few days.

Far away, yelling and cheering floated toward me. Miles out, yet. I turned my face toward it, searching for the source. Bo's and the barn were both that way. Ugh. Who knew what the hell the pack was getting into tonight. Bar fights were practically an everyday thing these days.

Then I remembered.

Silas had said Devon and Drake were fighting tonight.

My muscles tightened, indecision freezing me in place. Part of me was tempted to run over and stop it. But then I realized my urge had little to do with my human self. Mostly, my wolf wanted me to go. Not to avoid violence but to make sure she was the only contender for the role. My wolf wanted authority. And she wanted to take it from those who would threaten to steal it from her—the rightful choice to lead this pack.

Shoving her back, I forced myself to shake off her thoughts.

Another fight for alpha was only natural like Silas had said. And while Drake winning would undoubtedly have horrific consequences, I didn't know how to stop it. Not without using the alpha power I'd used last night. And I didn't have it in me to order anyone else to do anything. Not tonight, anyway.

I turned away from the sounds of cheering and raised voices.

My wolf urged me to turn around. To make my way to the barn and put an end to what she considered a complete waste of fur.

I smirked inwardly even as I refused her.

My inner wolf had no filter.

And she was making it clear that, for her, there was only one choice for alpha in this pack.

Little did she know, I could be as stubborn as she was.

Making a wide arc to avoid the barn or any of its current guests, I stuck to the perimeter of what I now knew to be pack lands. The closer I got to the border, the more aware I became of another presence.

Just ahead.

Right near the hexerei's lands.

Someone else was here.

My heart beat faster, my senses straining to catch a scent or some identifying movement.

Whoever it was knew to remain very, very still. Their heartbeat calm. Barely detectible to my sensitive ears.

My steps slowed.

The wind picked up, sending a breeze through my fur, and a strange scent reached my nose. Every nerve in me went on alert as I crept forward. The scent was vaguely familiar, but I couldn't quite place it. My wolf wanted to rip throats, ask questions later. I did my best to keep hold of the reins, inching closer to whoever waited.

Finally, the figure stepped out from behind a tree, and I stopped, too surprised to do anything but stare.

Hers was a face I recognized, though I never expected to see her here. Tiffany. The girl who always looked at Kai like he was still a possibility for her. Ugh.

What the hell was she doing here?

She looked right at me and said, "We need to talk."

13

Watching Tiffany warily, I debated shifting back to my human form, but a nude conversation with a girl who might be about to try to kill me in order to steal my boyfriend wasn't sounding smart right now.

Before I could decide, she said, "On second thought, don't worry about shifting. I can sense your discomfort, so I'll talk; just listen."

Bossy much?

I huffed a response, channeling Oscar and all of his non-committal grunting.

Tiffany took that as a yes.

"I've been hoping you'd come far enough out here that we could speak in private," she began, and I couldn't help but be impressed because she made it sound like she'd been out here a hell of a long time. Almost immediately, my suspicion kicked in. How did she know where to find me, though? These woods were massive.

"If you're wondering how I found you," she said, making me wonder if mind-reading was a thing, "I honestly don't know. I was on my way to the barn to see the fight, and I just…had a feeling, I guess. That feeling led me here. And then you showed up."

I stared at her, not sure what to think. Silas had said the same thing when he and Presley had shown up last night. It was starting to feel important.

"Anyway, look, I just want to say first that I'm totally happy for you and Kai being mates or whatever."

My eyes narrowed.

Her hands twisted nervously. "I really am," she insisted. "I know I didn't seem like it before, but the truth is I'm jealous."

I bared my teeth at her, my wolf ready to take this broad down if she so much as spoke another word about wanting my mate. But she put her hands up in defense and said quickly, "Not like that. I don't want Kai. Geez."

She blew out a breath.

"Please, just hear me out, okay?" she almost pleaded. "I promise I don't want to hurt you."

I forced myself to settle, and Tiffany went on, slightly more nervous looking. "The curse has been part of my life for so long; it's kind of all I knew. And I think part of me just accepted it would also be this way. Rowdy as hell, asshole guys. No loyalty. We throw great parties, sure, but that's only fun for a little while. The thing is… I want to find my own mate. And I think you can help me."

Okay, I couldn't take it anymore.

Shuffling behind a tree, I shifted.

"Wait," Tiffany hissed.

She moved to follow, but I re-emerged, crossing my arms over my breasts. Tiffany stopped short.

"Sorry. I thought you were leaving," she admitted.

"Not yet. But I have questions," I said.

"That's fair." Her gaze flicked to my arms, and her lips

quirked. "You don't have to cover up, you know. Nudity's no big deal."

"Noted." I didn't drop my arms.

Tiffany earned a few points by letting the subject drop and bringing her gaze back to mine where it stayed.

"How exactly do you think I can help you?" I asked.

"You're the curse breaker," she said as if that explained everything.

I shook my head, frustrated at how simple she made it all sound. "I'm not some guardian angel," I said. "I don't know who your mate is."

"No, but you can make it possible for me to recognize him."

The urge to tell her to fuck off was strong, but so was my empathy. I had Kai. Not just a boyfriend. Or a human relationship. I had a soul mate. A mate fated to belong only to me. What did Tiffany have? Besides resting bitch face and really judgy eyes?

"Look, the curse is already breaking down," I said. "That's why everyone feels an alpha call. I'm not sure what else you want from me."

"It's not like that," she said, and even in the darkness, I could see her cheeks flushing pink. "I mean, yes, I want you to succeed with breaking the curse. But what I'm saying is… I came out here to tell you something. Something bigger than all that." She hesitated, fidgeting now.

"Any day now," I prompted.

"I'm here to pledge myself to you," she blurted.

"Pledge yourself? What does that even mean?"

She exhaled impatiently, and I was pretty sure she rolled her eyes as she said, "It means I promise to have your back always, no matter who threatens you or who I have to fight. You're my leader. 'Til the end or whatever."

Her leader?

"Wait, isn't pledging something you do to your alpha?"

"Yes," she said simply.

Before I could fully process that, she dropped to one knee, leaning to the side so her neck was exposed to me.

"Tiffany," I began, backing away. "I'm not the alpha."

"Not yet," she said, looking up at me while managing to keep her neck exposed. "But you will be."

She didn't move as she said the words, clearly waiting for me to acknowledge the gesture.

I looked around, suddenly aware that anyone could spot us out here. And why did it matter?

"I can't just let you…this is crazy."

"Accept my pledge, Ash. You know you could use it."

Dammit. She clearly wasn't going to get up until I did as she asked.

"Ugh. Okay, yeah, I hear your pledge or whatever. Get up," I hissed.

Tiffany stood. "I heard what happened with Vinny," she said.

"What about it?"

She shrugged. "I'm not the only one picking a side. Vinny and the rest of those assholes chose Drake, which is a dipshit move if you ask me."

My mouth tipped up at that.

"I saw you take down Drake like he was a baby bunny or some shit," she went on. "So, my money's on you, the new girl."

"Thanks?"

"Anyway, my dad says this is how it works with alpha calls. You either feel the call to fight or you pledge yourself to the one you think will win."

I wasn't sure how I felt about that last part. My wolf preened, but I told her to stuff it and eyed Tiffany. "You think I'd win?"

Her brows rose like the answer should have been obvious. "Not if Vinny and those dumb asses catch you first."

I huffed at that, but the truth was she had a point.

"You need pack support, right? Well, you have mine. And there are a ton of others too. You only have to ask, and they'll come."

"What others?" I couldn't help but ask.

"Cade and Cody Marshall, Teddy, Miranda, Tori, both my parents, even Sherriff Copeland—"

"Okay, okay, you've made your point."

My heart was racing again but for different reasons. Kel had said lines would be drawn. At the time, I assumed she meant Drake. He'd recruited Vinny and the others to his side, and that side clearly wanted me dead. But this? Tiffany pledging herself to me? It was strange. I didn't know what to think.

"We all feel drawn to you, Ash. We know your wolf is the most dominant of us all. And we want the curse broken. We're behind you, whatever you need."

"I… it's not me," I said. But my argument was getting weaker and weaker. If literally everyone else thought I should be alpha—hell, even my own wolf knew it—my protests were sounding more and more like what I suspected they really were: fear. Cowardice.

In the darkest places of my heart, I felt the truth. There had only ever been one thing I knew how to do when things got hard or dangerous, and that was to run away.

Becoming alpha was the literal opposite of every urge inside my body.

I didn't know how to stay and fight.

Did I?

"Besides," I added, "even if I wanted it, Drake's challenged Devon. They're probably fighting right now. The alpha challenges are happening as we speak."

"First of all, the fight was postponed," she said.

I blinked. "It was?"

"Yeah. Apparently, Sheriff Copeland needed more time to finish investigating Drake's involvement in your attack last night."

"And?" I asked.

She shrugged. "That's all I know. The point is, the challenge period isn't over yet. You can still throw your name into the ring."

"I don't know anything about being an alpha," I said.

"You're Caleb's daughter," Tiffany said. "My parents and everyone else from that era all agree it's in your blood. Your birthright. And my wolf can't deny the call to follow you." She snorted. "Hell, I found you using some wolfish GPS or some shit. That has to count for something, right?"

I didn't answer.

Tiffany stepped back. "Well, anyway, I just wanted you to know you aren't alone. Whatever you need, just ask."

She turned to leave, but the words tumbled out before I could overthink them. "What if they reject me?"

Tiffany looked back at me, her blonde hair glinting in the moonlight.

"Your wolf..." she shook her head. "She's more powerful than you realize. In the end, I don't think anyone will be able to deny you as our alpha, but if you're worried about them accepting you, just show them."

"Show them what?"

"That you want this. It goes both ways, you know. We want you, but you have to want us too."

I watched her walk away, slipping in and out of shadows until she was nothing but the dark side of a moonbeam.

14

I woke the next morning to Oscar standing over me with a deep frown marring his features.

"What's wrong?" I asked, coming awake sharply as panic shot through me.

"You're late," he said and then headed for the door.

I sat up, rubbing my eyes. "Late? For what?"

"Work. Or are you giving up on that now too?"

"Excuse me?" I sat up, scowling. "I'm not giving up on anything," I said icily.

Was he referring to the alpha challenges? Because when I'd asked him last night, he'd made it sound like whatever I chose was fine. Although, when I'd returned from my run, I'd told him about running into Tiffany, and even I had to admit my protests against fighting for alpha were starting to sound like excuses.

Oscar hadn't said anything, though. He'd just gone to bed.

Now, he eyed me like he was biting back what he really thought.

"Prove it," he said and then walked out.

I listened as he opened and closed the apartment door. Then to the muted thuds of his boots as he descended the stairs. Then I fell back against the pillow, staring up at the ceiling.

Work.

Yesterday it had proven to be a nice distraction. Maybe I'd be lucky enough for another day of the same.

Unfortunately, that wasn't the case.

Every customer that came in asked me if I'd put my name in the running for alpha. By noon, I couldn't take it anymore. I spent my lunch hour hiding out behind a custom cruiser Oscar was rebuilding from scratch in his spare time. Oscar had disappeared into the office, once again on some mystery phone call. That was fine by me. I wasn't complaining about a little privacy.

"You look just like him when you're stressed out."

I looked up sharply at the sight of Mitch standing at the tool bench nearby. He gave me a sheepish look.

"Sorry, I didn't mean to startle you."

"No, it's fine."

Honestly, Mitch said so little; it was sometimes easy to forget he was there. His brand of quiet was nice, though. Companionable. He made it easy to be near. But now, his words wouldn't let me just sit in silence anymore.

"Look like who?" I asked.

"Caleb." He offered a crooked smile that vanished quickly. "You have those same lines on your forehead." He ran his finger across his forehead to demonstrate. "He always looked like that when he was deep in thought on a problem."

"You two were close," I realized.

"For a while. Then he met your mom, I guess. Didn't ever tell me who she was, but I put it together. Even saw them once. Stumbled on them while I was doing security one night. Never told him about it, though. I could tell his secret was important."

"You sound like a good friend," I said.

"I don't know about that. In the end, he was alone when he made his hard decisions." He hesitated and then added, "I wouldn't be able to forgive myself if I let his daughter go through it the same."

I blinked at him, surprised and then touched by his words. "Thanks," I said. "But I don't know that having another friend makes my decisions any easier. Feels like they were all made for me already."

"Nah, we've always got a choice. Your old man made his. Now you get to make yours."

"Even if they hurt people?" I asked.

"Honor yourself first," he said. "Then the chips can fall where they may, but at least, you'll be able to live with yourself."

He held up the wrench as if to signal an end to the conversation. Then he walked back to his workstation, leaving me to wonder just when the hell Mitch had gotten so damn wise. Or why I'd never noticed it before.

I was still sitting in that same hiding spot when Oscar returned. He looked down at me with a pointed look, and I groaned.

"I'm going." I pushed to my feet. "But for the record, old men on motorcycles are the nosiest bunch I've ever met in my life."

"Customers giving you trouble?" he asked.

"Not as long as I inform them of all my personal business before they pay their invoice. And then listen to them tell me who they think the next alpha will be and what I should do about it."

He frowned. "Take the afternoon," he said.

"No way, I can't just leave you hanging without a front desk—"

"Cody Marshall called earlier. Said if you needed any help with the front desk, he'd fill in."

"He did?"

Cody was a fifteen-year-old who worked at the gas station on the edge of town. I'd met him the day I arrived. When I'd been covered in my father's two-day-old blood. I hadn't spoken to him since. And I'd barely thought of him—until Tiffany had mentioned him as one of my "supporters" last night. Apparently, she wasn't lying.

"Yeah, I'll give him a call now," Oscar said. "You go on. Sheriff Copeland wants you to stop by today anyway."

My heart pounded with a weird mix of anticipation and nerves. Talking to Copeland meant trying not to say something that would get Kai into even more trouble. But it also meant possibly seeing Kai. Finally.

"Stay on the main road, though," Oscar warned."

"Thanks," I said, breathless.

I headed for the door, more urgency in my steps now.

"And keep an eye out for trouble," Oscar called to my back.

"Will do."

I was out the door and headed down the street before he could lecture me further. My senses remained alert as I walked the two blocks to the corner where I knew the jail sat. Yes, the jail was on the same street as a crystal shop, a tattoo parlor, and directly across the street from the town's only pharmacy. Ridley Falls was as small as they came.

But at least, that meant plenty of nosy onlookers to keep an eye out for Vinny or Drake or anyone else wanting to take a bite out of my throat.

Despite the possible danger, all I could think about

was Kai. Every cell in me hummed in anticipation at seeing him.

It had only been a couple of days, but even that was too long. My wolf was starting to go stir crazy.

The jail looked a lot like the other stores surrounding it. Well-kept, almost hipster in the updated siding and fresh paint. The signage was definitely government-issue and no-nonsense, though. I pushed my way inside, ignoring the "No Visitors" sign on the door.

The moment I walked inside, I felt the mate bond slam into me. A feeling so strong I could practically taste it. Kai was here. Under this roof. Inside these walls. And I was close enough to sense that he was struggling. Anxiety, stress—claustrophobia. It washed over me so thick I had to resist the urge to shift and rip this place down around me.

Why were they keeping him in a damned cell, knowing what his wolf would feel like? Weren't these cops wolf shifters too?

I steeled myself against the onslaught of emotion and made my way to the deputy sitting at the front desk. He looked up and frowned at the sight of me. I tended to have that effect. But I refused to let it dampen my anticipation.

"Can I help you?" he asked.

"I'm here to see Kai Stone."

"Did you make an appointment?"

"A… No." Was I supposed to?

"I'm afraid we don't allow walk-in visitors."

"I'm Ash Lawson," I began.

"I know who you are."

Irritation flickered, and I forced myself to take a deep breath. "Then you know I'm Kai's mate. That's different than some random visitor, don't you think?"

"Visitors are visitors," he said.

Okay, I officially didn't like this guy.

Before I could unleash all my favorite insults, though, he sighed. "Let me call my boss and see what I can do."

I waited while he made a call and listened to both sides because—wolf hearing.

Someone picked up on the first ring.

"Copeland," someone answered.

"Hey, boss. It's Rick. Listen, I've got Ash Lawson here to see Stone. You want me to let her through?"

"I'll come escort her. I've got a few questions."

"Sounds good."

Rick hung up and nodded at the wall of chairs behind me. "You can have a seat. Sherriff will be up to get you shortly."

Suddenly, the familiarity of the voice struck me. Sheriff Noah Copeland. The man who'd arrested Kai at the pack meeting was also the sheriff. Great.

"Thanks."

I forced myself to sit and look casual, trying to figure out the best way to play this. I'd already given away too much at that damned meeting. No way was I going to do the same thing again and get Kai into more trouble.

When a door at the back of the room opened and Sheriff Copeland strode into the lobby, I pushed to my feet, ready for battle. Instead, Copeland smiled broadly and extended his hand.

"Ash, it's good to see you again. Thanks for coming by." I didn't answer, but he didn't seem to mind. "Come on. I'll take you back."

I followed him through the back door and into a hall that ran the length of the building. Halfway down the hall, Copeland stopped at a reinforced door and swiped a key card. Something clicked, and then the door swung easily open.

Copeland motioned for me to enter first.

Inside was a small table with a chair on either side. The air was cool, almost cold. It looked like every interrogation room I'd ever watched on TV down to the scratches on the table and the scuffs on the cheap linoleum floor. My nerves sang beneath my skin.

"Have a seat," Copeland said from behind me.

I whirled. "You can save your interrogation for someone else," I told him. "I won't be answering any questions."

"Understood." He motioned to the chair again. "Please, have a seat."

I glared at him, but he didn't flinch and seemed content to wait this out. With a huff, I sat.

"I'd like to see Kai."

"Of course. First, has anyone spoken to you about the investigation?"

"No," I said warily. "Like I said, I'm not answering—"

"My questions, got it. The thing is, even with questions, there isn't much of a crime here, is there?"

"Excuse me?"

"Kai's only explanation of what happened is that he is and always will be protective of you. But there've been no details offered about what might have transpired between him and the man you call Vorack. I've received no information about a body, nor do any local hospitals in the area have a patient by that name."

"Okay," I said slowly, unsure of where this was going.

"At the end of the day, there's zero evidence of a crime," he said.

He sat back, assessing me.

I was too nervous to even hope that what he was saying was good news.

"What does that mean for Kai?" I asked.

He shrugged. "Charges will be dropped."

"But they could be brought up again in the future?"

"I guess that depends."

I didn't answer.

The idea of this hanging over us, of Drake being able to just dredge it up whenever he wanted, made me sick.

"I interviewed Oscar by phone last night," he said, which made me snap back to the present with the force of whiplash.

He had? Why hadn't Oscar said anything?

"Before you get upset with him, he was asked not to mention it for the sake of the case."

"I thought you said you had no case."

"Correct. I wanted to ask him about Drake. As his former employer, I wondered if Oscar might shed some light on the feud the two of you seem to have going."

"Feud is maybe the wrong word," I said icily.

"Yes, Oscar painted quite a picture for me. As did Silas and Idrissa when I spoke with them. I heard about the pack challenge he issued you. Or should I say Kai? And how well you handled it."

I squared my shoulders, refusing to incriminate myself with the wrong reply. "I did what I had to."

"You have a bad experience with cops or something?" he asked.

"As a matter of fact, I'm still recovering from watching my mate be led out in handcuffs for a bullshit crime," I said.

"For what it's worth," he said, his voice quieter now, "Even if there had been evidence, all signs point to self-defense."

I frowned but remained silent.

"Kai told me about what you looked like the day you showed up in town, Ash. The bruises. The swelling. Oscar corroborated his description along with Cody Marshall and several other pack members. If Vorack came here looking for you, his intentions couldn't have been kind. I'm sorry you had to deal with that alone." He leaned forward. "I hope that next time you need help, you'll feel you can call me."

My resolve softened a little as he talked about the beating I'd taken before coming to the Falls. I'd been so stricken with grief over losing my dad. I hadn't ever stopped to appreciate how much of that night I'd taken on my own shoulders. Even with Oscar in my life, I'd gone through a lot completely alone. The idea that I didn't have to do that ever again made my heart ache. Maybe if Dad hadn't kept us so isolated, he'd still be alive too.

I blinked back the tears that burned and focused on the present problems.

"Does that mean you'll be arresting Vinny and the others who attacked me and my friends the other night?" I asked.

"Is that what you want?"

"Uh, yeah. Why wouldn't I?"

He shrugged. "Say the word. I have plenty of evidence. Although, they'll just be held until the new alpha can be chosen, and then they're no longer mine to deal with. Pack law. Attacks against fellow pack members are punished by the alpha."

The way he said it made me feel a certain expectation.

"Tiffany and I spoke the other night," I said, watching his expression for some kind of clue.

"Did you?" he asked knowingly.

"She said you support me—for alpha."

"I do."

"Why?"

"You see things differently than those who've spent their lives as a lone wolf. And I think we need that perspective in our next leader. But more than that, my wolf recognizes you as its alpha."

"What does that even mean?"

"It's ... not something I can put into words. My wolf just feels called to follow you."

I exhaled heavily at that. On second thought, I didn't want to have the alpha conversation again.

"Does that mean you can do something about Drake?" I asked.

"Unfortunately, there's no evidence that he told Vinny and the others to attack you. Personally, I suspect their wolves have chosen him to follow, and that breeds the kind of loyalty my questioning can't breach." He pinned me with an intense look as he added, "The only way to remove Drake from the equation would be to challenge him for alpha."

I didn't even know how to respond to that.

Telling him no didn't feel right. Not after my conversation with Tiffany. In fact, the more I tried to summon the word, the less my wolf felt inclined to let me speak it.

"Okay," I said finally. "Thank you for everything. I just have one question."

"Shoot." He grinned. "Sorry, police humor. What's your question?"

"Well, maybe I'm missing something here, but if you've dropped the charges against Kai, why is he still in a cell?"

"That's a very good question."

..*

. . .

Copeland swiped his key card over the digital reader and then stood back. I stepped up to the cell door, now unlocked for me. It didn't have bars but was instead made of solid metal with a single window in the center. I could only imagine how confining that felt to be inside. But at least it would offer us some privacy now.

"Just knock when you're finished," Copeland said quietly.

I nodded and then pushed open the door and stepped inside.

The room was small and gray.

Gray walls, gray floor, and, you guessed it, gray ceiling. In the midst of all that gray was Kai.

His white shirt might have made him stand out except for the way he'd hunched his shoulders and hung his head like he was trying to fold in on himself.

He didn't even look up when I walked in, though I could sense through the mate bond that he'd recognized me. What the hell?

Behind me, the door clicked shut.

"Hey," I said.

His head came up slowly.

Our eyes met, and in his dark gaze, a storm raged.

I watched as his hands gripped the bench seat, his knuckles white with the effort. He didn't get up and approach me. If anything, he seemed to be gripping the bench so he wouldn't get up.

"Hi," he said in a ragged voice.

My heart squeezed for whatever had made him sound so wounded.

I sniffed suspiciously. "Are you hurt?"

"No, I'm fine."

He wasn't fine, though. He was so damn far from fine it wasn't funny.

"Kai." I took a step forward and watched as he tensed.

"What are you doing here?"

I stopped, completely at a loss. He'd never rejected me like this. Not even before when he was pretending to hate me. Even then, I'd always known part of him wanted me. But this… I didn't even understand how he could do it when I could tell his wolf wanted so badly to close the distance.

"What's wrong?" I asked.

"We should talk," he said quietly.

"Okay, so talk." I sank onto the L-shaped bench seat. It ran the length of this wall and then curved around to the far one where he sat. But I didn't use it to slide closer. Instead, I remained perfectly still, desperate for him to just explain himself.

"Cherise came to see me yesterday," he began, and my wolf instantly went on alert. My hackles rose at the unfamiliar name.

"Who's Cherise?"

"A friend," he said, which only made me more triggered. I forced myself to breathe deeply, knowing full well Kai could sense my rage. He did nothing to calm it. "She told me about the alpha challenges," he said, not quite meeting my eyes.

"What about them?"

"She said you hadn't added your name to the challengers yet."

"I haven't," I said.

His eyes met mine again, something painful sparkling back at me from their dark depths. "But you will, right?"

"I don't know. What does this have to do with us, Kai?

Or with you volunteering to remain locked in a cell? Let's go home. Talk about this—"

"My name's been added," he said.

I blinked. "I mean, that was pretty much a given after Drake challenged you in front of the pack like that."

"It's not just Drake's challenge." He shook his head, hung it low again. When he raised it, his expression was stony. He was bracing himself. "I want this. My wolf feels the alpha call, Ash."

"Okay," I said, drawing out the word as I tried to understand the problem. "Again, we can talk about this when you're not in a jail cell."

"Ash," he snapped, and I fell silent at the abruptness of it. "You're going to add your name to the challengers. You have to because that's how the curse is broken. And my name has already been added. Do you not understand? We'll have to fight each other. For alpha."

"Get real." I huffed, rolling my eyes at the ridiculousness of it all. "I'm not going to fight you, Kai. That's insane."

"Is it? These alpha challenges are sacred, Ash. If you and I make it to the final round, we'll be forced to fight each other." He shook his head. "I should have rejected Drake's challenge."

"Is that why you're still in this cell?"

"I can't fight Drake if it means fighting you."

"Kai, you'd make a great alpha. I'm not going to stand in your way."

"Well, you should. Don't you get it, Ash? If you're not alpha, the curse can't be broken. But my wolf, it wouldn't let me turn it down. I feel called, Ash. I didn't think that could happen. Not when your wolf is the rightful choice."

"This is why you're upset? Because you think you're

taking something away from my wolf? Kai, I don't want alpha. I never did. That's you."

"What about the curse?" he shot back, eyes flashing with a temper I still didn't understand.

"I don't know. We'll figure it out."

"There's not another way, Ash. This is a curse, not assembly instructions for IKEA furniture. There are rules."

"I don't give a fuck about rules," I said, my voice rising.

We were practically yelling now. I didn't care. This was stupid. All of it. Kai voluntarily sitting in this cell. Our fight. The fact that everyone kept pushing this on me.

"Do you give a fuck about me?" he yelled back.

"Of course I do. I wouldn't come to jail and yell at just anyone."

"You know what I mean."

"And so do you," I said.

He scowled, and the temper I'd been working to hold back finally sprung free.

"How can you even ask me if I care?" I demanded. "You're it for me, Kai. Or didn't the whole claiming mark thing give it away?" I huffed, unable to stop the words from tumbling out. "I've lost everything. My parents, my home—hell, I never even fully had one of those. And more than that, I lost my place in the damn world because it turns out I'm not even human. And you are the only thing that has kept me sane through all this. But the one thing I won't lose is my free will. I refuse to fight for something I don't want.

"I will find another way to break the curse because I will not be forced into one more damn thing in my sad fucking life. Now, if you want to punish yourself, be my guest. I'm not going to sit around and feel sorry for myself about my lack of choice. Where there isn't choice,

I will create one for myself. Because that's what the fuck I do."

I got up and headed for the door, but a hand snaked around my wrist, spinning me around and pressing me into the wall. Kai's eyes blazed with fury and determination unlike anything I'd ever seen. But the temper was matched by something else. Desire.

Lust curled in my gut.

My breath caught.

I hadn't even known he could move so quickly. And now, all I wanted was for him to never move again. For us, for this, to be all there was.

"Ash," he whispered, his breath ragged, his expression tortured.

"I miss you," I whispered back.

With a desperate sound, he crushed his mouth to mine. The kiss was bruising. Angry. I could feel his frustration in the way he held me against the wall and in the force of his tongue invading my mouth. I wrapped my arms around his neck, burying my fingers in his hair, and kissed him back with the same temper-filled passion.

By the time we broke apart, my legs had somehow become wrapped around his waist. But when Kai pulled back, I lowered my feet to the ground again, reading his eyes as if they were an open book.

Despite the kiss, and all I knew it meant to him, the feelings coming through our bond were unchanged. He was here because he thought it would protect me. Not from Drake or some other outside threat. From him.

Angry and sad and irritatingly horny, I shoved him off me and whirled toward the door, pounding on it with my fist.

"You're wrong," Kai said quietly from where he stood behind me.

I didn't bother to turn around. "About what?" I snapped.

"You do want it," he said. "You just don't think you deserve it."

I opened my mouth, a litany of curses and denials at the ready. But nothing came out.

The door opened.

I walked out.

15

Idrissa answered her front door dressed in a towel, her bright red hair wet and tangled.

"Hey," I said.

"Hey."

Sharp barking began, and I caught sight of a Chihuahua racing up the hall straight for me. I might have enjoyed the enthusiastic welcome if the dog wasn't already baring its teeth.

"Oh, no you don't."

Idrissa scooped him up just before he could launch himself at my ankle. She held him in one arm as he growled at me, head tilting right then left.

"Hi, Galileo," I said.

He growled.

"Shut up before I put you in a purse," Idrissa told him.

He stopped growling.

I lifted a brow. "Impressive."

"He bit the sheriff yesterday, so I'm not taking any chances."

I bit my lip, fighting a smile at that. "Kinda wish I'd seen it."

"Definitely entertaining," she said.

My smile slipped as I remembered the real reason I was here. "How's Isaac?"

"He's in his room, sleeping. My mom's with him."

"Is he—?"

"He's nearly healed now," she assured me, and the relief in her eyes was proof she meant it.

I exhaled. "Can we talk?"

"Sure. Is everything okay?" she asked. "It's late."

"I couldn't sleep."

Truthfully, I hadn't tried. After my trip to see Kai earlier, I'd gone home and paced the apartment until I'd practically worn a hole in the floor. Oscar had made me tell him everything and then promptly ordered take-out rather than asking me to cook dinner like usual. I hadn't eaten more than a bite, though. In fact, the more time went on, the less okay I felt about everything.

Idrissa stepped back. "Come in."

She held the door wide, and I stepped into the quiet foyer. All the lights in the back of the house were off, and I couldn't hear any movement upstairs. Idrissa motioned for me to follow her up, but I hesitated.

"I don't want to wake everyone," I said.

"Give me five." She turned and dashed upstairs, leaving me standing alone in a house that smelled like a family of werewolves and the family Chihuahua.

My eye caught on the wall of photos lining the hall. I smiled at the sight of Idrissa and Isaac as kids. Isaac with a flamingo print swimsuit and Idrissa with a baseball camp on backward over her messy hair—still dark like Isaac's back then. Amberly and Warren stood behind them, both smiling into the sunlight.

They looked happy.

Warren's expression was so open, friendly. Nothing like the pinched look he wore every time I saw him. I wondered what had changed for him?

The curse, maybe?

I kept going, studying each of the photos, which gave a chronology of the twins' childhood. Dirt bike competitions for Idrissa. Dance for Isaac. The last photo was from high school; a collage of pictures that included a group shot with several other familiar faces. Kai, Silas, and Presley all stood together with the twins. Every one of their gazes held secrets and chaos. The same secrets and chaos I'd stumbled upon when I'd come to this town.

I'd heard Idrissa talk about how they'd once all been friends. Now, seeing the photographic evidence of how much the curse had changed them all, I wanted to do something to help bring them back together again.

Kai's words echoed in my head: *you do want it. You just don't think you deserve it.*

I blinked, shoving his words out of my mind as footsteps sounded on the stairs. Idrissa appeared, her jeans and tank both black and her hair pulled up into some kind of intricate knot on her head.

"Come on," she said and slipped out the front door.

I followed her over to the detached garage and waited while she unlocked it and turned on the lights. I'd only ever seen the garage portion, which had been covered in nothing but motorcycle parts and various tools meant to put them together again. But this time, Idrissa bypassed that and led the way up a narrow flight of stairs that opened up into a loft above.

It was decorated with funky artwork that offered a strangely attractive blend of motorcycles and classy women. Marilyn Monroe on a cruiser except she was dressed in coveralls and giving the camera the finger. A sculpture of a woman's bust made from what looked like an exhaust pipe. Somehow, it all worked. And it was very Idrissa.

"What is this place?" I asked.

"My hideaway," she said. "I'd move out here, but that would mean Isaac finding new space for his art, and I can't bring myself to evict him."

"Wait. Isaac made all of this?"

"Yeah. He sells most of it online. Makes a killing too."

"Wow, I had no idea." I took a closer look at the sculpture, intrigued. And impressed. "This is incredible."

When I looked up again, I caught Idrissa studying me.

"Something happened," she announced.

I frowned. "Can't I just want to come hang with my bestie? For fun?"

"You're here after dark. Alone, even though half the pack is trying to off you. And you want to talk about phallus-shaped artwork my brother sells on Etsy. Something's wrong."

"I care about my friends' lives," I said, not even sure why I was bothering to have this argument. But it made me feel better for reasons that were probably very, very lame when said aloud.

"And we care about yours," she shot back. "Which is why, respectfully, I have to tell you what an idiot you are for being out alone like this." Her eyes narrowed. "Does Oscar know you're here?"

"He's the one who told me to go out," I said.

"You know I can smell when you lie, right?"

"No, you can't."

"Okay, but if I could, it would be badass."

I rolled my eyes. "Vinny and the others are being held

in the county jail. Just so you know, you don't have to worry about me being out there alone."

"No shit?" Her grin faded, and her eyes widened. "Damn, girl. Okay, spill it. What have I missed playing nursemaid to the whiniest patient ever?"

I took a deep breath and tried to figure out where to even begin. "I had a meeting with the sheriff today," I said.

"Yeah, I had mine yesterday over the phone. He wanted to talk to Isaac too, but he just ... wasn't in good shape." Her voice dipped low, and I reminded myself he was going to be okay. "Anyway, how'd it go?"

"He offered to arrest Vinny and the others," I said.

"Good. They deserve worse."

"It's a temporary fix," I said, "But it gets them off our backs for now."

She nodded. "And what about Kai? He doesn't have shit on him, you know."

"I know." I looked down at an ashtray made from nuts and bolts welded together. "Kai's charges were dropped."

"Ash, that's great. Wait. Why do you look like a kicked puppy? And why aren't you at his place having a conjugal?"

"He's still in jail."

"Sorry, what? I thought you said—"

I met her eyes, my temper pressing at my skin. "He's there of his own volition."

"Explain."

I gave her the short version of everything Kai had said.

"So, basically, he wants alpha, but he wants you and he wants you to want alpha."

"I can't even believe I understood that," I said. "But yes."

"So, what are you going to do?"

"Nothing," I said, exasperated. "I don't know how many more times I can say that I don't want to be alpha."

"Why not?" she asked, her face scrunching in an expression I couldn't decipher.

"Why not what?"

"Why don't you want to be alpha?"

My eyes narrowed. "Now you sound like Silas."

"I don't think you meant to insult me that badly just now, so I'm going to ignore it. Answer the question, Ashes." She put emphasis on the nickname she knew I hated.

I gave her a dirty look. "I don't know. Maybe because I don't want to be in charge of an entire town full of assholes?"

"Not even if those assholes would be happier because of it?"

"No one is happier with me in charge," I muttered.

"Ah." She lifted her chin knowingly. "Now we're getting somewhere."

"What the hell is that supposed to mean?"

"It means we're getting down to the daddy issues of it all. Come on." She made a motion with her hands that resembled pulling a rope out of my chest. "Keep talking. Why aren't we happier with you in charge, Ashes?"

"I'm going to rip your nipple off if you call me that again."

"So violent." She gasped with mock fear. "Tell me how you really feel."

"This is bullshit," I said, frustrated. "I came here for support."

"I support you. I mean, I think I made that clear when I attacked my fellow asshole townspeople for you just the other night." She smirked. "I just want to understand you."

"Fine." I threw my hands up, exasperated and pushed

far enough that the words came tumbling out. "I'm no one, okay? I'm Ash Langford, daughter of a drunk. I'm a drifter. A loner. Friendless. No social skills. Hell, I'd never even been on a date until Kai and never had a real friend until you and Isaac. I have zero political experience. I didn't even fit into a social hierarchy in high school, that's how invisible I was.

"I'm not a leader, I'm a runner. When things get hard, I run away. Start over. Pretend myself into a new life. And when something happens to threaten that life, I pack up and run again. Then I do it all over and over. That's not alpha leadership. It's cowardice. And I refuse to bring my toxic baggage to an entire pack. It's not their problem; it's mine."

"And there it is, folks. Finally. The moment we've all been waiting for. Ash Lawson—because first of all, that's your real name—is now self-aware, and what do the kids call it these days? Oh yeah. Woke. Congratulations."

"Shut up."

Idrissa's expression softened. The teasing vanished, and she smiled gently. "You're not a runner, Ash. You're a warrior."

I snorted.

"I mean it. You have always had one thing to protect: yourself. And you did it the best way you knew how. The only way your parents taught you. To retreat. But since you stepped foot in the Falls, you've never once retreated or backed down from anyone. Hell, I thought you were going to whoop Silas' ass that first day in Bo's bar. Guaranteed, he'll never throw a single tray at someone's head ever again."

I fought off a smile at the memory of that. Silas had been terrifying back then—okay, sometimes he still was—but I'd refused to back down against someone like that.

"And don't forget about Vinny," she added.

"Screw that guy," I muttered.

She snorted. "I'm glad you finally understand why I punched his lights out that day. But I will never forget the look on your face when you saw what I'd done to him. Ash, you cared. You worried about him, a complete stranger. Hell, you were ready to fight me to defend him."

"That wouldn't have ended well for me at the time," I said, my mouth lifting in a half-smile.

"Damn right, but you were ready anyway," she said with a laugh. "You fight back, Ash. You see what you want, and you find a way to get it. That's what I love about you. Frankly, I couldn't be friends with someone less fierce." She shrugged. "I'd terrify them."

"You do have a point about that," I admitted.

She reached out and covered my hand with hers, a rare show of affection for Idrissa.

"Forget everyone else, Ash. Forget your fear. Forget your past. Forget all the forces conspiring to bring you to this moment. And for shit's sake, forget the damned curse." Her eyes caught mine and held fast. "What do *you* want?"

"I don't even know anymore," I admitted, my insides churning with it all laid out there.

"Fair enough." But Idrissa wasn't letting me off the hook, not like everyone else had. "What does your wolf want?"

"Ugh. Oscar asked me the same thing."

"And? Did you ask her?"

"She's kind of a bitch," I admitted.

Idrissa laughed. "Why's that?"

"She wants everything. Her mate. A family. Friends. A home."

Idrissa's eyes glittered like I'd just said whatever it was

she wanted to hear. "What about alpha? Does she want that too?"

"You mean does she feel the alpha calling?"

Idrissa nodded.

"Maybe," I admitted. "She doesn't want anyone else to have it, that's for sure. How do I know if that's what this is?"

"You'll know when you're ready to," she said simply.

I tried not to think about it. Mostly because wanting it would mean everything Kai had said was truly the problem he was making it out to be. If I did want it, where would that leave us?

I wasn't quite ready to figure all that out. Besides, another issue still had me at a loss.

"About the alpha call," I began, "is it possible that others can feel it within me? Like, they can sense the alpha in me even if I can't?"

"Like supporters?" She nodded. "You saw all those wolves attack us on behalf of Drake, so I'd say yes. If they can pledge themselves to a weak sack of shit like him, anyone can sense it in anyone else, I guess."

I bit my lip.

"Why?" she prompted, watching my face warily now. "Did something happen?"

"Tiffany offered her undying fealty."

Idrissa's confusion overtook her suspicion. "What?"

I sighed. "I went for a run last night. Tiffany found me in the woods and knelt in front of me and then bared her throat for me."

Idrissa's eyes widened, and I had zero doubt she knew exactly what that move symbolized.

"Seriously?"

"Seriously. And she said there are others. Members of the pack who support me for alpha."

"Okay, not to look a gift horse in the mouth—and that's not the first time I've called Tiffany a horse, by the way—but what's in it for her?"

"Her true mate, I guess."

"Does she know who it is?" Idrissa's voice jumped sharply.

"No, I mean, I don't think anyone does yet. But she wants to. She says she wants me to do whatever it takes to finish breaking the curse so she can find him. They all do." I sank onto the couch against the wall and picked up a coaster made from some kind of metal.

"Wow. Okay, you're in a girl gang with Tiffany. Gotta admit, didn't see that coming."

I snorted. "You and me both. Hell, I didn't see a single bit of this coming."

"Yeah, destiny's a sneaky bitch."

I looked up sharply. "You think being alpha is my destiny?"

"I think there's destiny's plan and there's your free will. If you want something, take it."

I leaned my head back and stared at the ceiling, trying to think past all the swirling thoughts filling my head.

"It's not that complicated," Idrissa said.

I looked up. "Sure feels like it."

"How about this: Do you like us?"

"Us who?"

She shrugged. "Me. Isaac. The assholes in this town."

I smiled. "You're the best friend I've ever had," I said. "And I'd say that even if I had a best friend before you."

She grinned. "Damn right you would. And do you want to stay with us?"

My smile fell. "Yes," I said quietly.

"Seems like the logical step is to fight for what you want."

"Logical," I agreed.

"See? Simple."

I snorted. "Except for Drake challenging Kai. And the hexerei wanting to kill us all. And the fact that Drake is fighting Devon to the death as we speak."

Idrissa's eyes widened. "I'm sorry, the fuck?"

"You didn't hear?"

She shook her head and pointed at me. "Speak."

"Drake challenged Devon to an alpha duel."

"But Drake already challenged Kai."

I shrugged. "I guess he got bored waiting around for them to release him."

"No wonder Kai chose to stay put." She shook her head. "If he's locked up, he can't fight. And he doesn't have to forfeit."

I hated to admit that I understood his strategy, as crazy as it seemed.

"So, Devon and Drake are fighting," Idrissa said. "Tonight."

I nodded. "Silas told me about it. I just figured you already knew since I'm always the last to know anything around here."

Idrissa stood up, heading for the stairs. "Don't just sit there, let's go," she called over her shoulder.

"Wait." I stood and hurried to follow her down the stairs and outside. "We can't show up there. Vinny might be arrested, but there could be others—"

"Drake's little minions can fuck right off," she declared, striding over to the dirt bike propped in the corner. "Besides, we already took them down once, which Drake knows, so if he's smart, he'll watch himself."

"Right, but is *this* smart?" I pressed. "You and me going in alone?"

Clearly, Idrissa wasn't interested in smart. She

wheeled the bike out the door and into the moonlight. Then she looked back at me.

"I'm not worried about Drake's little soldiers, and neither are you. What we are worried about are the alpha challenges—and keeping our eye on the frontrunner. Drake's wolf shouldn't be stronger than Devon's, not from what I've seen out of the two of them in the past. But if Drake's challenging him, that means the asshat thinks he can win."

"You think Drake has something up his sleeve?"

"Doesn't he always?" She held out a helmet to me. "You riding with me or running?"

I took the helmet.

"Silas won't be happy I'm showing up there," I said, remembering what he'd said about lying low until I figured out what I wanted.

"Silas can go to hell," Idrissa said as I climbed on behind her. "Wait. How did you say it before? Oh yeah. He can kiss my Ash."

She kickstarted the bike, and we sped off.

16

Even over the noise the dirt bike made, I heard the roar of voices coming from the barn before we'd come to a full stop. I climbed off the back and slid my helmet free, setting it aside as Idrissa started for the barn. I hurried to catch up, bracing myself for the reaction of the crowd when we walked in. Would Drake order someone to kill me again? Would he still be alive? Would Devon?

But Idrissa stopped short of the main door and motioned for me to follow her around back. The whole thing felt uncomfortably familiar. Last time I'd been here, I'd hidden out back and spied through a hole in the wall. Now, thanks to getting caught doing just that, the wall was a hole.

Someone had boarded it up, I realized when we crept around the corner. A terrible job, for sure, considering the scrap sheet of wood was riddled with splinters and rusted nails. But it held.

And sure as shit, it offered another gap just like before.

Idrissa didn't stop there, though. She crept past the

patch job and around to the far corner where a rickety ladder had been bolted to the main support beam.

I lifted a brow. "I thought you didn't care about Drake and his minions?"

Idrissa winked. "Damn right. But we need to make an entrance."

An entrance. Of course.

Why had I expected anything less from Idrissa?

She had to jump to reach the first rung, but after that, it was an easy enough climb to the loft access above.

I followed her lead until we were both standing in the open loft. Really, it was nothing more than a long, narrow space enclosed on the two longer sides but completely open to the elements on either end.

From the front, I could see past Bo's bar at the other end of the field and out over the trees that seemed to run on for miles and miles.

The wind stirred, bringing an unfamiliar scent with it. But there was no time to wonder about it before Idrissa motioned for me to follow her again. We crept deeper into the loft, yet the voices of the crowd below rose right over us. Idrissa reached down and peeled back a small block of wood that sat loosely against the others. It came away like a puzzle piece being removed from the very center.

This hole offered an even better view than the one on the back wall. And a hell of a lot more cover. Too bad I hadn't known about this particular hiding spot the first time.

Below us, the barn was crowded with people. They'd packed themselves inside but were now pressed against the walls, still yelling as they shrank back from the center attraction.

One glance, and I could see why.

Two wolves faced off in the middle of the dirt floor. Both were bloodied, but my nose told me the blood belonged only to one of them. Drake's wolf was easy to recognize, especially after watching him move through the woods the other day. The wound I'd given him during our fight had healed, and he moved with a strength and speed I didn't remember him having.

My attention turned to Devon.

I spotted a fresh wound on his left side—deep from the looks of it. And with every step and feint, he grew slower. Clumsier. Devon's wolf was strong. Even my own wolf could feel its dominance. An obvious alpha candidate, I realized.

But Drake's wolf was clearly stronger.

In fact, from the looks of it, Drake was only toying with him now.

Prolonging the inevitable.

When I realized what was coming, I reached for Idrissa's hand and held it tight. She looked at me, our eyes meeting and conveying everything my words could not. I didn't know Devon personally. Not beyond our one personal encounter which involved him flirting with me and Kai nearly kicking his ass for it. But he didn't deserve this. And he was a damn good guy compared to Drake.

When Drake finally delivered the killing blow, I winced and bit back the howl of protest my wolf wanted to utter. The rest of the crowd groaned and booed, but a round of cheers rose over the rest.

I followed Idrissa's nod and spotted a small group of supporters on the left, all of them cheering for Drake.

My stomach clenched in disgust and rage.

This wasn't right.

It was division, not unity. Wasn't having an alpha supposed to bring everyone together?

"This has to stop," I choked out.

Idrissa looked up at me with a look in her eye I didn't recognize at first.

"Hell yeah, it does," she said.

And then she waited, watching me expectantly. Like it was my move now.

She'd done this on purpose, I realized.

Brought me here. Given me a front-row seat to witness Devon's death. Because she knew if I saw it, there'd be no more sitting on the sidelines. No more wringing my hands over the pack's problems while pretending I could stay out of it.

It wasn't the pack's problem.

It was my problem too.

And it was time I started acting like it.

Had Idrissa manipulated me—again? Yes. But was it the push I needed? Apparently.

Squaring my shoulders, I let go of Idrissa's hand. "This ends now," I said.

Idrissa's lips curved in a devilish smile. "Ready to make that entrance?" she asked.

"Let's do it."

She stood and reached for a handle I hadn't noticed before. This time, when she peeled back the wooden hinge, it revealed a trap door more than big enough for my body to fit through. A set of stairs lay folded to one side, but I didn't bother swinging them down.

Instead, I grabbed either side of the opening and swung myself through it to the ground floor in one clean swoop.

My feet landed with a hard thud right in the center of the fighting arena. Directly in front of the crowd.

And Drake.

He'd shifted back to two legs, and someone had given

him a pair of gym shorts to wear while he basked in the victory glow.

At the sight of me, the cheers died abruptly.

The first face I focused on was Silas.

He gave me a hard look, but he didn't tell me to get out. In fact, he didn't say a word. No one did.

Just like Idrissa, they were all waiting.

For me, I realized.

Their wait was over.

"Drake," I called.

He turned away from his admirers, and when he saw me, his eyes immediately narrowed. There was no trace of nerves or worry as he stalked toward me.

"You here to challenge me, Ashes?" he asked.

The alpha energy rolled off him stronger than I'd ever felt from him.

I tensed as my own wolf rose to the surface, ready to do battle if and when it came to that.

"I'm here to stop the unnecessary fights," I said. "The pack should be coming together, not ripping itself apart."

Some cheered at that. Some yelled their disagreement.

Idrissa dropped to the floor beside me, her expression daring anyone to come any closer.

"Drissa, hey. I hear your brother ran into some trouble the other night," Drake said.

"Ash, either you kill him or I will," Idrissa said between clenched teeth.

Drake looked at me, brow raised. "You sure you're up for another round?"

"I'm sure I could send you running, tail between your legs, just like I did your little kill squad," I told him.

His smile disappeared.

One point for Ash.

But the power rolling off him never dimmed.

"You forget I've already issued my challenge," he said. "And it still stands. I'll fight Kai for alpha. And until that's done, I have nothing to say to his mate."

I felt my wolf straining to get out. She wanted this. To end it all now. To put Drake down like he deserved. But something held me back. Whatever power Drake had now, it hadn't been there last time. He'd done something. Found a way to get stronger.

It didn't make sense.

Still, it was either this or let Drake tear the pack apart.

"Kai's not here," I said. "You'll have to settle for me."

"Are you sure about that?"

Drake's question, and the smug-ass look on his face, threw me.

"Why wouldn't I be?" I demanded.

But Drake's attention had already shifted.

A hum of commotion began near the door. The crowd parted as someone else walked in.

I knew him by smell alone, which was just as well since he was nearly unrecognizable through the layers of grime.

Kai.

His clothes were covered in dust and dirt. His hair was matted to his forehead, and my wolf nearly lost her shit, trying to get to him to make sure he was okay.

Shoving people aside, I raced across the space and slammed into him, wrapping my arms around his neck and pulling him close.

I didn't care who was watching.

His arm came around me, squeezing me tight. "I'm okay," he murmured against my ear. "I'm okay."

I forced myself to relax. But then the reality of this moment hit me, and panic seized my heart, squeezing it painfully. "What the hell happened to you? How are you here?"

I pulled back, more questions tumbling out before he could answer.

"I heard about the fight tonight and decided it was time to go," he said, eyes flashing as he glanced past me at something—or someone—that made his jaw tick. "Since the deputy had left for the night, I made my own exit."

"You..." My jaw dropped. He'd broken out of prison? "Why? I mean, you can't—Drake is here. He killed Devon, and he—"

"I know." His expression was grim and devoid of a single thing except for violence.

Drake sauntered up beside us, wearing a satisfied smirk on his disgusting mouth. And I realized he'd done this. Somehow, he was responsible for Kai being here now.

This was all Drake manipulating everyone else. And now, he'd have the fight he wanted so badly.

"Ready?" he asked Kai.

"You have no idea," Kai said, eyes sparkling with the need to kill.

The roar of the crowd was deafening as Drake backed away to a far corner to wait. Silas came forward, cutting off any chance at a conversation between me and Kai before this shitshow went down. My heart hammered so hard I worried it would beat right out of my chest.

"Kai," I began, not caring that Silas was listening.

But Kai stopped me. His hands cupped my cheeks. "Ash, this has to happen. Drake's challenge—it can't be taken back."

"I don't get it. You said you didn't want to fight each other."

"And if I hadn't shown up tonight?" he pressed. When I

didn't answer, he said, "You were going to fight him in my place, weren't you?"

"The killing has to stop," I said.

"I agree. But I can't let you fight him. And I can't forfeit. You do understand that, right?"

"Yes, but his wolf... Something's different, Kai. He's stronger."

Kai frowned. "You think I can't beat him?"

"Of course you can. I just...Kai, if anything happens to you—"

"You'll die," Silas said.

I flinched, suddenly remembering he was here. "What?"

"If one mate is killed, the other doesn't usually survive very much longer," he said.

"Shut the hell up, man," Kai groaned.

Silas looked at Kai. "You didn't tell her any of this?"

"Of course not," Kai said. "I'm not an idiot."

"Debatable," Idrissa grumbled from my other side.

Ignoring her, Kai looked back at me. "I'm not going to lose."

"Kai, you need to know something," I began. "About being alpha. About me."

My stomach swirled. Fear, urgency. He needed to know that I'd decided to compete. That his fight with Drake was going to pit us against one another.

"Are we fighting, or are you going to stand here and hug your girlfriend all night?" Drake demanded.

The crowd went wild.

Kai shook his head. "We'll talk after," he said quickly. "I promise. As long as you want. I have to do this, Ash. Please understand."

The worst part was that I did understand. Now that I'd

admitted I felt the calling too, I couldn't imagine resisting it. And I wouldn't expect Kai to do it either.

He pressed a kiss to my jaw, and then he was dropping his hands from my face and turning to face Drake. His alpha challenger. Over his shoulder, he called out to Silas, "make sure she doesn't interfere."

"Kai," I said, but he was already walking away.

Silas scooted in closer to me, but I ignored him, keeping my eyes fastened on Kai's back.

My stomach twisted at the idea of what was to come next.

"Begin," Silas called, his voice a roar above the rest.

Drake's form shimmered once, signaling his change. Then, he was on all fours. Covered in fur. Stalking toward Kai.

Kai's form pulsed, and I braced myself as he shifted, mid-stride.

They leaped at the same time, claws and teeth clashing violently.

I grabbed Silas' arm as Idrissa appeared on my other side.

"What happened to Drake?" I asked, watching as the wolves circled and leaped and did their best to rip each other apart. "His wolf," I said. "It's bigger."

Silas didn't answer, but his expression was pinched with either confusion or concern.

Even Idrissa looked lost. "I don't know, but it's bullshit," she said. "He's cheating."

In the center of the room, Drake pinned Kai and I sucked in a sharp breath as Drake's teeth narrowly missed Kai's throat. Kai twisted and slid out, his teeth ripping a gash in Drake's back leg.

Drake growled, no sign of pain.

My wolf was restless now.

I had a feeling the first show of blood was going to push her over the edge.

I couldn't take this.

It should be me.

The thought startled me. I didn't want to take this from Kai. His rightful place. But it was my place too. Somewhere between Tiffany pledging herself to me and Drake's campaign to keep me from breaking the curse, I'd begun to believe I belonged here. Not just in the Falls. But as the pack's alpha too.

Tiffany had called it my birthright.

And for the first time since hearing the words, standing here, watching Kai fight for something I wanted, I knew I couldn't just stand aside.

I let go of Silas' arm and took a step toward the fight.

"Oh, hell no, you don't."

Determined, I broke into a run, but Silas grabbed me around the waist, lifting me clean off my feet.

"What the hell, Si? Put me down," I demanded, kicking my legs and flailing my arms.

"You can't intervene," he said, struggling to keep from getting punched or kicked. "Pack law."

"There is no pack law," I argued. "Not without an alpha to enforce them. Now put me the hell down."

"Okay, then. Kai's law." He tossed me over his shoulder and started for the back of the room.

Idrissa was screaming at Silas too, but he ignored both our protests and kept marching. With my head hanging upside down and eyes facing Silas' back, my view of the fight was completely obscured. When a sharp yelp rang out between the two wolves, I lost it.

Using my nails, I reached up and sank my fingers into Silas' neck. My nails cut his skin as they raked downward, and Silas hissed. Probably more in surprise, but it didn't matter. His balance wavered, and I threw myself sideways, sending us both falling to the ground in a mess of limbs.

I was up again before Silas could recover, sprinting toward the fight.

Blood.

I didn't know who it belonged to, but I no longer cared. Rules be damned, Drake was getting his throat ripped out, and there wasn't a damn thing in the world left to stop me.

But a howl from outside split the air, and I froze.

Up ahead, so did Kai.

Even Drake faltered.

We all looked at one another, and I knew we were thinking the same thing. Whatever had made that noise, it wasn't one of ours.

And it wasn't friendly.

But the power rolling in from outside was unmistakable.

Another howl went up. Then another.

The sound of the joined voices made the hairs on my neck stand on end.

"What the hell," Silas said roughly, and I didn't know if he was talking about my getaway stunt or the howling.

"They're close," Idrissa said, rushing up to me.

I looked at Silas.

"They're not ours," he said, confirming what I already knew.

"Keep everyone inside," I said. "Kai."

He was already at my side, pressing me toward the wall with his furry body.

Yeah, right.

"I'm going out there," I said, meeting his large yellow eyes with a glare of my own to match. "You can fight me or come with me to make sure everyone else is safe."

He huffed but then turned for the door.

I walked beside him, Idrissa and a few others behind us. I could hear Silas asking everyone to wait until we checked things out. Some were hanging back, but most of the crowd fell into step behind Idrissa.

Outside, a fog had fallen over the grass, making it nearly impossible—or it would have been without wolf senses—to discern the shapes rising up from the ground.

Cars.

A few motorcycles.

A wolf.

My stomach jumped as I spotted a single wolf stalking toward us in the tall grass near the trees. Kai had gone absolutely still beside me, and I knew if I saw it, he did too.

I reached for him, my fingers grabbing a fistful of his fur. Probably not acceptable wolf interaction, but I couldn't let him throw himself at whatever creature was approaching. And I knew that's what he'd do because it's exactly what I wanted to do too.

But the wolf was moving slowly. Not a threat. Especially considering how outnumbered it was. The scent reached me, and I realized it was the same as the one I'd noticed earlier in the loft. How long had he been out here?

"Is it someone from the pack?" I asked Idrissa.

"Nope," she said with zero hesitation.

"You're sure?"

"My wolf knows the scent of every single shifter in the Falls," she said. "That's not one of them."

I watched as the wolf came to a stop a safe distance away. It didn't shift or attempt to communicate. It simply...waited. A moment later, more movement caught my eye.

Two more wolves stalked out of the woods and into the grass. They stopped beside the first.

One of them shifted but not before I noticed even more wolves still moving inside the trees. They emerged in larger groups now, not bothering to hide themselves.

My gut tightened with a sense of danger.

The shifted wolf now stood on two legs.

A man.

Broad shoulders. Sinewy muscles running down his arms and legs. His skin was tanned and showed signs of being in the sun for many years. His beard was peppered with gray. And his eyes—those were sharp as a predator's.

"Ash Lawson?" he asked.

A ripple of shock ran through me. Behind me, murmurs went up.

"Who's asking?" I called out.

"I'm Baron Asheville. This is my pack."

He gestured to the wolves now flanking him on either side. I stared, letting his words sink in. His pack? As in, he was their alpha? What the hell?

"Do you know this guy?" I asked Idrissa, who'd gone noticeably quiet.

"I've heard of him." She swallowed hard and looked at me. "He's one of the most powerful alphas in the country, Ash. He's not someone to mess with."

Well, damn. That didn't sound great.

"Okay. But what's he doing here?" I whispered back.

She shook her head, her eyes wide.

"What's your business here?" Silas demanded.

For once, I was grateful for Silas' tough-guy demeanor. With Idrissa's words ringing in my ear, I wasn't entirely sure I could have pulled it off.

"I'm here to speak to Ash Lawson, alpha-heir to the Lawson pack," Baron said.

"This is the Lone Wolf pack now," Silas said.

"Yes, I knew all about your curse and the alpha who abandoned you." The man's eyes flashed with disgust, and my hands balled into fists at the insult to my father. I mean, sure, it was true. But that didn't mean this asshole could say it.

"If you know about our curse, then you know we have no alpha-heir," Silas shot back. "No alpha either."

"I hear that's all changing," he said. "You've lifted the curse, and your pack now feels the alpha call. And that means there will be an alpha of this pack once again."

"I don't see what business that is of yours," Silas said. "This is pack business."

"Not quite," Baron said, "This is alpha business." And then his hard gaze landed on mine. "Ash Lawson?"

I lifted my chin. "Yes."

"I, Baron Asheville, challenge you, Ash Lawson, for the role of alpha of this pack. Do you accept?"

"I…" I stared at him, stunned. "You're serious."

"I would never joke about an alpha challenge."

The crowd had gone completely silent.

"Ash isn't a contender for alpha of this pack." Drake's voice rang out loudly against the quiet. Out of the corner of my eye, I could see him moving toward us.

Baron's eyes snapped to where he approached.

"It's down to me and Kai Stone," Drake added, nodding a chin toward where Kai stood beside me.

Baron glanced at Kai and then back to Drake, eyes narrowed as he assessed them both.

"My wolf challenges who he perceives as the strongest," Baron said finally. "I've said what I've come to say."

Drake's expression twisted into rage.

"She's not the strongest," he snarled. "I am."

"My wolf has chosen," Baron said, his tone harsh and

impatient. He looked back at me. "Do you accept or forfeit?"

Drake let out a string of curses that Baron ignored.

Beside me, Kai growled, letting me know exactly what he thought of this entire debacle. I could feel his shift coming. And the moment he was back on two legs, I knew he would do his best to put a stop to this. Even if it meant challenging Baron himself.

I couldn't let that happen.

For the first time since Drake's alpha challenge, I understood how Kai felt. And why he'd accepted.

With hands shaking, I met Baron's gaze as steadily as my freaking-out heart would allow and gave him my answer.

"I accept."

17

An hour later, I stared blankly at a flyer on the wall that advertised a potluck dinner with "cake walk" printed in big blue letters. The date for the event was over three years ago, and the edges of the flyer were crinkled or missing. Yet, here it remained. Tacked to the wall of the pack's meeting hall. Like some last remnant of a community that no longer existed.

Sure, the pack remained. But the spirit of togetherness this flyer suggested had long since been abandoned. Kind of like the potluck flyer.

Through the closed doors that separated the foyer—and me—from the actual meeting space, I could hear Warren's deep voice droning on. The words were muffled, but the vibe was very much "lecture," and I had one guess who he was talking about when I caught words like "responsible" and "good for the pack."

Behind me, the front door opened.

I didn't bother to turn.

The mate bond alerted me to Kai's presence with more

than enough emotion behind it. I didn't need to look at him, too. That would only make me feel worse.

Kai stepped up beside me. I could feel his eyes on me, but I refused to look over. After Baron's challenge to me earlier, the Asheville pack alpha had left to await news about the details of our impending fight. Kai had gone with them, taking Silas and Presley along to make sure the Asheville pack cleared our borders without attempting any kind of harm. It was noble of him, but I couldn't get past the feeling that he'd left me to deal with everything alone.

Idrissa had brought me here on her dirt bike before returning home to check on Isaac. Oscar had met me at the door to the meeting hall, hugging me tighter than he ever had. And then Warren and Amberly had arrived, and they'd locked themselves in the meeting room to deliberate. Whatever the hell that meant.

"Hey," Kai said.

I kept my eyes on the wall. "Hey."

"Can we talk?"

"I'm in a meeting," I said.

"Yes, I can see that." His tone was dry, and my temper flared at it.

I glared at him, noting again that his clothes were covered in dust and dirt. "Shouldn't you be in jail?"

"I decided to stop wasting tax dollars," he said, and something about the words suggested a story behind them. But I refused to take the bait. He'd shut me out, not the other way around.

"Congratulations. Did Cherise advise you on that too?"

He opened his mouth, about to respond, then shut it again.

I turned back to the flyer and the bulletin board it was tacked to. Other flyers hung beside it. Advertisements for home cleaning, a truck for sale, puppies free to a good home. It was all here. The idea of a town you might want to live in. Instead, what you got was Ridley Falls, full of lone wolves who liked to fight and cause chaos.

I wanted this version of the town. The one where the crystal shop held yoga in the garden out back on Saturday mornings and the thrift store hosted a trunk sale in the fall.

But none of this existed anymore. It was all gone. Maybe it was too lost to get back. I sure as hell knew nothing about being a part of a town like the one on this bulletin board.

"Was this ever real?" I asked.

"What?"

"The stuff on this board." I pointed at the flyers. "Did this version of Ridley Falls ever exist?"

I looked at Kai, and he shrugged.

"Yeah, of course."

"And what happened? Everyone just woke up one day and lost their shit?"

"It was a slow descent," he said on a sigh. "The cake walk was ruined when Cade Marshall got drunk and threw a pie at Presley's head. He missed, and it hit Amberly instead."

My eyes widened as I tried picturing that.

"What happened to Cade?" I asked.

"Idrissa happened," he said, and I didn't really need much more information than that. My mind conjured a full enough picture with those two words. "Needless to say, that was the last potluck ever held."

He glanced at the board, his expression softening as his gaze turned distant. "I used to love those dinners, though. When I was a kid, we held them once a month on the full moon. Did a pack run and everything. Watching the entire pack change at once like that..." He shook his head. "It was pretty incredible."

I bit my lip, feeling nostalgic for something I'd never even had.

"If you're alpha, you have to reinstate pack dinners, okay? And a cake walk. They need a fucking cake walk in their lives. Promise me."

"Ash, what the hell are you talking about?"

"I'm talking about the future of the pack, Kai. Someone needs to put things back together. It's about more than just being alpha. Honestly, choosing an alpha is the beginning, not the end. These people deserve better."

"Why are you talking to me like it's all on me?"

I didn't answer.

"Ash, you're stronger than Baron Asheville."

I snorted. "Did you see that guy? He's a tank. And he's been an alpha for longer than I've been alive."

"And he challenged *you*."

"Wow, is this your idea of a pep talk?"

"Listen to me. Alphas only challenge the strongest. Anything weaker than them, and their wolves don't feel a threat, so they don't even bother." He huffed impatiently. "Do you get it? He didn't challenge me, and he damn sure didn't challenge Drake. Only you. That means his wolf sees you as the strongest here."

"I get what you're trying to say, but all I heard is the fact that an ageless, undefeated predator has chosen me as its next prey."

His eyes flashed. "You're not doing this."

"Doing what?"

"Backing down. Feeling beaten. Letting him in your head."

"How can I—"

"Ash, look at me. Do I look scared for you?"

"I don't know."

"Use the bond. Feel into it. Do you feel fear from me right now? Worry?"

I frowned. "No."

"Exactly, because I know you can handle this."

He grabbed my hand, probably because he could sense how badly I wanted to turn and walk away from this whole conversation. He held tight, refusing to let me.

"Your wolf feels the call. I know it. I can sense it. Just admit you feel it too."

"Fine." I bared my teeth at him in a flash of temper. "I feel it. My wolf feels it so sharply she wants to rip the throat out of anyone standing in her way. That could even include you, Kai Stone."

"It doesn't."

"How do you know for sure? You said it yourself. Hell, you stayed in jail so you wouldn't be forced to face my wolf."

"I was wrong."

"Ugh. Stop being nice to me right now."

His lips twitched. "You want me to be mean?"

"Yes," I insisted.

"Why?"

"Because it's easier to be mad."

"Because you're used to it."

I scowled. "Whatever."

"Ash." He stepped closer, closing the gap between us. He still held my hand with his, but with his other hand, he brushed his thumb over my cheek. My skin tingled, which kind of just pissed me off more. This was not what I'd meant when I told him to be mean.

"Kai, I don't want to lose you. You're the first thing that's felt like home to me in a long time. I can't take any of this without you. And I refuse to take it from you either."

"You were right," he said quietly. "I was wrong. We'll figure it out."

"What if—"

"No more what-if. We deal with what's in front of us. That's all we can do."

"We'll have to fight each other."

"We'll find a way."

"I feel the alpha call," I said again, not even sure when the tables had turned and I'd become the one voicing all the reasons this wouldn't work.

"I know. It's kind of amazing."

"How is that amazing?"

"Because you feel connected to this place. These people. You want to fight to keep them. And I know you've never had people in your life. Not like this. So, it's amazing to see you choose it now. I'm so proud of you."

My eyes filled with tears.

Kai leaned in and brushed his lips over the one tear that slipped down my cheek. "Don't cry, Ashes."

"I just… I don't know if anyone's ever said that before."

"That they were proud of you?"

I nodded, not trusting my voice.

"Well, now they have. And get used to it. I'm going to say it again when you whoop Baron Asheville's crotchety old ass."

I smiled through the tears. "He's in his prime, Kai."

"Maybe until he met you."

I shook my head. There was no telling my mate anything right now.

"What's the verdict in there?" he asked.

"No idea." I sighed. "It's kind of irritating having them talking about me while I'm supposed to stay out here, but then I remembered that if I was inside, I'd have to actually listen to Warren's bullshit."

He grinned. "Great point."

"I've gotten to the point where I don't really care what they decide, so it doesn't matter anyway."

"Wait. Decide what? Idrissa said they were just discussing the logistics of our two challenges and a security detail to watch Baron's pack for the next couple of days."

"Apparently, they're adding a third item to the docket. Whether or not I get to stay in the Falls until an alpha is chosen."

"What? Why in the hell is that even a question?"

"Drake's little army has filed formal pack complaints about me. Apparently, Oscar has been on the phone, trying to head it all off, but I guess tonight was the tipping point."

"Baron challenged *you*. How is that your fault?"

"Who even knows. Drake's trying everything he can to remove me from the challenges. As for the rest, I think Warren just wants control, and he feels it slipping away after all these years."

"You're defending him?"

Anger leaked through the bond, and I watched as he turned and headed for the doors leading inside. I reached out and grabbed his wrist.

"Kai, it's fine. You'll only make it worse."

His eyes flashed angrily. "You're one of us, Ash. They can't just kick you out."

"Look, even if they do, it's only temporary. Besides, I'm half-hexerei, Kai. I can't ignore that, and I can't ask them to, either."

"You're pack. That's all that matters."

"I'm starting to think that's not entirely true."

"What are you saying?"

"I'm half-witch, Kai. I don't know what that means for magic, but I can't deny it's part of me. I'm done pretending or lying. If they ask me to leave, I'll go."

One look at his stormy expression told me what he thought of my words. Before he could respond, the doors opened, and Warren leaned out into the foyer.

His eyes landed on me. "Ash, you can come inside now. We've made our decision."

He disappeared inside again. I started to follow, but Kai stopped me.

"Do they know?" he asked.

"Know what?"

"About the hexerei losing their magic?"

"Oscar knows," I said. "And the twins."

"You told them." I nodded. "What about the oath?"

"Immune," I said, "You?"

He shrugged. "Not interested in finding out."

Kai took my hand, and together, we followed Warren down the aisle to where the other elders waited at the front of the room. Oscar shot me a look, his expression strained, though I had no idea what it meant. Mitch, who'd arrived with Oscar earlier, looked uncomfortable in a crowd as usual, and Amberly offered a tight smile that could have gone either way, honestly.

Beside Amberly stood two other guys I'd never seen before. One of them had a sandy-colored head of hair with a bushy mustache to match. The other had a neck tattoo of what looked like a large spider. Neither of them looked particularly friendly in this moment. I hadn't even seen them arrive.

Kai glared at them all.

"You called Clem and Hector? This is bullshit," he said.

Warren was quick to cut him off. "You're a guest at this

meeting, son. You'll behave accordingly or you'll be asked to leave."

"Warren, you're an obsolete idea," Kai said. "This whole thing is completely irrelevant. The pack doesn't even listen to you anymore. What makes you think Ash or I will?"

Warren's hands shook, and I tensed, wondering if Kai had just pushed him too far. But Amberly put a hand on his arm, and he reluctantly relaxed just far enough to regain control.

"This council is the only thing standing between what we once were and complete chaos," Warren said, his cheeks flushed. "I won't stand aside and let us lose ourselves. Not when we're so close to regaining what we lost."

"If you kick Ash out, you're only feeding that chaos."

Warren snarled, and I realized his wolf was much closer to the surface than I'd thought. He leaned toward Kai as Amberly jumped forward to get between them.

"Kai, wait outside," she said in a voice I'd never heard her use before. Not angry, just firm. It reminded me of my mother. A complete force when she wanted to be.

Kai didn't argue, only glared. Then he glanced at me. "I'll be right outside." But the words were meant for Warren and sounded a lot like a warning.

I nodded and watched as Kai stalked out. He slammed the door behind him with enough force to shake the windows.

"Warren, relax," Amberly said in the same forceful voice. "Go sit down. Take some breaths."

Warren turned to her, blinking. She gave him a hard look, waiting as he slowly turned and sat down on the nearest bench. I watched in surprise at the way he obeyed her command. I didn't think Warren listened to anyone like that.

Satisfied, Amberly turned to me. "Warren's wolf is having a harder time holding its humanity than before," she said. Her tone was matter-of-fact, but the words startled me. "This isn't him. I know that doesn't help much, but the version you've met, it's not the Warren I know."

"How is this happening?" I asked. "I thought the curse was breaking."

"Warren and I lost our mate bond years ago, but our commitment to one another seemed enough to... Anyway, it's breaking down. All of it. The alpha call might have returned, which has helped some of them, but the rest of us are losing it faster than we were before."

"We need these alpha challenges to happen—and fast," Mitch said.

He gave me a pointed look.

"In the meantime," said the stranger with the mustache, "we could get on with this damn meeting." He gave Oscar a pointed look.

Oscar cleared his throat, glancing at me. "Right. Ash, this is Clem and Hector." Oscar motioned to the mustache and then the tattoo.

"Hi," I said uncertainly.

"She's young," the one with the dark hair said. Hector, maybe. Oscar hadn't been specific about who was who.

"She's old enough to have triggered the first wave of the curse's release," Amberly said. Something about her tone suggested this wasn't the first time she'd defended me.

"Have you figured out the challenge logistics?" I asked, impatient with all of the comments.

"We have," said Oscar. "Your challenge with Baron will happen two days from now in the field outside the barn.

It's the largest space we have for something like this and the one we can control easiest."

"And security?" I asked.

"We're putting together teams," he said. "I've made some calls, and they're on their way over."

As if on cue, the doors at the back opened, and in walked Idrissa, Isaac, Silas, and Presley. I zeroed in on Isaac, who looked completely recovered from his injuries. He shot me a wink and a thumbs-up as if to confirm. I smiled.

"Thanks for coming," Oscar said as they made their way up the aisle. "You can have a seat, and we'll be with you in a moment."

Idrissa shot me a questioning look as she slid into the second row with the boys. I shrugged and turned back to the council members.

"With all of that settled, we need to talk about your place here," Warren said. He'd gotten to his feet again and looked slightly less ready to take a bite out of someone.

"What about it?" I asked.

"It's come to our attention that you are descended from a hexerei," said Clem.

Yeah, we were going with Clem for the sandy mustache and Hector with the neck tattoo.

"She doesn't know that for sure," Oscar snapped, and I realized whatever they'd decided, he'd already been arguing against it. That didn't bode well for me.

"Do you know your mother's lineage?" Hector asked me.

"No," I said. "I don't. She never told me about any of this. Neither did my father."

"But your father was Caleb Lawson," Warren said.

"Yes, we've established that." I couldn't help the bit of sarcasm leaking in. This was repetitive. And after the whole thing with Kai a moment ago, I was losing my grip and my patience. The council was one thing, but these two assholes were strangers, and I didn't like them poking their noses in my business. Or worse, getting to decide my fate.

"Look, Oscar let me stay here when I first came to town. I learned about my wolf side, and I fought for my place in the pack, fair and square. I have a right to be here."

"That's true for shifters," Clem said, nodding, "But we don't allow hexerei in the Falls. For everyone's safety. I'm sure you understand."

"I'm not hexerei," I said. "Not in the way that makes them… them. I have no magic. I'm not a threat to anyone's safety."

Except maybe his if he tried to make me leave.

"That's not proven," Clem said, looking to Amberly instead of addressing me directly. Asshole. "And unless we had definitive proof she was one of us—"

"I'm mated to a member of this pack," I snapped. "Is that definitive enough?"

Clem didn't answer.

Hector looked thoughtful.

"Are we really having this conversation?" Idrissa asked. She stood up, crossing her arms and glaring at Hector and Clem. Amberly started to answer, but Idrissa cut her off, turning her glare on her mother instead. "And since when do Clem and Hector get a say?"

"They're on the council," Warren said.

"They haven't been active for over a year," Idrissa shot back. "Hector moved to Franklin three months ago."

"We realized this particular circumstance required the wisdom of the entire group," Clem said, and I looked over in time to see Isaac roll his eyes.

"The council's a figurehead at best, and you know it," Isaac said. "If you try kicking Ash out, you're going to have a riot on your hands."

"From what I've heard, we already had one over letting her stay," Hector pointed out.

I could feel the mood swinging out of my favor, and my wolf howled at me to stop it.

"We'll need to vote," Clem said. "All in favor of Ash relocating until this curse business can be resolved?"

"Aye," Hector said.

"Aye," Warren said which earned him a slap from Amberly. "What? It's for her safety," he insisted.

"Aye," said Clem.

"No," Oscar said in a hard voice.

"No," Amberly said firmly.

"Mitch?" Clem looked at him expectantly.

I realized, with dismay, he was the tie-breaker. I'd known Mitch since my first day on the job at the Throttle, but other than telling me I looked like my dad, he'd barely said more than two words to me. To be fair, he barely said more than two words to anyone but still. We didn't exactly have a bond.

"Ash stays," said a firm voice from the second row.

Everyone turned to look.

My eyes landed on Silas.

He'd stood and was meeting the stares of the council without a blink.

"Excuse me?" Clem frowned at him. "Silas Hale. You're not on this council."

"The council is a fucking joke," Silas said, shoving his way out of the row where he sat and marching up until he was face to face with Clem. Behind him, Idrissa and Isaac approached too. "The only way the council will ever carry the weight it once did is if Ash breaks the curse, restoring our ability to choose an alpha. And even then, it'll only happen if that alpha decides to give you a voice again. Otherwise, you're just a bunch of old men with superiority complexes."

"And women," Isaac pointed out. At Amberly's glare, he winced. "Sorry, Mom. Trying to be inclusive."

"Silas," Idrissa hissed.

"No, they need to hear this." Silas met Hector's eyes steadily. "Do you hear that, or have you lost your wolf hearing in your old age?"

"Watch it, kid," Hector snarled.

"Listen." Amberly's eyes were lit up with interest.

Her head cocked as she concentrated. The others did the same.

My wolf hearing clued me in a second later, and I recognized the dull roar of voices. Lots of them. All congregated nearby. Maybe even directly outside from the sounds of it.

"What is that?" I asked.

"Supporters," Idrissa said, smiling at me.

"Supporters of what?"

"Of you," she said simply. "We saw them when we came in."

All eyes swung toward me.

My stomach clenched with nerves. Did she mean—?

"Who's out there, exactly?" Warren demanded.

"Tiffany. Cade and Cody Marshall. Even Sheriff Copeland. There are about a dozen or so, and all of them are demanding Ash stay until her challenge is complete." Idrissa looked at Hector and Clem and then, finally, her father. "They've promised to burn this building to the ground if you kick Ash out."

"You can't be serious," Warren said. "That's insane."

"Aren't we all?" Idrissa shot back in a voice so innocent and not-Idrissa I smothered a laugh.

"Even the sheriff?" Hector asked to no one in particular. He looked more surprised than upset. Like he was trying to wrap his head around it all. Join the club, dude.

"Drissa's right," Silas said. "Those wolves out there are untethered. Unbound. They don't listen to you. They haven't for years. You need to realize they will only get wilder and more out of control unless the curse is broken and they can tether themselves to an alpha or a mate. If not, one of these days, your pretend-council is going to piss off the wrong wolf, and they'll turn on you."

Hector and Clem were noticeably silent.

Silas went on. "Our rule about fighting for your place here is the one thing the entire pack honors. If you go against that, you risk them turning on you sooner rather than later. For *your* safety, Ash stays."

I stared at Silas, stunned.

Agreeing to spy on Drake to collect evidence of his douchebaggery was one thing. Standing up to the council for me was another.

"No," Mitch said into the silence.

It took me a minute to realize he'd just voted to let me stay.

I exhaled.

"Tiebreakers always go in favor of the accused," Amberly announced, not bothering to hide her excitement. She smiled at me. "You can stay, Ash. And I'm very sorry for the inconvenience we've caused you tonight. Especially when you have much more pressing matters to think about."

"Thank you," I told her, reeling a little.

Conceding defeat, Clem and Hector gave a curt goodbye and then left quickly. Warren waylaid Mitch and

Oscar, and I overheard him trying to convince them of his reasoning in trying to vote me out as protection. I wanted to be angry at him. But then I thought about what Amberly had said, about this version of Warren being so different than who he really was.

I hoped so.

And I hoped he could return to normal soon.

Idrissa tugged my sleeve, and I trailed behind her and the others as we made our way back up the aisle. Kai was waiting for us in the lobby when we exited, but I held up a finger to ask him to wait a moment. Then, I caught up with Silas.

"Hey," I said.

His brow furrowed in either impatience or irritation. "What?"

"Thanks," I said. "You didn't have to do that."

"Rules are rules," he said with a shrug. "I'll see you around."

18

At the sight of Kai and me, the crowd outside went wild. Cheers, clapping, sign-waving. I wondered if this was what celebrities felt like. Well, aside from the pressure of dying or killing someone sitting like a weight on my chest. I stopped on the top step, taking it all in and trying to figure out what the hell I was supposed to do now. I sucked at speeches, but I also didn't want to ignore them either.

Without a word, Kai stepped up beside me. His hand slid into mine and squeezed. I squeezed back gratefully. We might not have been on the same page about the alpha challenges—or anything else right now, for that matter—but he was still here. Standing next to me. And in my world, that counted for a hell of a lot.

My heart warmed, and together, we faced the crowd.

One step.

Then another.

We descended slowly. I wondered if Kai did that for my benefit. If he could sense how wobbly I was over this entire crazy-ass scene unfolding. Someone screamed my name and waved a sign in the air with "Ash for Alpha" painted across it in glittery lettering. They were... campaigning for me? It felt surreal.

"Ash," called a little girl I'd never met before. Her blonde hair fell into her eyes, and she pushed it back with a quick slide of her palm. The careless movement revealed a face that couldn't have been older than four or five. She pushed her way through the crowd and held out a stuffed llama.

Behind her, a woman was doing her best to catch up—and looking frazzled for her efforts.

I bent down so that the girl and I were at eye level. When her mom reached the front of the crowd, her eyes widened at the sight of us, and she slowed to a stop.

"Hi," I said to the girl.

"You're Ash," she said, awed.

"I am. What's your name?"

"Callie."

"It's nice to meet you, Callie. What can I do for you?"

"I brought you a present. This is Rosie, my llama. She's so you don't get scared when that bad man tries to be mean to you again."

My gaze flicked from Callie to her mother, who was wincing apologetically as she came forward. "So sorry about this," the woman said. "She overheard me telling someone about Baron's challenge to you, and, well, she has a mind of her own as you can see."

I grinned, looking from her to Callie and then to the llama. "You know what? I think it's a fantastic idea. Thank you, Callie. This will help me a lot."

"It will?" her eyes went wide.

"You bet. If it's okay with you, I'll bring Rosie with me to the challenge. I could use a good luck charm."

"She's real good luck," Callie told me. "One time, I

thought there was a monster under my bed, but it was only mommy and daddy making funny noises. Rosie is a good protector, though."

Callie's mom's face flushed a deep red. Beside me, Kai coughed, and I pressed my lips together to keep from laughing.

"She's obviously the best protector," I said, trying like hell to keep a serious face. "I'll take good care of her."

Callie squealed and threw her arms around me, nearly knocking me off my feet. I managed to catch myself and hold us both upright for the cutest hug I'd ever gotten. Kids had never really been my thing before. Not that I'd spent any time around them. Having a drunk dad and living on the run didn't exactly lend itself to situations with little people. But in this moment, Callie's easy acceptance of me—and more, her support—touched my heart in a way nothing else in this town had.

I thanked her and let her mother peel her away, Rosie the llama tucked carefully into my arm.

"That was different," I said, pushing to my feet and rejoining Kai as he led me past the rest of the crowd. Some of them high-fived Kai or stopped and hugged me. Every one of them felt genuine with their support. But it wasn't until we'd eventually left them all behind that I finally realized the support hadn't been all about me.

"You have a lot of admirers back there," I said, feeling strangely jealous.

My wolf wasn't threatened by the females. Not in that way. But she also hadn't missed how many of them had used Kai's name and the word "alpha" in the same sentence.

So, I wasn't the only one with a fan club.

"So do you." Kai shot me a glance.

"Kai," I said, but he stopped me.

"Come home with me." He stepped closer, his breath warm against my cheek in the moonlight. "Let me put my arms around you. I promise we can fight the rest of the night if you want. But just let me hold you first."

I nodded, unwilling to trust my voice. Feeling his arms around me was all I wanted. Well, okay, maybe I'd have to take him up on the fighting thing, but we could always have make-up sex after. And if he kissed me like he had in that jail cell, I didn't mind at all.

"Okay," I said.

I shot Oscar a quick text and then fell into step with Kai just as a car engine approached from behind. We both looked over, and I spotted a familiar white Mustang.

Isaac grinned from the driver's seat. "You two crazy kids need a ride?"

Beside him, Idrissa looked worn out. I imagined she hadn't slept much lately. It felt rude to impose. I opened my mouth, ready to tell him no, but movement caught my eye, something dark and furry stalking toward us through the trees just ahead.

Drake.

"Yeah," I said as Kai tensed beside me. "Thanks."

I tugged Kai toward the car. He glared at the wolf, who'd stopped to stare right back at us, not even bothering to hide his presence. But he didn't make a move to come closer either.

"Now's not the time," I told Kai.

"I just want to end this," he said in a low voice.

"I know, but there's something off about him. I want to know what."

My wolf wanted to rip his throat out too, but I knew better. Even from here, I could sense it. Just like earlier in the fighting arena, his wolf felt different. Bigger. Enhanced, maybe. Was that a thing?

A lifetime of surviving among people stronger and more dangerous than I was had taught me to proceed cautiously. And never start a fight you weren't sure you could win.

Kai and I climbed into the backseat together.

"Thanks," I told Isaac when we were settled.

"Don't thank him yet," Idrissa said, stifling a yawn that sparked one in me too. "He drives like a grandma. You'll be lucky to get home sometime this century."

"I drive responsibly," Isaac told her sharply.

Idrissa shook her head. "You don't have to stop at every crosswalk."

"I don't," he argued.

"You came to a complete stop at the corner of Fifth and Cherry the other day. There was no one around and not even a yield sign there."

I sat back against Kai, listening to the twins' bickering. It was usually enjoyable—or at least ignorable—but tonight, their banter had an edge to it that I'd never heard before.

Then again, we'd all been through hell the last couple of days. It made sense we were all short on patience.

By the time we pulled up at Kai's though, their arguing had gained steam. Kai and I sat quietly, unwilling to get into the middle of something that had undoubtedly existed long before I knew them. The twins had a specific vibe that, when crossed, felt a lot like breaking and entering. Still, this was next-level.

Isaac slammed the car to a stop much sharper than necessary, and Idrissa shoved her door open, climbing out.

"Was that necessary?" Idrissa demanded.

"Is your tone necessary?" Isaac shot back.

"You do not want to fuck with me right now, Isaac. I've

had less sleep than a vampire, and my level of hangry is unfuckwithable right now."

"Is your heart frozen like a vampire's too?" Isaac shot back. "Because you're being a complete bitch."

Idrissa's eyes widened, and I felt the change in her energy as I ducked out of the backseat into the night air.

"Uh-oh," Kai said under his breath.

Idrissa straightened, hands balled into fists as she backed away from her side of the car so she could stand in front of the hood and glare at Isaac. "The fuck did you just say?"

"You heard me," Isaac yelled from inside the car.

"Why don't you come say it to my face, little brother."

Idrissa's words were like poisonous darts.

Isaac shoved out of the car.

Oh, shit.

Bull's eye.

Kai and I exchanged a look.

"Isaac," I began, "why don't we—"

"Not now, Ash. This is between me and the she-devil," Isaac said.

I hurried up to Idrissa. "Why don't you come in? We'll order pizza—"

"Fuck off, Ash."

Idrissa eyed her brother angrily.

I watched as they faced off, the air between them rippling with tension and their beasts—too close to the surface. Holy hell, would they shift and fight? Right here in Kai's yard?

"Guys, this isn't like you," I began, but Kai tugged me back just in time.

The twins both exploded in a blurry mess of fur and fabric. I screamed, barely avoiding a claw as it whipped past my face and raked across a snout. Growls. Snarls. The entire thing was unbelievably vicious.

I watched from where I'd fallen on my ass. Inside my skin, my wolf howled at the wrongness of this.

"Kai, we have to do something," I said, scrambling to my feet.

"You stay here," Kai said, already stepping out of the shorts he wore.

"Kai," I said.

"Just stay." His eyes held mine, pleading. "If you get hurt, I won't be able to remain neutral, and I don't want to hurt either of them. Do you understand?"

I nodded.

He shifted and then jumped right into the middle of the chaos.

"What the hell?"

I whirled at the sound of a voice and spotted Presley coming up the drive. He looked at me like he expected me to make sense of it all.

"They're losing it," I said because what other explanation was there?

He growled and then shucked off his jacket and jeans before shifting too. Then he leaped straight for Isaac, who Kai was apparently struggling to keep off Idrissa.

It took them both to break it up, and I bit my lip as Kai's wolf flashed its teeth at Idrissa's throat. My wolf strained to shift and help, but I remembered Kai's words and knew exactly what he meant. If one of the twins accidentally hurt either of us, our mate bond wouldn't allow anything but immediate retribution. The last thing I wanted was for one of them to get hurt.

Finally, Presley and Kai managed to subdue the twins. Or maybe they'd just run out of steam. When they all finally broke apart again, Presley was literally sitting on

Idrissa, who was looking ready to maim him permanently for it.

She nipped at his hip hard enough that he let up, though barely.

Kai stood between Isaac and Idrissa, his large wolf eyes boring into Isaac's. A wave of power flowed from Kai to Isaac, and I watched as Isaac slowly lowered his head and bared his neck to Kai in full submission. Looked like I wasn't the only one who knew that trick.

Presley was the first to shift back.

He remained standing over Idrissa, clearly ready for round two if needed. He looked from her to Isaac and Kai, and then, finally, to me.

"Well? What in the actual fuck just happened?" he demanded.

While the rest of them shifted back, I told Presley what had happened. When I'd finished, he stared at Idrissa like she had three heads.

"Am I missing something here?" he asked her. "You fought because he agreed that you're a bitch when you're hungry?"

"Shut up, Pres." She stalked to the trunk of the car and popped it open. I watched as she grabbed a pair of shorts and pulled them on then did the same with a tank top.

"Here." She tossed Isaac and Kai each a pair of shorts.

"Thanks." Kai slid into them, still watching Isaac and Idrissa warily.

Idrissa slammed the trunk and sighed. "I think we need to talk about the alpha challenges," she said.

"What about them?" I asked.

"Isaac," she prompted.

He nodded, and I could see whatever was going on, they'd both figured it out during their epic brawl just now.

"My wolf is kind of losing his shit," Isaac admitted.

"You don't say?" Presley drawled.

"Fuck off," Idrissa snapped. She looked at Kai. "Thank you." Her tone was genuine enough that he nodded.

"You want to fill us in on what made the two of you go at it like rival packs?"

Idrissa shot me a look. "The curse," she said wearily. "It's getting worse like my mom said. I think…we're out of time."

"Dris is right," Isaac said. "It's like I could feel my wolf losing control, but I couldn't do anything to stop it. Like I was a bystander in my own body. That shit was weird."

"Kai, your alpha power knocked us back to sanity," Idrissa said.

"Yeah, thanks for that, bro." Isaac clapped Kai on the shoulder.

Kai shot me a nervous look.

"Thank you," I told him.

"This is bad," Idrissa said. "If the curse caused Isaac and me to go at each other, imagine who else might be losing it." She turned to me. "We need to end this, Ash. The challenges. Choosing an alpha. Whatever else we need to do, we're out of time. It has to happen now."

Something crept into her eyes. An emotion I'd never seen on Idrissa Close before.

Fear.

"I don't want to hurt my brother," she said quietly. "Please help."

I grabbed her arm, squeezing encouragingly. "I've got you," I assured her. "Whatever it takes, okay?"

She nodded, still looking shaken.

"Okay, tell you what," Presley said. "Isaac, you're with me tonight. You can help me run perimeter for the alphas-to-be here. That'll give you and your sis some space and keep you from killing each other for a while."

I fully expected Isaac to tell Presley to go to hell. They'd never exchanged anything remotely friendly in front of me before. But Isaac nodded.

"Yeah, that sounds good."

"Are you sure about this?" I asked him as he passed.

He pressed a quick kiss to my cheek. "I'm not sure about a single fucking thing. Except that if anyone can make all this okay again, it's you. Goodbye, lover."

Kai snarled softly.

"I was talking to you, Kai," Isaac called over his shoulder.

Then he and Presley disappeared into the trees across the road. Farther down, my gaze caught on something distant and gleaming. For a split second, I swore a pair of yellow eyes peered out at me from the darkness. But then I blinked, and whatever I'd seen was gone.

Still, I shuddered as I turned to see Idrissa and Kai both watching me expectantly.

"Let's go inside," I said. "You can both tell me how to beat Baron Asheville."

19

I started for the door and then glanced back when I realized only Kai had moved to join me. Idrissa stood in the yard in her shorts and tank, her car key clutched in her hand.

"You're not coming?" I asked.

She shook her head at me. "I'm going to take a raincheck."

"What's wrong?" I asked, worried her wolf was going to snap again.

"Nothing. I'm good." She eyed me then Kai. "Better than the two of you," she added when I started to argue. "Besides, a full night's sleep in my own bed is something I can't really remember having right now."

My shoulders fell.

Kai's gaze burned my cheek, but I refused to look at him. Suddenly, the idea of being alone together left me feeling all kinds of awkward.

"Okay," I said, out of reasons to tell her to stay.

"I'll be back bright and early tomorrow for training,"

she added, and I wasn't sure whether to be relieved or scared. Either way, what came out was a groan.

Idrissa grinned. "Glad to see my training methods left such an impression before." She opened her car door and then paused to add, "See you crazy kids later," before sliding inside.

The engine turned over, humming as she backed out of the driveway. I watched her go until she was out of sight, thinking again about the flash of something I'd just seen in the woods. Nothing had caught my senses. No scent. No movement. For all I knew, I'd imagined it.

Idrissa would be safe. So would Isaac and Presley. I had to let go of the worry.

Then Kai's voice was at my ear.

"You okay?"

I looked up at him, blinking at the sight of his stubbled jaw so close to my face. His closeness sent a wave of longing through me.

"Ash?"

"Yeah, I'm fine," I said. "Just tired."

"Come on."

He took my hand and led me inside. The sound of the front door clicking shut behind us felt louder than normal. Maybe I was just tired. Or maybe this moment felt heavier than it should. I mean, when your boyfriend willingly stayed in jail to avoid you, that was a problem, right?

"Presley is the answer you were looking for earlier," he said which was so far out of the scope of things I was expecting, all I could reply with was a lost look. "You asked me how I got out of jail," he explained. "The answer is Presley."

"Presley did that to you?" I asked, referring to the grimy clothes he'd first arrived in earlier.

"Not exactly. First, I nearly tore my cell apart because apparently James, the deputy, had gone home for the day, and my wolf got a little desperate once it decided to leave."

"Why?" I asked. "I mean, you'd been there for days. Why tonight?"

"You," he said. At my confusion, he explained, "James, the deputy, told me about the alpha fight this morning, and while I hated to think of Devon at risk like that, it was better than having you at risk."

I couldn't bring myself to be pissed at that. If it had been a choice between Devon and Kai, I hated to think it, but I would have let Devon fight too.

"So, what changed your mind?" I asked.

His eyes flashed as he said, "Something in the bond changed."

"The bond. But we were too far apart."

He cocked his head at me. "I felt you the entire time I was locked away, Ash."

"You did?"

"Why the hell do you think I allowed myself to stay there? You really think I would walk away from you for that long without knowing if you were safe? I tracked you every second I was inside that cell."

"I don't... I didn't feel you," I said, trying to understand.

"Are you sure about that?" he asked.

I frowned, thinking back to the last few days. The stress. The sadness. The desperation to do something—anything—to stop the runaway train that Drake had started by challenging Kai.

"Did you question if I was safe?" he prompted.

"No, I ... just knew you were I guess." I shook my head. "But that was it, Kai. I didn't feel anything else from you.

No worry or sadness or fear or anything that would have made sense for someone locked up."

He simply watched me like he was waiting for me to put it together.

"Are you saying it's because you weren't feeling those things?"

"Did you ever doubt that I loved you?"

"No."

"It's all I felt," he said. "The entire time I was in that cell, I sent you love, Ash. I knew you'd worry. Hell, I was half-terrified you'd mount a full-scale attack in my honor. But the entire time, I focused on remaining calm and steadfast. I wanted to make it easy on you, or as easy as I could, considering. Shit, it's the least I can do after the hell I put you through."

The bond had grown, and I hadn't even noticed. What did that say about me? I was so quick to blame Kai for all our problems. But none of this was one-sided.

"So, what changed?" I asked, "If you were sending love and all that, what made you want to suddenly leave that cell?"

"I felt your decision," he said. "To fight for alpha."

Well, shit. I hadn't planned to tell him that part.

"You felt that?" I asked quietly.

"And I knew where you'd go," he said. "I started to lose my mind. Rick had apparently left for the night. No matter how loudly I howled or screamed, no one came. I think I dented the door before it finally opened and I saw Presley standing there with Rick's key card."

"Presley got you out," I said. "But how did he know to come?"

He shrugged. "He says he sensed me and came to check on me."

I frowned. "Sensed you how?"

"No idea. I guess it probably has something to do with how he found us in the woods the other day."

"And how he and Silas found me the night Vinny attacked."

And Tiffany.

The list just kept on growing.

His expression tightened. "Presley filled me in on what Vinny tried to do. Why didn't you tell me?"

"Me?" My eyes narrowed. "You were in a cell. Charged for murder because of me. And then when I came to see you, I found out you weren't charged with murder. In fact, you were charged with nothing and using the place as your own personal hostel. Kai—"

"I know, I know, shit. I'm sorry. I shouldn't have done that. I was just..."

"Protecting me?"

He sighed.

"It sounds lame as hell now."

"It sounded lame then too."

He looked up and caught my eye.

I smirked.

He exhaled.

"I owe you a lot of apologies."

"You don't owe me anything," I said.

"Bullshit."

He closed the distance, pressing his palm to my cheek.

"I owe you everything." His words were like gravel scraped over my skin.

My breath caught at the wave of emotions coming through the bond. Even without it, though, I would have felt it through his gaze. Kai Stone's love was like a hurricane complete with stormy waves crashing to shore. And I was that shore—getting sucked right out to the chaos of the sea with every aching look he gave. And I wanted it.

Dammit, I wanted it all. To be swept up. To lose myself in the squall. To drown in the depths.

Before I knew it, I'd lifted onto my toes and pressed my lips to his.

He growled and grabbed me by the waist, pulling me against him with the force of a tidal wave. All at once, I was sucked under.

His hands gripped my hips, pressing our bodies together, but it wasn't enough. I wanted more. Needed it. I rocked my hips against his, shuddering at the feel of his hardness against my core. My hands locked around his neck as he lifted me up and carried me to the couch without ever removing his mouth from mine.

He sat, settling me on top of him so that my legs straddled his and my core ground against his erection. I couldn't breathe, but I had no interest in remedying that.

Kai was my oxygen now.

His hands trailed up my sides, grazing my breasts, as his tongue dove into my mouth, exploring, claiming. I made a small sound that only caused him to hold me tighter and kiss me harder.

My skin burned where he touched. And still, it wasn't enough.

I felt for the edges of his shirt and pulled it over his head. Kai broke the kiss as I peeled his shirt away. But instead of picking up where we'd left off, he looked up at me with his hurricane gaze that pinned me where I sat.

"Ash," he said, breath ragged as his fingers snaked up my neck and into my hair.

But I leaned down and held a finger to his lips, eyes pleading as I said, "Please. I don't want to talk. Not tonight."

"I need you to know that everything I did was because I love you."

His words were forceful like he was willing me to take them. To understand. And the thing was I did understand. Kai's way of showing love wasn't exactly perfect, but I didn't exactly have room to talk either. Hell, neither one of us had ever seen any good examples, so I couldn't be surprised when we both sucked at it. Screwing up was kind of to be expected.

I wanted to tell him that, but, in this moment, right now, I knew the best way I could deliver the message was to show him. Neither of us was great at communication. Not verbally, anyway. But this—giving him my body? Using it as a symbol to show him I'd also given him my heart and soul—this was something I could do.

"I know you love me," I said softly.

At my words, some of the desperation left his expression. He exhaled and angled his forehead until it was pressed to mine.

His hands cupped my cheeks. "That's good. Because I'm not the best at showing it sometimes."

"Oh? You mean like that time you stayed in jail when you could have been here with me doing this?"

His lips quirked.

"Yeah, that's one example."

"I'm not great at it, either," I admitted.

"You're way better at this than me," he argued.

I sat back and arched my brows. "Want to make it a contest?"

His mouth curved in delicious mischief. "I'm willing to do whatever it takes to come out on top."

I grinned. "No problem, I'll take bottom."

Kai grabbed me and picked me up, flipping me over so that I was on my back, pinned underneath him. The move happened so fast I was breathless by the time he was looking down at me.

I pressed a palm to his bared chest. His skin was warm. I wanted that warmth against me. His hands trailed over my body, and I arched my back to help as he eased my shirt over my head and tossed it aside. My heart thudded wildly as he stood and peeled my pants off each leg. His fingers trailed over my skin so slowly it made my thighs ache.

I wasn't sure how to feel about the slow pace. It made the emotions too big to ignore. Gone was the urgency. The feverish need. This felt different. Like letting myself be seen in a way I never had before.

"Kai," I said, my voice thick with emotion.

"What's wrong?" he asked.

"Nothing, I—"

I blinked, surprised and horrified when my eyes stung with tears.

"It's okay," he said, his voice gentler than ever before. He leaned over me, brushing my hair from my face and planting small kisses on the tip of my nose then the underside of my jaw.

I took a shaky breath.

"I thought I was losing you," I said in a small voice.

"You'll never lose me," he said. When he lifted his eyes to meet mine again, I saw it there, the absolute truth of his words. "I swear it, and it's a promise I know I'll keep, no matter how many times I fuck up the rest. You'll never lose me, Ash. And it's not the mate bond or duty or anything else. I belong to you, and there's nothing in this entire world that could change that. Not shifters, not hexerei, and for damn sure, not some stupid curse. Do you get that?"

"Not yet," I admitted. "But eventually..."

"We have until eventually," he assured me.

The curse doesn't.

I didn't say it out loud. It was a conversation we could have tomorrow. For tonight, I wanted to practice believing that love like this existed. That Kai Stone felt it for me. That he saw me. And that, even though we weren't perfect, we were still choosing each other. Maybe that was all love was anyway. A choice, over and over again, every day.

"I love you, Kai Stone."

"I love you, Ash Lawson," he said, eyes glittering as he lowered his mouth to mine and finished what we'd just started, slowly enough to let me feel every emotion and every touch.

My back arched as he slid inside me, pleasure rocketing through me. I moaned and Kai's hot mouth captured mine, swallowing the sounds. His pace was slow torture, building toward a release that, when it finally came, emptied me. Even then, he didn't stop, and when I cried his name, shudders wracked his body as he finally came with me.

20

I blinked, woken by the cheery sunlight streaming in through Kai's bedroom window. It was stupid, the amount of light these blinds were letting in. Didn't the sun know I was still exhausted?

"Rise and shine, sleepyhead."

I groaned, rolling away from the sound of Kai's way-too-chipper voice. He padded across the room and sat on the edge of the mattress, bringing with him the smell of fresh coffee.

I rolled back toward him, squinting through messy hair and sleepy eyes.

Kai grinned and held out a steaming mug.

"For me?" I asked, my voice not much more than a desperate croak.

"For you," he confirmed.

I sat up and took the mug. "You're my favorite," I said, sipping gingerly.

"I heard that," Idrissa called from somewhere else in the house.

"She's already here?" I whispered.

"Heard that too," she yelled, cutting off Kai's reply.

I winced.

"You can win me back with breakfast," I shot back.

"Ha!"

I looked up at Kai, who watched me with a look that felt way too heavy for this early in the morning.

"How'd you sleep?" he asked.

"For the three hours I got, it was heavenly." I yawned, which prompted another sip of coffee.

"I would apologize for that, but I'm not sorry."

I smirked. "Trust me, no apology necessary." I pressed a quick kiss to his mouth. "For anything," I added.

He sighed, clearly not willing to let my comment be enough. "Look, I know we didn't get a chance to talk much last night. I was thinking today—"

"Knock-knock." Idrissa pushed the bedroom door open wider and peered in at us.

"What's up?" I asked.

"Training," she said, tapping a non-existent watch. "Starts in twenty."

'Ugh." I groaned as she walked out, grinning maniacally. The only thing that could cheer up a monster like Idrissa was physically torturing me with training. I knew that because this wasn't the first time she'd had the privilege.

"Get dressed," Idrissa ordered me as she left again.

I grimaced. "I guess those eggs won't make themselves." I threw the covers back and scooted to the edge of the bed.

Kai stopped me.

"Ash, can we please talk about this alpha problem?"

His tone was sharp, and I knew he was losing patience. Last night had been about everything except talking. But now, with my alpha challenge looming in less than forty-eight hours, I didn't have time to sit and work through our countless obstacles.

"I don't know what to say," I admitted. "Is that what you want to hear? I'm avoiding this because I have no freaking clue how to navigate this situation. I—"

"Kai! Ash! Get your pretty asses out here now," Idrissa called.

Her tone—not angry but more warning—sent an alarm through me. Kai ran from the room with me right behind him.

In the living room, which was now missing a rug thanks to our little situation with Vorack, Idrissa stood staring out the window through the open blinds.

Something outside had drawn her attention.

"What is it?" I asked.

"Look." She nodded, and Kai and I both joined her at the window, peering out into the morning sunshine. I scanned the empty yard and Idrissa's Mustang parked in the driveway until my eyes landed on what had drawn her attention.

Whatever I'd been expecting, it hadn't been this. Limping across the road and into the yard was a large, brown—and very bloody—wolf.

My breath caught at the sheer amount of blood coating its fur. From the looks of it, I was surprised the beast was still standing. This wolf wasn't one of ours. His scent was foreign and, more than that, my wolf just... knew. Mental note to ask about that weirdness later.

"Who is that?" I demanded.

"I don't know," Idrissa said. "Otherwise I would have let him in." She shot Kai a look. "What do you think?"

"He's a mess," Kai said grimly. "I can smell the blood from here. It's more than a little bit."

"He seems to be alone," Idrissa said, scanning the trees

that lined the road across from the house. "I don't smell anyone else."

"I'm going out," Kai said.

"Wait." I grabbed his arm. "What if he isn't alone? What if the blood is covering their scent? It could be a trap. Drake—"

We all looked over in time to see the wolf outside collapse at the bottom of the porch. Kai pulled his arm free, and I let him go, following him to the door and outside onto the porch.

We all paused to inhale the air, but Idrissa was right. I couldn't smell anyone or anything else waiting to pounce.

Kai was down the steps first.

He crouched beside the wolf and put his hand gingerly against its throat. The wolf huffed but didn't protest a touch that should have felt like a threat.

I wrinkled my nose as the blood smell became stronger to my wolf senses. Crouching beside Kai, Idrissa leaned in close and examined the wounds slashed across the wolf's ribs and chest.

"These are deep," she said. "They look like puncture wounds—from teeth. And claws." She looked up at Kai sharply. "He was attacked."

My stomach clenched.

"Challenges and official fights have been prohibited until the alpha challenges are over," Idrissa added. "This guy must have found someone willing to duel anyway."

I looked to the trees again, wondering what the hell had happened to this wolf. And just as importantly, how bad off was the other guy?

"Let's get him inside," I said, a strange feeling of being watched raising the hairs on my neck.

"Inside?" Idrissa looked ready to protest. "Are you sure that's a good idea?"

"He's clearly not a threat in his current state," I said. "Besides, there are three of us and one of him. And if we don't..." I trailed off, unwilling to say the words. "We can't just leave him out here unconscious."

"Ash is right," Kai said. "Let's get him inside so we can see what we're dealing with."

It took all three of us to lift-drag the injured wolf up the steps and into the house. I eyed the thick trail of blood we'd left in our wake. The only benefit of trashing the rug was not having to do it again now.

Inside, Idrissa shut and locked the front door. "I'm going to stay at the window and keep an eye out," she said. "You two see what can be done for him."

"Call Isaac," I said. "He and Presley are supposed to be coordinating security patrols. Maybe they saw something."

She pulled out her phone, dialing quickly and then scanning the trees outside as she held the phone to her ear.

"Should we call an ambulance or something?" I asked Kai.

"Human medicine can't do anything for him," he said. "And according to Silas, the pack doc has his hands full with Vinny's injured friends." He shot me a glance, and I stiffened, recalling all the damage we'd done to their side.

"I think this one's on us," he added, taking a step back from the unconscious wolf.

"What are you going to do?" I asked.

Kai looked up, his mouth flattening into a grim line. "I'm going to shift and see if my alpha powers can wake him."

"Why would you do that?" My heart raced, not just for what he was about to do but because the look on his face suggested this plan involved no small amount of danger.

"He's not healing," Kai said, his words coming faster, urgent now. "The more blood he loses, the longer he's unconscious, the harder this will be for him to recover from. We need him to wake up. To fight this. To heal."

"What if he tries to hurt you?" I asked.

His brow rose. "You'd let that happen?"

"Hell no," I growled.

His lips twitched. "There's my girl. If he tries anything," he said with a shrug, "protect me."

My eyes narrowed, but I said nothing as Kai stripped and then shifted. At the window, Idrissa left a voice mail for Isaac and then dialed someone else who I suspected was probably Presley. Between dialing, she kept her gaze glued to the yard.

Turning back, I watched as Kai's wolf approached the injured one. Kai bent low and used his nose to shove gently at the wolf's cheek.

Nothing.

Kai growled and bent down again, this time, fastening his yellow eyes on the injured wolf's face in a silent call. I felt the alpha power rise and roll off Kai—directed intently at the injured wolf. It was strong. And for some reason, that made me proud.

My wolf rolled her eyes at that.

She was stronger, she'd already decided. But she wouldn't tell our mate she thought so.

The injured wolf stirred with a weak growl. Its eyes fluttered open then closed again. Kai bared his teeth, redoubling his efforts. The power coming from him increased.

Still, the wolf only stirred before falling back toward unconsciousness.

I watched the wounds, but they remained unchanged.

Kai was right.

He wasn't healing. And he wasn't waking up. Not even with Kai's alpha power prodding him.

My wolf stirred again, straining to help.

I bit my lip, determined to give it time. Finally, my own wolf snarled, the sound escaping me without warning.

Kai looked up at me sharply, a look of curiosity in his wolf eyes.

Part of me fought whatever instinct my wolf felt, but with no other solution in sight, I gave in and let her do… whatever the hell she was going to do.

First, I stripped out of my clothes. Then I let the change come over me.

The moment I shifted, my wolf leaned toward Kai and nudged him.

Try again.

Kai blinked and I wondered for a split second if he'd heard the mental words.

He leaned forward again, and together, we sent alpha power toward the injured wolf. This time, the wolf opened his eyes and bared his teeth.

I pushed harder. Kai did the same.

The wolf lifted its head off the floor, snarling at us.

But I barely noticed its sharpened teeth or extended claws.

Instead, I stared at the wounds that were, impossibly, beginning to heal. Slow as hell but definitely healing all the same. My wolf preened, full of satisfaction. I leaned in, licking at the wound on the stranger wolf's paw, knowing my wolf was helping the healing even if the human in me was about to vomit all over this entire room.

The snarling stopped.

The wolf lowered its head to the floor again, apparently deciding to accept our help rather than fight off our attempts.

Trying not to be human, I let my wolf do her thing.

Between the licking, snapping her teeth, and whatever weird combo thing Kai and I were doing with our alpha power, the injured wolf was clearly on the mend by the time I felt the first tug of exhaustion hit me.

"Presley's here," Idrissa announced after what felt like hours.

Kai nudged me, nodding toward the bedroom, and I grabbed my clothes in my teeth before heading for privacy so I could shift and change.

When I emerged again, Presley was standing in the living room with a human-looking Kai and pensive Idrissa. They were all staring down at the injured wolf, who was fully conscious and whining his way through healing the worst of its bloody wounds.

"Any idea who he is?" Presley asked.

"We were hoping you knew something about that," Kai said.

"Did you see anything last night?" Idrissa asked. "During patrols?"

"No." Presley shook his head. "It was completely quiet all night. Silas relieved us this morning, and I sent Isaac home a couple of hours ago to get some sleep. Hell, I was headed that way myself when you called."

"Did you call Silas?" I asked.

"Yeah, he said everything's…" Presley trailed off as his eyes landed on me.

Kai and Idrissa both stared as well.

"What?" I asked.

"You're glowing," Kai managed after a moment.

I looked down, wondering what the hell she meant. My eyes landed on my necklace, and my breath caught.

Idrissa was right. The moon part of the pendant was literally glowing as if powered by some internal light.

"Has it always done that?" Presley asked.

"Uh, no," I said, frowning as I gingerly picked it up off my chest. It was warm to the touch. What the hell?

"Where did you say you got that thing again?" Idrissa asked.

"My mother. She left me this when she took off. My dad made me swear to wear it always. Otherwise, I'd..." I fell silent as another thought occurred to me. "This symbol," I said. "Kel told me it's my mother's coven symbol. The one they would have used if she'd taken over. Do you think...do you think it has magic in it?"

"In it or just detecting it," Kai said.

"What do you mean?" I asked.

"Ash, I know you felt it. What we just did for this wolf." He glanced down at the wolf who was watching us all with wide eyes.

He could hear every word of this, I knew, but I couldn't bring myself to worry about it. Not when everything I thought I knew about this worthless piece of jewelry was being challenged.

"We helped him heal," I said, feeling strangely defensive. "We used our alpha powers to wake him so he could heal."

"Yeah, but combining our alpha power?" He shook his head. "I've never heard of two alphas being able to work together like that."

His eyes were sharp on mine. Through the bond, I could feel the full impact of his words. An impact he was trying to downplay, probably for the benefit of listening ears.

"I didn't know," I said. "My wolf—she wanted to help. I

could feel her idea of working together, and then we just did it." I shook my head. "I just went on instinct."

"It was the right instinct," he said, grabbing my hand and squeezing. "It healed him."

"But you think.... My necklace...."

"I don't know," he said, answering the question I hadn't been able to voice.

I could feel the wheels turning for us all as we tried to understand this. Especially me. I'd worn this necklace for weeks and nothing. Why now? I looked down at it again, struck by the glow it emanated. I'd only seen a shade of white like this once before, and even then, it had only been a vision. A projection of someone else's vision. Or so I'd thought.

"We need to talk to Kel again," I said.

"Wait, who's Kel?" Presley asked.

I shot Idrissa a look. Then the injured wolf.

Except, he was no longer injured. Or barely. His wounds had closed enough to stem the bleeding. He watched us from the floor with a look of full awareness, and I could hear his heartbeat, steady and strong now.

My wolf tensed, but I refused to acknowledge him as a threat. He'd given us no reason to. Not yet.

Instead of answering Presley, I addressed the wolf.

"I'm Ash," I said. "This is Idrissa, Presley, and Kai. You're safe, and you're going to recover just fine. If you want to shift back, we can find you some clothes, and we can help you get back to wherever it is you're supposed to be."

The wolf stared up at me, considering.

I could feel the tension rising from the others as they braced themselves for an attack. But the wolf stood awkwardly, its knees wobbling slightly before it steadied.

Then, it stepped back and shifted.

For a long moment, no one spoke. I could feel the others' shock matching my own as we all stared at the shifter we'd just saved.

The wolf—now a man—was the first to break the silence.

"It seems a thanks is in order."

"You're…." Idrissa trailed off, and I realized it was the first time I'd ever witnessed her struck speechless.

Kai and Presley weren't much better.

I tried to think of what to say, but my brain had somehow disconnected from my mouth.

"Baron Asheville," he finished, looking slightly amused if I was reading his expression correctly. "I'm the alpha of the Asheville pack. And I think we need to discuss what just happened, don't you?"

21

None of us answered. Baron didn't seem to mind; I had a feeling the question had been rhetorical anyway.

"Ash, Kai, I owe you a great debt," Baron said. "My life, in fact. Thank you for what you did."

His eyes flashed with awareness, and I watched as he brushed his hands over his still-healing wounds. Then he looked back at me, and I realized with a growing sense of dread how much he'd just overheard.

"Whether you fully understand your capabilities or not, you are very powerful. Together, the most powerful alpha duo I've ever met."

He stood before us, still too bloody and bruised for me to fully notice how naked he was, thank the moon goddess for that. But the questions… I had so many.

"What happened?" I couldn't help but ask. "To injure you so badly? Alpha challenges have been suspended until the scheduled time."

"I was attacked," he said, his expression tightening. Rage flashed, his fists tightening at his sides. Despite his obvious exhaustion and weakness, he looked ready to rip heads off.

"By who?" Presley asked.

He looked just as pissed as Baron, though I suspected Presley was taking this incident personally since he was supposed to have been on watch against it.

"One of yours," he said darkly. "The one who calls himself Drake. And when I find him, I'm afraid I'm going to have to kill him myself."

Kai, Presley, and Idrissa all let out curses.

"I thought you were supposed to be watching him," Idrissa demanded in a heated whisper.

"We have been," Presley argued. "So far, he hasn't done anything incriminating."

"Are you seeing what I'm seeing?" she demanded.

Presley didn't answer.

Baron ignored them and kept his eyes on me.

Something about the way he watched me felt different. No more animosity, not like last night when he'd arrived at the barn, ready to tear me apart. Now, he looked cautious, like he was trying to solve a mystery.

Maybe it was the same mystery I was trying to solve.

While the others speculated quietly about Drake, I spoke directly to Baron.

"Was Drake injured at all?"

Baron's expression tightened again, and he hesitated. The others all tuned in, suddenly interested again.

"Not that I'm aware," Baron said stiffly.

The curses and mutterings stopped as we all tried to digest the fact that Drake had done so much damage to Baron without getting a scratch on himself in the process.

"Seriously?" Presley said, awe lacing his irreverent tone.

Baron looked ready to murder something rather than answer the question.

"Was there anything off about him?" I asked. "Drake, I mean."

"Besides the fact that he's serial killer crazy," Idrissa put in.

"He's different." Baron frowned. "Last night, I felt no threat from him. My wolf dismissed him easily as a possible challenge. But when he approached me last night, he was stronger. Much more powerful than before." He shook his head. "It makes no sense."

"I've felt it too," I said. "He's done something to himself. To make his wolf more dominant."

"Like what?" Idrissa asked.

"He shouldn't have been able to beat Devon as easily as he did," Presley said, "That's for damn sure."

"I smelled the death in your barn last night," Baron said.

"That would have been Drake's handiwork," I told him.

"Still, my wolf did not think he was even worthy of us." Baron looked just as perplexed as the rest of us.

"It's not possible," Idrissa said, "for him to have gotten this much stronger in what—twelve hours?

"It shouldn't be," Baron agreed grimly. "I've fought in dozens of alpha challenges in my lifetime. I've never lost, and I've never once felt the surge of power that came from Drake. It wasn't natural."

"Something unnatural yet overpowering," Kai said slowly. His eyes gleamed, and I realized where he was going with his theory just as he said the words, "The only thing that can do that is—"

"Magic," we said together.

Baron's gaze whipped from Kai to me again.

"I haven't encountered magic in a pack in decades," he

said, eyes narrowing slightly. "And now I find it twice. Shouldn't be surprised it's your father's pack again."

"Wait. What do you mean *again*?" I asked.

He let out a breath and winced, holding a hand up to the wound over his ribs. "Mind if I sit?"

"Yeah, of course." Kai gestured to the couch.

Idrissa reached over and grabbed a throw blanket, holding it out to the large alpha.

He wrapped it around his waist like a towel and sat.

Idrissa whispered to Presley about coffee, and the two of them disappeared into the kitchen. I suspected it was more about giving me privacy so I could grill Baron about my dad.

"You knew my dad?" I asked when Baron remained silent.

He looked up thoughtfully, his lips curving in a wry half-smile. He looked almost friendly when he did that. Or he would have if his giant body wasn't the size of a bread truck. A very bloody bread truck at the moment.

"Yes, I knew Caleb. We were friends…of sorts."

"Our packs were rivals from what my dad used to tell me," Kai said, clearly not convinced.

Baron snorted. "Yes. We were that too."

"I don't understand," I said.

"Caleb and I were competitive as hell. But we were nothing compared to our own fathers." Baron glanced up at me. "Your grandfather, Henry, and my old man had some bad blood long before I was born. Apparently, my mother was supposed to be mated to Henry—until she recognized my old man as her one true mate. Henry was salty about it. Rightly so, I guess. Anyway, Caleb and I were raised to see each other as enemies, but it never quite stuck with us. We were competitive, sure. One-upping each other on everything."

He chuckled, remembering as he talked. "Caleb was a hell of a fighter. Fought dirty too. You could never predict his next move. And the alpha power…" He shook his head. "Unmatched."

"Sounds like the apple doesn't fall far," Kai said, and I looked up sharply as I realized he meant me. "Don't look so surprised." He chuckled.

"I guess I didn't stop to think that he was actually good at being alpha. All I can see is that he walked away. No word. And no way for someone else to lead in his place."

"Yeah, that's partly my fault," Baron said, and even through the blood staining his skin, I could see a light flush in his face now.

Holy shit.

Was this brick house of an alpha embarrassed?

"Why's that?" Kai asked.

"Caleb and I had a bit of a falling out right before he left." Baron eyed me with what looked like regret. "I knew he'd been seeing someone. His mate, he'd called her. I never questioned it. Sure, it was strange that he was keeping her secret, but I just figured he didn't want anyone else messing with her until they were ready to announce things. Who could blame him after what happened with our own fathers? But then I found out she was…"

"Hexerei," I finished for him.

He sighed. "I was an ass about it."

"You were against it," Kai said.

Baron nodded. "I was afraid it would cost him the treaty."

"I'm sure he understood you were trying to protect him," I said.

But Baron shook his head. "The last time I saw him, he asked me to step into his place. Become alpha of the pack."

"He told you he was leaving?" I asked.

"He knew Warren would fight for it, but according to him, Warren was too much of a politician. A people pleaser. Anyway, I told him if I became alpha, we'd have nothing to do with those damned hexerei. They're trouble." His expression darkened with the words, and I could see the disdain in his eyes. It was enough to make my defenses go up.

"He didn't want that kind of alpha," I said, finally beginning to understand at least a little bit of my dad's decision to cast this curse.

If he couldn't trust any of the alphas to lead properly in his place, he'd make sure no one did. And without magic, the witches couldn't hurt us either. Except that, in the end, the wolves were just hurting themselves.

"No, he didn't," Baron said, shoulders sagging. "He wanted peace."

"What's so wrong with that?" I asked, strangely defensive of my father; a man who, the more I learned about him, the less I felt I knew.

Baron shook his head. "It's a nice idea in theory, but I can't ever see either side being truly capable of it. Can you?"

We fell silent.

My heart ached at the memory of my father. The person he'd been. A version I'd apparently never really known. The kind of guy who'd decide no leader was better than a bad one. I wasn't sure if he'd been brilliant or reckless in the end. But I no longer saw him as the villain.

"Why'd you come here and challenge Ash if you knew Caleb was her father?" Kai asked. "She's strong; I know you can sense that. Maybe even stronger than you."

"Kai," I whispered as Baron's expression hardened again.

"She's gifted," he said, "You both are. But she's half spook, and that's not something I can allow in a position of leadership. Not in a pack that rivals all others in strength and will. The Lawson pack needs a pure wolf as an alpha, regardless of how I feel about it personally."

Anger speared through me at that. "You're wrong. The pack needs unity, not separation. We need to understand our enemies, not attempt to destroy them. That kind of mentality only leads to loss and pain."

Baron's brows lifted at that. "You think you know a better way? Better than all the wise alphas that have come before you?"

"I'm not my father. I didn't fall in love with a witch. And I'm not you. I don't let hate drive me."

I backed away. Mostly because my wolf had decided we weren't going to be friends with Baron after all. And I didn't want to reopen wounds that had just now begun to close. Not when I'd worked so hard to save his ass.

"You should go," I said. "We'll alert our people to Drake and have him secured until after our fight. If you'd like another day to heal before our challenge, we can arrange it."

Baron stood, towering over me. "No," he said. "I'll be ready."

Kai walked to the door and pulled it open for Baron. "We'll see you tomorrow then."

Baron left without another word.

Kai closed the door behind him, and Idrissa and Presley nearly fell on each other as they tumbled back into the room.

"Holy shit, you just alpha'd his ass," Idrissa crowed.

"What?" I asked, still reeling from it all. The healing. The necklace. Standing up to Baron. It was a lot to take in. Since when did I do magical, badass shit like it was no big deal?

"You healed him then made him open up to you then sent him packing," Idrissa said. She grinned. "That's my girl."

"We need to find Drake," Kai said, devoid of all the exuberance Idrissa gave off.

He looked positively murderous, and now that Baron wasn't here to distract us, my thoughts turned to what Drake had done.

"We need to be careful," I warned. "Drake's not what he seems. I think Baron's condition is proof of that."

"Baron would have died without your intervention," Presley said. "Speaking of which, are we going to talk about the whole glowing bit or just tuck that into our pockets for later?"

Before I could answer, his phone rang. "Silas," he said then looked up at me and Kai. "What are we telling him?"

I hesitated and then said, "Everything. We tell him everything. But no one else. At least, not about the necklace and all that."

"Isaac?" Idrissa asked, eyes wide. "Can I tell him? Because he knows when I lie, the little fucker."

Shit. "Yeah, okay, Isaac. But that's it."

My phone rang next, and I checked the caller ID then groaned.

"Who is it?" Kai asked, leaning in.

"Oscar." I glanced at Kai as I answered the call. "Him too. Then no one else," I added.

Kai's lips quirked. "Got it."

I wandered away from the others to speak to Oscar, who basically interrogated me like this was a fifteenth-century inquisition.

"No, I'm not alone... Yes, I'm safe... No, I'm not going to run away again... I'll be home in an hour for work."

"Don't worry about your shift," he said. "I've got it handled. You need to prepare for tomorrow night."

Too tired to argue, I mumbled a promise to check in later and ended the call.

By the time I hung up, exhaustion clung to every muscle and movement. This wasn't the lack of sleep kind of tiredness I'd felt when I'd woken earlier. This was something different. I turned toward the group again, who was apparently still discussing what to do about Drake, and swayed.

Grabbing the wall for support, I blinked until the dizziness passed.

"Whoa." Kai appeared beside me, grabbing my hips to hold me steady. "You okay?"

"I don't know. I feel strangely drained."

"Let's sit," he said, steering me toward the couch before I could protest.

Not that I would have.

Sitting seemed good.

"Better?" he asked when I was settled on the couch.

"Um, the room's only slightly spinning now, so, yes?"

"Something's wrong with Ash," Kai called.

Idrissa and Presley broke off their conversation and came over. Idrissa crouched in front of me, peering up at me with sharp blue eyes. I did my best to focus on seeing only one of her.

"Your pupils are dilated." She looked up at Kai.

"We should have the doc take a look at her," he said.

"I called him when Baron showed up," he said. "Never heard back."

"Dammit," Kai muttered.

"Silas said he has his hands full," Presley said. "I don't think he has time for house calls.

Kai's mouth twisted in frustration. "I have to meet with Warren about my challenge with Drake."

Shit. I'd forgotten all about that meeting. They were setting their fight for the day after mine.

"We can't tell Warren," I said, fighting through the brain fog that threatened to make me forget everything that was at stake here. "About the alpha thing. And the necklace."

"I won't," he promised me. Still frowning, he looked up at Idrissa. "Can you take her for me?"

"I can't. I told Oscar I'd interview for Drake's mechanic spot."

"Dris, that's great," I said.

She beamed at me. "Maybe I'll get out of my own garage and into one that actually pays me."

"You're a lock," I told her.

I knew how much she wanted to work on bikes for a living.

"I can take her," Presley said. "I need to run by Silas' to give him an update. I can just tell him to meet me at the doc's instead."

Kai hesitated. "Fine," he said. "Straight there. No stops. Text me when she's safe."

"Of course, dude," Presley said. "I won't let anything happen to her."

"Here." Idrissa handed over her keys. "Take my car. But if you scratch it, you deal with Isaac."

Kai looked only slightly convinced by Presley's promise of my safety, but I knew he didn't have a choice. If he missed his check-in with Warren, he risked forfeiting the challenge.

"Will Drake be there?" I asked. "At this meeting."

"Yeah, he has to if he wants the challenge to happen," Kai said.

I took the necklace off, my fingers clumsy with the clasp. Finally, it came free, and I handed it to Kai. "Take this."

"Ash, what—"

"Get as close as you can," I said.

"Why?"

"If it glowed for my magic, maybe it'll glow for his."

"You think he's using magic?" Kai asked.

"What else would send him to the hexerei? His wolf is changed, Kai. I can feel it. We need to know how before he hurts someone else."

Someone like you.

Kai nodded, wrapping his hand around the pendant, and then immediately dropped it with a sharp hiss. I looked down at where he clutched his palm. A burn had been seared into his skin.

"What happened?" I asked.

Gingerly, Kai picked up the necklace, touching only the chain, and handed it back to me. "I think this thing doesn't like to be borrowed," he said.

I took the necklace back, my hands closing over the pendant without a single sizzle to stop me.

"It reacted to your skin," I said, not even sure how I could feel surprised anymore. Not after everything that had just happened.

"You better hang on to it," he said.

"You're okay?" I asked.

"Fine." He held out his palm to show me the burn was already hardening and beginning to heal.

I exhaled, relieved.

"And I don't need the necklace," he added, getting to his feet. "Drake's not leaving that meeting unless it's in handcuffs. Sheriff can keep him out of our hair at least until Baron's dealt with."

That sounded good to me.

"Call me if you find anything," I said as he left.

Idrissa slipped out a moment later, and then it was just Presley and me.

"My lady," Presley said, gesturing to the door where Idrissa's Mustang waited for us. "Your chariot awaits."

22

Presley readjusted the side mirror for the fourth time. I could barely keep my eyes open, but I didn't miss the way he kept glancing behind us in the rearview as we neared downtown.

"Is there a parade back there?" I asked.

"Huh?" He glanced over, frowning. "What do you mean?"

"You keep looking behind us." I stifled a yawn. "Are we being tailgated?"

He didn't laugh. "Something like that."

The sound hit me then.

Exhaust.

Loud as hell too.

Only one kind of machine sounded like that.

Motorcycles.

I forced my eyes open and glanced into the side mirror, my jaw dropping a little at what I saw. Motorcycles, two across and at least twenty deep, tailed us in a long line of leather-clad riders. They were riding our ass with no intention of passing even though the way was clear for them to do exactly that.

I caught the one on the right staring at me as he edged closer and closer to the Mustang's bumper.

"Holy shit." I sat up straighter, alarm spearing through me. "That's some Fast and Furious shit right there."

Presley didn't answer.

Something about watching Presley worried into silence undid me.

"Do you know who they are?" I asked.

"No. They're not lone wolf riders." He frowned. "The emblem on their vests reminds me of another pack's symbol I once heard about, though."

"Another pack?" I asked. "Are you sure they aren't Asheville? Baron's people might be pissed about Drake and taking it out on us."

He shook his head. "Not Asheville. See the rising star over the wolf's head? The story I heard about that symbol was for a pack up north near the Poconos."

"Please tell me the story is a friendly one," I said as one of the bikers revved his throttle and the others followed suit.

"Not exactly." He shot me a glance. "It involves two brothers betraying each other and their pack. Violently."

At his words, the bikers sped up. A couple of them pulled into the lane beside us, the one for oncoming traffic, and rode up next to us. Through his sunglasses, his eyes were fastened in an angry glare.

I gripped the armrest, my panic spiking.

Ahead, an oncoming car sent the two bikers back to their original places at our bumper. Presley watched it all with sharp eyes. The exhaustion had receded for the moment thanks to my burst of adrenaline, but I also knew we couldn't fight off this many of them. Not alone.

"How bad is this?" I asked.

"I don't know," he admitted. "They're clearly here for us or they would have gone around by now."

My pulse sped as I tried to decipher what they wanted from us. Something hot pressed against my leg, and I looked down to see a glowing light emanating from my pocket where I'd stashed the necklace. I pulled it out and looked down at the crescent moon pendant. Sure as shit, the thing was glowing again.

"I don't know if it's a good idea to lead them straight to Doc's," Presley said. He glanced at me then back to the road. I followed his gaze. Up ahead, a flashing yellow light marked a four-way intersection. I knew a right would take us into town. But he had a point. The doc's office was full of injured werewolves—not much help in a fight with a biker gang. If it came to that.

"Take a left," I said.

"What's that way?" he asked.

I gripped the necklace tightly in my fist, feeling urgent now. "You'll see. Just trust me. Take the left."

Presley muttered something about secretive women and took the left. At high speed, the force of the turn pressed my body against the door, and I shut my eyes as the world whirred by and the tires squealed against the pavement.

When we straightened again, I opened my eyes to see half the bikers hadn't made the turn. The ones that had were filling in the gaps, though. Fast.

"Remember where you found me and the twins the other night?" I asked.

"You mean when Vinny decided a sample wasn't enough and tried making you the main course?" He snorted. "What about it?"

"Take us there," I said. "Pull off, and then we'll shift and run."

"That's your idea?" Presley looked at me like I'd lost it. "Are you fucking with me, Ash? Because those guys behind us can shift and run too, ya know. Not the best idea as escape plans go."

"Give me your phone," I said, ignoring him.

"Why the fuck—"

"Just do it."

He handed me his phone, and I scrolled through until I found Silas in his contacts. He picked up on the second ring.

"What?"

"It's Ash," I said, talking louder as the bike engines revved closer.

"What the hell," Silas demanded. One question that required several answers.

"Presley and I made some new friends," I said.

"I knew it," he muttered cryptically. "Where?"

"Highway eighty. Same place as with Vinny."

"I'm on my way."

The line went dead before I could tell him to bring backup.

"Faster," I told Presley as several of the bikes tried veering into the lane beside us again. If they did that, they could cut us off.

"This car isn't faster than their bikes, you know." Presley gripped the wheel with white knuckles.

"Just drive," I said.

"This is—"

"Shut up so I can concentrate!"

He clamped his mouth shut, and I twisted in my seat, pulling my necklace free from the pocket where I'd hidden it. The stone pulsed with warmth, and I crossed my fingers I wasn't wrong about my suspicions. If the magic in this thing wasn't real, we were so screwed.

Focusing on what I wanted—to lose this biker gang for good—I whispered to whatever hexerei magical gods or goddesses there might be and asked for help.

The pendant heated and glowed brighter, and for a moment, that was it.

My hope sank to the bottom of my stomach like a brick in the ocean. Feeling heavy with disappointment, I turned around again and sank into my seat. It had been stupid to think it could be that easy, I told myself. Magic was complicated. And not something you could just pick up and perform. If it was—

"Holy shit, what'd you do?" Presley demanded.

I looked back in time to see the bikers drive clear off the road and into the grass. Most of them slid and crashed at the sudden loss of traction. The ones who didn't only managed to remain upright by braking hard and stopping just before their bikes left the pavement.

No one managed to recover either.

Every single one of them was continually slammed sideways by some sort of invisible force. No matter what, they couldn't point their motorcycles in the direction of our bumper and remain on the road.

The last of them disappeared around a bend, and I turned and looked at Presley, eyes wide.

"What the hell just happened?" he asked.

I grinned. "Magic."

The high of our victory wore off way too fast. By the time Presley found the pull-off and we exited the car, I was running on fumes and fighting the urge to just lie down and sleep right here on the forest floor. A bed of pine needles sounded damn delightful right about now.

"Whoa, Ashes." Presley hurried over and looped an

arm around my waist, hauling me off before my knees could buckle.

"Sorry, I'm just so damn tired."

"Now is not the time to go all Sleeping Beauty on me."

I snorted. "Good because if you try to kiss me, I'll kill you."

"If a kiss is what it takes, why are we headed away from your mate? Hell, even Idrissa would probably do it if you asked nicely."

"We're going to see a hexerei," I said.

Presley jerked to a stop. I grunted as he pulled me to a halt with him.

"The hell did you just say?" He looked me over, frowning. "Are you unwell? Is there fever in your brain? Because that can drive a person insane, I heard."

"What the hell is wrong with her?"

The harshness of the voice made me jump. Or maybe it was the fact that Silas's presence was an automatic irritation.

Pres adjusted his grip as we both turned to see Silas striding toward us, looking angry enough to fight an entire biker gang on his own.

"She's fine," Presley assured him, but Silas marched right up to me and peered at me closely as if gauging for himself.

I yawned widely, and he made a face, straightening again.

"Just tired," I finished.

Silas looked at Presley. "Explain."

Presley gave him what should have been the short version except that he tried drawing the car chase part out into something that sounded like it belonged in an action movie. By the end, Silas was rolling his eyes and looked ready to punch something.

"You think they were here to challenge someone?" he asked when Presley was done.

"No idea, but we didn't feel compelled to stop and ask," Presley said.

"I passed them on the way in," Silas said, glancing at me again. "They're still stuck on the road, unable to follow you here."

"How long do you think it'll hold?" Presley asked.

"No idea. We need to get you back to town before whatever you did wears off."

"Not yet," I said, lids drooping.

"What?" Silas demanded.

"I have to see Kel." My knees buckled again. "Promise me." I forced my eyes open. "Promise," I said again to Presley. "If I pass out, take me to hex lands and ask for Kel."

He scowled.

I looked at Silas. "Swear it."

"You're insane," he said.

"They won't hurt us. Just ask for Kel," I repeated.

He glared at me with something in his gaze; a look I'd never seen on him before. Something almost...wistful. Then he blinked, and it was gone.

"Silas, I'm serious. Whatever's wrong with me—it's because of the magic. I need to know..."

I wanted to tell them about the hexerei's lack of magic. To assure them we'd be safe. But my tongue felt heavy. The words wouldn't come.

Silas sighed. "Fine. I swear it. Just don't fucking ask me to..."

I never heard the rest of it before sleep swallowed me whole.

..*

Air heavy with smoke wrinkled my nose as I stirred awake. Stiff limbs protested my movements, but I forced my arms into a stretch as I sucked in a breath that tasted like woodsmoke. My head felt clearer than it had earlier, and the lingering exhaustion had finally become manageable. The sound of a fire crackling sent my eyes snapping open. I sat up quickly, intent on scrambling to my feet to face whatever new threat awaited.

"Whoa."

Presley was there, hands out as if to help me up. Or maybe just to shove me down again. Who knew.

"What happened?" I asked.

"You're okay," he said. "Take a beat."

I looked around, heart racing as I tried to get my bearings.

I brushed my hair out of my face—it was a hot, tangled mess from the feel of it—and sat up. The first thing I noticed was the trees. We were deep in the woods somewhere I didn't recognize. A fire crackled steadily a few feet away. Someone had stacked a pile of wood beside it. The heat was welcome against the chill of the afternoon air.

I looked down at the feel of heavy wool underneath my hands. A blanket lay between me and the pine-needled ground. Presley watched me take it all in warily. Slowly, he eased back down onto the log he'd been using for a chair.

"Where are we?" I asked.

Maybe *when* was a better question.

The sun sat higher in the sky than I remembered from before.

"Hexerei lands," Presley said, looking none too happy about it.

"How did we...?"

"Silas carried you all the way in," he said. "You were passed out worse than my uncle Fred at Thanksgiving. I thought your snoring was going to get us shot at."

I glared at him. "I don't snore."

He grinned.

"Where's Silas?" I asked, looking around. Now that I was awake, I could sense the presence of others nearby. And my nerves were not going to calm until I knew who was out there.

"He's keeping watch," Presley said. "Along with—"

"You're awake."

I looked up as Kel strode into view. Her long hair was braided in what must have been her signature style. Like before, she wore fitted pants and tall boots that made her look like some sort of goth supermodel. But the sight of her startled me more than it should have. I hadn't even heard her coming.

What the hell?

Silas trudged behind her, his expression taut and full of things he probably wanted to yell at me for. But he'd done what he promised. He'd found Kel and brought me out here to meet with her.

Maybe I'd let him yell at me later just to call it even.

"We were beginning to wonder," Kel said.

"How long was I asleep?"

"Almost three hours," Presley said, sounding personally offended by it.

Three hours? I blinked. Kai would be worried sick.

"Relax, I called Stone," Presley said. "He's only going to kill me a little bit, but he's fine."

I exhaled. He was going to kill me too, but that was a problem for future me.

"I heard what happened," Kel said, crouching beside me.

"Which part?" I asked.

"Healing, glowing, and collapsing," she said. "Does that sum it up?"

"Yeah, that's pretty much the highlights," I said.

Lips twitching, she looked into my eyes and then scanned the rest of me as if her gaze was some sort of medical machine designed to read my vitals.

I glanced at Presley, who just shrugged.

"How are you feeling?" she asked.

"Better," I said. "Like I can finally keep my eyes open. The exhaustion before… I've never felt anything like it."

"Magic does that," she said so matter-of-factly it silenced me. She gave me a wry look. "You're surprised to hear me say that, and yet you knew to come here for help."

"I… I wanted answers. But it's crazy, right? I think I would have known if I had magic."

"Would you?" she asked. "You didn't know magic was real until a few weeks ago. We tend to see what we believe rather than the opposite. Who's to say you didn't have magic and simply dismissed it as coincidence?"

"I've never been this tired before," I said, which felt like a stupid argument but seemed to make Kel reconsider.

"Where's the necklace?" she asked.

"Here."

I pulled it out of my pocket and held it up. Kel didn't move to take it, which already told me she knew more than we did.

She peered at it for a long moment. "Has it done anything other than glow?" she asked finally.

"Kai tried to hold it, and the pendant burned him," I said.

"Hmm."

She frowned, her forehead creasing, and I felt my impatience bubble up. "Kel, if you know something about this, you have to tell me."

"Relax," she said. "I'm not holding out on you. I'm just trying to think."

"Well, think fast," Presley said.

She shot him a look. "I told you we're safe here."

"And I told you nowhere in hex lands is safe for us," he shot back.

I glanced back at Silas, fully expecting him to jump in and add his two cents, but he stood silently, eyes scanning the woods. His shoulders were stiff, and the muscles in his forearms were flexing so hard I thought they might snap.

"If Kel says we're safe, then I trust her," I told Presley.

He huffed, clearly not convinced.

"We're safe," Silas said with a force of conviction that surprised me.

We all turned to look at him, but he continued scanning the trees. I frowned. If we were so safe, what was he looking for?

At a loss, I looked back at Kel. "How is it possible I have magic and never knew until now?"

"First of all, that's entirely possible if someone sealed it."

"Sealed it? What does that mean?"

"Like a Ziploc bag?" Presley asked.

Kel rolled her eyes. "Sealed it inside the necklace, you dumbass."

"So the necklace is like a Ziploc bag," Presley said.

Kel looked at me.

I shrugged. "He's pretty."

She snorted.

"Hey," Presley protested, but Kel ignored him.

"To get the answers you want, we need to ask the right questions." She looked down at the pendant again, studying. "For starters, the necklace—where did you get it?"

"My mother left it for me when she..."

I didn't bother to finish, not with how intense Kel looked. Her head snapped up, her eyes meeting mine and boring into them. "Your mother, the hexerei, gave you this. And you didn't think to mention that up front?"

"Why would I?" I asked. "I had no idea what she was at the time. It felt like some lame-ass consolation prize from a woman who would rather live alone than see my face every day."

Kel sighed. "May I?" she asked, gesturing to the necklace.

"It could hurt you," I warned.

"I'll take my chances."

I held it out, and she picked it up, turning it over in her hands. I bit my lip, waiting, but she didn't react. All at once, the pendant began to glow. Kel's eyes lit with a gleam as she stared into the stone.

Finally, she handed it back to me, and our eyes met.

"Magic senses magic," she said with a secret smile.

I felt a strange tug of recognition then. Like she and I shared a common bond. It felt nice, having a connection like that. Like...family. Shaking that off, I focused on the necklace again.

"It didn't burn you," I pointed out.

"The magic has spelled itself against anyone not a match."

"Not a match," I said. "You mean anyone without magic?"

She nodded.

"So, to anyone without magic, it's, like, booby-trapped?" Presley asked.

"Exactly." She looked at me. "That necklace is the key to everything."

"How do you know?" I asked, my hand closing around the charm.

"Remember the vision I had last time?" she asked.

"The one with all the light around us?"

She nodded. "Magic has a signature, and the feeling I had in that vision is the same feeling I get when I hold that. There's definitely magic in that thing. A fucking lot of it too from the sense I got. You don't know where your mom got it? Or why she gave it to you?"

"No."

I tried not to feel the full weight of that particular goose egg. More blame to heap at Mom's feet. Ugh.

"Well, I think the answers you want are tied to that pendant."

I sighed. "And to the one person who refuses to show up and face what she's done."

"Speaking of people and what they've done," Presley said. "You know anything about one of ours slumming it with the hex's?"

Kel's eyes narrowed, and I jumped in.

"He means Drake," I said. "Brown hair. Shifty eyes. Handsome but creepy. Power-hungry douchebag. We saw him sneaking onto hexerei lands the other day."

She shook her head. "I don't know anything about that. But Cohen has his hands in things he knows I wouldn't approve of. I'll ask around."

"Thanks."

"Don't mention it." She glared at Presley. "I mean that literally, lupin."

Presley snorted. "Relax. Bragging about roasting s'mores with a hex-betch doesn't exactly score me any cool points back home."

Kel shot him a murderous glare.

"Presley," I hissed.

Kel's gaze swung back to me.

"Pretty," she repeated through clenched teeth.

"Pretty," I agreed.

She growled, and Presley, wisely, said nothing.

"About the magic…" I said.

"I don't know any more than what I told you. But you'll figure it out," she said.

My eyes narrowed. "How can you be so sure?"

"Because your blood swore it." She smirked. "And I can feel your determination in my veins. Besides, you're a hexerei now. An Archer. And we never give up."

23

Silas was silent on the walk back from Kel's camp. At first, I just felt grateful he wasn't yelling at me, but the longer we walked, the more pronounced his withdrawn demeanor became. He seemed distracted, and that was the least Silas-like thing he could have been.

"What is it?" I asked finally.

He looked over sharply, seemingly startled by my words. "What?"

"Something's bothering you," I said.

"Bullshit," he muttered.

You're being weird," I said. "You haven't yelled at me once about recklessness in coming out here, and you didn't even threaten Kel back there. Something's wrong."

Silas scowled at me, but Presley spoke up.

"She's right, bro. You're off."

"Maybe I'm preoccupied with the fact that the entire world is going to shit and the only way to stop it is some magic fucking necklace."

"There's the asshole we all know," I said.

He glared at me, but for some reason, the force of it didn't rub at me like it usually did.

"You were looking for something," I said. "What was it?"

"What are you talking about?"

"At Kel's camp. You kept scanning the trees."

"I was watching our backs for a threat. We were in enemy territory. I'd be an idiot not to pay attention."

"You said we were safe, though," I said.

"You did say that," Presley put in, which earned him a look that promised violence. "Geez, calm down." Silas swatted at him, and he ducked out of reach. "Well, you did say it."

"This is bullshit. I save your ass and all you can do is come at me."

"I'm not coming at you. I'm just..."

"What?" he demanded.

"I'm trying to be your friend, you jackass."

He didn't say anything to that, but my temper had already snapped.

"Both of you came to me," I said. "You wanted to help. To prove yourselves."

"We did prove ourselves," Silas said. "When Vinny attacked, we felt your distress. We found you and, fucking hell, Ashes, we would have killed them for you if you'd needed us to."

I blinked, struck silent by that.

Silas huffed.

"What do you mean you felt my distress?" I asked.

Silas didn't answer. I looked at Presley.

"Kai said you just knew he needed your help," I said. "When he couldn't get out of his cell, he said you showed up."

Presley shrugged. "My wolf knew he needed me."

"And Silas?"

Presley sighed. "Silas' wolf feels called to protect you. Not Kai."

"Silas' wolf chose me?" I stopped, completely at a loss about what to do with that.

"So fucking what?" Silas groaned. "Dammit, Pres, why did you have to run your mouth?"

"What's the big deal? Everyone's wolf is picking someone. It's not like we have a choice, anyway. Our wolves just decide." He looked at me. "For the record, this doesn't mean I don't support you for alpha. It just means my wolf senses Kai's needs instead of yours."

I looked at Silas, still shocked. Kel's comment came back to me. About lines being drawn. Had Silas chosen *my* side of the line?

"But you hate me," I blurted.

"I don't hate you," he said.

Then again, speaking the words through clenched teeth kind of detracted from the message.

"So, then, why are you acting like such a huge dick?" I demanded.

"It's none of your damn business," Silas snapped and then increased his pace until he'd put distance between us.

Fine by me.

I forced myself to start walking again. Presley fell into step beside me.

"Don't take it personally," Presley said.

I looked over sharply. "Too late."

"Nah. Seriously. He always acts weird out here," he explained.

"What do you mean out here?" I asked. "In the woods? Or just at Kel's camp."

"That camp back there is a sort of loophole," he said.

"What kind of loophole."

"If you look on the boundary maps, the way the lines are drawn, that spot doesn't fall inside either of our borders."

"So, it's like neutral ground?"

He shrugged. "More or less. Although, it's not like we've ever tested the theory. Until today."

"What does that have to do with Silas being an extra asshole today?"

Presley hesitated. I knew full well Silas could hear every word of our conversation, so I didn't expect an answer.

I'd all but given up when Presley said, "Silas camps there sometimes. That's all I know."

Silas' hands fisted, but he never looked back.

Presley didn't say anything else.

But the silence that followed only made all of my own worries more pronounced. I didn't want to sit in my thoughts. Not when they all felt like a dead end. My mother was the only one who could tell me about this stupid necklace, and I damn sure didn't want to spend the entire walk back thinking about her.

I looked over at Presley. "What was the story?" I asked.

"What?"

"About the two brothers. And the pack with that symbol we saw on the biker's vest. You told me you'd heard of that symbol in a story."

"Right. Well, it's more of a legend, really. I never really believed it before—but the symbol is the same."

"Tell me," I said. "I just need a distraction."

"Legend says there were two brothers born to the same alpha. The youngest was raised in the shadow of his older brother, the true alpha-heir. The younger was always compared to the older. Always measured against his sibling and found wanting. And that shadow he lived under became a darkness that swallowed him whole. He became hungry. Desperate for power of his own. He wanted recognition. Without the comparison to his older sibling. But he wouldn't get it. Not while his older brother was the alpha heir."

"What happened to him?" I asked, caught up in the story. "The younger brother."

"They say he traded his soul for the power to steal a wolf's essence. And he stole and stole until he became strong enough to challenge the alpha-heir. When it came time to fight, the alpha-heir was clearly stronger, despite the dark methods of the boy, but the alpha-heir couldn't bear to strike down his own brother. So, instead, the alpha-heir used his superior strength to scar the boy. Scratch after scratch. Bite after bite. Cut after cut. The alpha-heir marked his brother so that even if he healed, everyone would know what he'd done. That he'd used the darkness to betray his own blood. And then, the alpha-heir banished his brother forever."

"Where did he go?" I asked.

"Many shifters looked for him. Watching the alpha challenges across the country for years after. But there was no one who matched the description of someone with so many scars. They say he died. Or that he came so close to death that he lost his humanity and became stuck as his wolf, wandering in search of a pack who would accept him."

"That's terrible," I said.

"It seemed like nothing but a story meant to warn off anyone who would be tempted to gain power through nefarious methods." He glanced at me. "But the symbol on those vests is the same as the one from the story. The pack emblem."

"You think it's really them? That the story's real?" I asked.

"Who knows. I mean, what would they want with us anyway?"

"Good question." I bit my lip, letting my mind wander over a problem that felt far less personal and, honestly, far less dangerous than the ones I should have been worried about.

Up ahead, Silas whistled sharply.

I looked up, the legend forgotten as my wolf scanned the trees for some threat. But Silas glanced back and waved us forward, posture relaxed.

"What is it?" I asked when we caught up.

"Kai's here," he said at the same moment the bond alerted me.

I pushed past the others, following my heartstrings. Up ahead, Kai and the twins were making their way toward us. When he saw me coming, Kai broke into a run and scooped me into his arms, lifting me off my feet as he held me close.

"Good goddess, it's like something out of a Hallmark movie." Idrissa sounded disgusted, but I just grinned as Kai set me on my feet again.

"You watch Hallmark movies?" I asked her.

"When I'm sick," she said with a sniff. "Don't judge me."

"If they do, it won't be for that," Isaac said, and everyone tensed. "Relax, it's just sibling banter," he added. "I'm not going to bite her face off."

"How'd the meeting go?" I asked Kai.

"Besides the fact that Drake denies ever attacking Baron and without proof, Sheriff refused to arrest him?" His expression darkened. "Fucking peachy."

Presley snorted. "You sound like Isaac."

"Pretty sure he's rubbing off on me," Kai said.

"Uh, Ash is the only thing rubbing you, trust me," Isaac said. He gave Presley a pointed look, and I paused, trying to decipher what exactly was passing between them.

"We should get moving," Silas said abruptly.

He was staring into the trees, still tense, despite the fact that my senses told me we were alone.

"I heard about your entourage earlier," Idrissa said.

"What happened?" Kai asked me.

"I'll tell you while we walk," I said, pulling him into step beside me. "But you have to promise not to be mad."

"Why would I be mad?"

"Because my story involves magic and hexerei and passing out in the woods in the middle of enemy territory. Basically, lots of danger."

He gave me a wry look. "I willingly chose jail over being with you, so I don't think I get to be mad when you make executive decisions about your own life."

"No argument from me," Idrissa piped up.

I shot her a look.

"Oh, is this not a group discussion?" she asked.

"Come on," Silas said, and it took me a moment to realize he was talking to Idrissa.

"What is it?" she asked.

"I'm going to shift," he said. "Keep an eye on the way ahead. Make sure we're clear."

"What does that have to do with me?" she asked, and he glared at her. "Right. Okay. Got it. I'm here to help."

She and Silas broke off from the rest of us, disappearing into the trees together.

"What the hell was that about?" Isaac demanded.

"No fucking clue, man. Your sister's weird," Presley said.

"Your mom," Isaac shot back.

I caught Kai's gaze and smiled, pressing a kiss to his mouth as we walked. He slid his fingers into mine.

"Tell me everything," he said.

"Okay, but Presley will have to fill you in on some because, apparently, I slept through half of it."

"Bro, she was like Sleeping Beau—Whoops, bad example. No kisses were involved. Not one. So you can just relax and don't worry about anything."

Kai looked from Presley to me.

"Should I be worried?" he asked.

"I mean, he is pretty," I said, laughing way too hard when the look he gave me was such a match for Kel's withering expression earlier.

"Are you going to tell the damn story or insult me all day?" Presley demanded.

"Pretty is not insulting," Isaac said. He winked at me, adding, "Besides, I think she can do both."

..*

"I guess training is out," I said as I watched Idrissa drive off with Presley. We'd made it back to the road without running into anyone, although the exhaustion from earlier was starting to creep in again. A pot of coffee sounded perfect right about now. Maybe a direct IV drip straight into my veins would do the trick.

"You don't need to train," Kai said.

I looked at him in disbelief. "You do remember who I'm facing tomorrow, right? Body like a Mack truck. Muscles the size of watermelons. Ring a bell?"

"Your wolf is an alpha, Ash. She's got this. You just have to let her."

"Like, give in to her completely? Kai, she wants to eat squirrels, it's gross."

Isaac smothered a laugh.

Presley looked surprised. "You've never given in to your wolf fully before?"

"I don't know. I sort of did the other night with Vinny, but it was just for a moment so I could do that whole alpha-command thing on them. And when I ran home, I felt her kind of take me over for a minute."

"Damn, girl." He shook his head. "You're missing out."

"How did it feel?" Kai asked me. "When you let her out to run?"

"Good," I said, thinking back. "Free. Like nothing else mattered for a moment."

He nodded. "Our way of life isn't just about shifting at will. It's becoming one with our wolf's soul. Its spirit is part of us just as much as our humanity. If we don't embrace it, we risk exhausting ourselves by fighting against it constantly."

He gave me a meaningful look, and my eyes widened.

"You think my exhaustion is from fighting my wolf?"

"Maybe. Either way, a run would do you some good. Especially after the day you've had."

I bit my lip. He had a point. And a run sounded amazing.

"Come with me?" he asked.

I glanced over at Isaac and Presley.

"On that note, we're going to go," Isaac said.

"We are?" Presley frowned.

Isaac elbowed him, and he grunted. "Right. We are."

"We're going to check in with the security teams and see if anyone's spotted that pack from earlier," Isaac said.

"And Drake," I said. "Make sure someone's on him at all times."

"We've got people on him," Presley said, "But so far, he's clean."

I doubted that but let it go.

A moment later, Isaac and Presley left in Isaac's car, leaving Kai and me alone.

"Ready?" Kai asked.

"Not yet." I pulled my necklace out of my pocket and re-fastened it around my neck. The pendant felt cool against my throat, but when I looked up, Kai was watching it like he expected it to do something.

"Kai?"

"This morning," he said, looking up at me again. "We didn't have time to talk about it then, but ... you were in my head."

I blew out a breath. "I know. Is that— Was that magic too?"

"That was shifter magic," he said.

"Is that a thing?"

"Well, no. But telepathic communication hasn't happened to our pack in generations," he said. "So, I'm calling it shifter magic." He shrugged. "Might as well be."

"When we first realized we were mates, you said something about a mental bond."

"Mental bonds are an extension of our emotional bond. Usually, that means increasing our connection in terms of distance. Some mated pairs have been able to sense general ideas or mood but never specific words like this."

"So, we're freaks," I said.

He kissed my cheek. "We're special."

I didn't answer. Between the magic and the alpha challenges, I didn't have any more room for weird shit.

"Do you think you could do it again?" Kai asked.

I looked up at him. "I guess it depends on how it works. Do you get to hear everything I'm thinking, or can I pick and choose?"

"Worried I might hear something bad?" he asked.

"My head is not always a sane space."

He looked amused. "We'll save it for another day. Come on, you still feeling up for this?"

"Let's run," I said.

"First, strip."

My eyes narrowed at him. "Was this all an elaborate ploy to get me naked?"

"I'm insulted," he said in mock offense. "That you would even think I need an elaborate—"

I cut him off with a kiss.

His lips curved into a smile against my own, and his hand circled my waist.

"Is it working?" he whispered.

I laughed. "Definitely."

Pulling away, I stepped back and made a show of slowly peeling my shirt over my head. Kai's gaze darkened, and he barely even blinked as he watched me strip out of my clothes. I purposely kept my movements slow and sensual, enjoying the game between us.

My heart rate picked up as he began to follow my lead, stripping out of his own clothes with the same slow pace.

At the sight of his cut muscles, inky black tattoos, and that perfect V-shape where his hips dipped, I realized my mistake. I'd meant to tease him, and that plan was seriously backfiring on me right now.

"Everything okay?" Kai asked, amusement lacing his words.

I blinked and licked my lips, hoping I hadn't drooled noticeably. "Huh?"

He grinned. "You look a little lost."

"Not lost. Just…thirsty," I managed.

He took a step toward me, and my bones became soft and liquidy at the sight of all that gorgeous muscle headed my way. But then he slipped past me, his fingers only grazing my ass.

"What the…"

"Tell your wolf to come and get me," he said over his shoulder.

"Are you fucking serious?" I demanded.

He laughed.

Laughed.

I cringed, disgusted to realize women could get blue balls too. My thighs ached. My stomach churned.

"You're playing with fire," I called to his back.

But Kai just kept on walking into the trees. "Come and get me, little wolf. And I promise to let you do whatever you want when you catch me."

I took a step toward him. Then another.

"Whatever I want?" I asked, my imagination already running wild.

Kai turned, giving me a full view of everything he was offering. When my eyes finally found their way back to his, he was smirking. "You just have to catch me first."

My wolf didn't hesitate.

The moment Kai shifted and raced off, she rose up. I shifted, mid-step, and took off after him.

The next few hours passed in a blur of animal senses.

Sights. Sounds. Scents.

Presley had been right.

I'd never given in like this before, and I'd been missing out. Letting my wolf take the lead was freeing. Every problem dropped away. And the ones that remained—the ones my wolf considered worthy of her time—became simpler.

She wanted to be alpha, and so she would fight for it.

For my wolf, the decision was as easy as wanting something and feeling worthy of going after it.

Her strength and determination felt like a missing piece to my human soul. Outwardly, I kept my focus on chasing Kai. But inside, I went through an entire metamorphosis of what it was to be Ash.

By the time I caught up—something I wondered if Kai let me do because, damn, he was fast—I'd found a sense of peace about it all. And on top of that, my wolf was more than ready to claim her prize.

Kai finally fell still long enough for me to get close. I pinned him, feeling triumphant, but my victory was short-lived when Kai reached up and dragged his long tongue across my entire snout.

My wolf huffed and snarled as I scrambled back.

Kai shifted mid-laughter.

I shifted too and glared at him. "You're going to pay for that," I said.

His eyes glittered. "I can't wait."

I threw myself at him, taking us both down with a grunt. But Kai's hands were gentle around my shoulders and hips, rolling me so that I came out on top again.

He looked up at me with complete love and devotion in his dark eyes. "Well?" he said. "What is it you want?"

I leaned down, whispering, "You," just before I kissed him.

This time, I lost myself to my human senses, and when Kai slid inside me, the pleasure of his body moving with mine sent me over the edge with a sense of freedom that had nothing to do with shifting and everything to do with experiencing destiny in physical form.

24

The woods surrounding the barn were full of wolves. I could smell them and hear them almost as much as I could feel them. A pulsing of wild energy. Some of it felt familiar—the members of the pack I'd come to know. More than a few of them bore minor wounds from various skirmishes. Idrissa and Isaac weren't the only ones turning on each other, according to the stories I'd heard. Idrissa had been right. We were out of time.

Today counted for a lot.

As if I didn't have enough pressure, Tiffany had brought her own little entourage. They'd all made a show of staking out space directly behind me. Like my own little fan club. It was flattering. And weird. Especially when they saw me frowning and backed up a ways. Like they'd read my discomfort.

The rest of the energy felt foreign—the Asheville wolves, though I was getting better and better at identifying our pack from theirs. They'd held up the rules, despite Baron's attack, and hadn't set foot on our pack lands until today's appointed time.

The level of respect they'd displayed was more than I could say for some of our own people. Not to mention the foreign pack Presley and I had encountered yesterday. Despite security patrols, no one had seen them since. It was strange. But I wasn't going to complain. We had enough problems without adding some mysterious pack of legends to the mix.

One wolf, in particular, stood out to me above the others already assembled here.

A shudder ran through me as Drake's wolf emerged from the trees. I almost didn't recognize him, and if it hadn't been for scent, I probably wouldn't have. His wolf was noticeably larger than before. Hell, his paws alone were the size of dinner plates. And the power he was sending toward me now was no joke. I swallowed hard, heart racing as I let his attempt at dominance wash over me.

He wanted me to cower.

But mostly, he wanted to make sure my wolf knew who would win should she be so inclined to challenge him to a fight.

Asshole.

I brushed my fingers over the pendant at my throat, double-checking it was tucked out of sight. With Drake this hopped up on whatever he'd dosed himself with, I didn't want to take any chances at someone in the crowd noticing that my moon pendant doubled as a glow stick.

There'd be time for that explanation later.

Provided I lived long enough.

We'd all agreed my magic had to stay hidden for now. At least, until I got through today. If Baron had reacted that strongly to it, who knew what the council or any others would do if they learned what I was.

Drake strode past, deliberately ignoring me, and found a spot near the edge of the fighting space. His paw just barely grazed the line, in fact; a deliberate move meant to put me on edge. He knew that I knew he'd dodged, well, everything. The sheriff wouldn't arrest him and Warren refused to bar him from today's challenge. The smugness he exuded was him simply twisting the knife.

Gritting my teeth, I looked away.

A moment later, two figures broke off from the crowd and strode toward where I waited in the center of things.

Oscar and Warren.

Beyond where they'd stood, Baron waited.

He'd already undressed and stood with arms crossed, surrounded by his pack leadership. From here, I probably could have squinted to take in the details of his massive body. But I definitely wasn't into that idea.

Instead, I looked away and braced myself for what we were about to do.

One of us wouldn't make it off this field.

As much as I didn't want it to come to that, I was damn sure determined the one left lying here wouldn't be me. My father hadn't been willing to let Baron have his pack, and neither was I.

And if anyone tried intervening—looking at you, Drake—my backup would be ready. I resisted the urge to glance behind me toward the barn where I knew Kai had hidden himself in the loft.

We hadn't talked about the alpha problem. In fact, we hadn't talked about much at all in the last twenty-four hours. We'd spent a good chunk of it in wolf form. And yes, I'd even eaten a squirrel. Presley had insisted—and then laughed his ass off when I finally did it. Kai had eaten it with me, but apparently, Idrissa preferred rabbit.

They'd all—except for Silas, who hadn't spoken a word to me since leaving that campsite—taken turns running with me. According to all of them, the longer I stayed in my wolf's skin, the better equipped I'd be for today. And they were right.

My wolf felt sharper than ever.

My senses were heightened. The bond with Kai felt stronger. And my strength had returned, no more exhaustion.

Even now, if I tuned in, I could feel Kai's adrenaline through our bond. Pressing the lid down on my awareness of him, I focused on the two men approaching me. Scratch that, I focused on Oscar, the friendlier face.

"Ash," Oscar said, and in that one word was all his worry and fear and anxiety. For some reason, knowing that made me feel better. "How are you doing?"

"I'm ready," I said, despite my heart hammering inside my chest loud enough for the entire crowd to hear.

"Baron says he'll give you a five-second head start to shift," Warren said.

I glared at him then past him to Baron. "No, thanks."

"Are you sure?" Warren frowned. "It's more than fair."

"Is it?" I turned my ire toward Mr. Close. "You think so little of my chances that giving me a head start seems *fair?*"

"I was only thinking of your best interest—"

"Doubtful," I snapped; then, to Oscar, "I'm ready. We can begin as soon as you've both cleared the field."

Oscar stared at me. For a moment, I thought he would just nod and retreat, strong and silent as usual. But then he grabbed me and pulled me against him in a stiff hug that stole my breath.

Then he stepped back, hands on my shoulders, gripping tightly as he leaned in so that we were eye to eye. "Give him hell, kid. Do you hear me? Don't hold back."

"I hear you," I said, breathless and fighting back a teary-eyed smile.

Here I was about to face off with the strongest alpha on the eastern seaboard, and I was getting all warm and fuzzy about how my strong-and-silent uncle had just hugged me in front of the entire pack.

Then, Oscar was snapping at Warren to move his ass, and they both strode away.

I blinked back the soft emotions and focused on the fight. Adrenaline and pure determination pumped through my veins as I turned to face the largest alpha I'd ever seen—and prepared to kill him.

Sweat coated my palms, turning them clammy. My breath turned shallow as I watched Baron exchange a few words with Warren and Oscar. Then, he headed this way. Every step he took was like a drumbeat signaling the end.

Or, for the winner, a beginning.

My wolf, however, was not nearly so panicked. She grumbled at me to stop being dramatic.

Let's skip to the ass-kicking part, shall we?

Her voice in my head was wickedly confident. And more importantly, fearless.

Rather than attempt to argue with her, I prepared to shift.

My wolf wanted to run the show, and I wasn't going to stand in her way.

Human Ash didn't stand a chance.

Wolf shifter Ash just might.

But the closer Baron got to where I stood, the more obvious it became that he didn't intend to shift at all.

When he neared, I noted the strange expression he wore.

Something was wrong.

I braced myself.

"Ash, may we speak?"

"Is everything okay?" I asked, frowning as I let myself look closer at his chest and arms. "Are you not healed enough for this?"

"It's not that." He shook his head. "That wolf over there." He nodded to my left. I glanced over and scowled before turning back to Baron.

"Drake?" I said, the name bitter on my tongue.

"He's the one who demanded I challenge him at the barn the night I arrived."

"Yes," I said, unsure if that was meant to be a question. "The sheriff decided there wasn't enough evidence to arrest him. I know that's frustrating. He's been allowed here only as a spectator. But if you'd prefer, I can have him removed—"

"That's not it." He looked from Drake to me, still clearly troubled. "His scent. It's different today than it was before."

I nodded. "I've noticed it too. Something's off. We're looking into it."

He hesitated. There was more going on here, something beneath the surface. Something he didn't want to tell me.

"If you have information about Drake," I began, but the rest of my words were drowned out by a vicious growl.

I looked over to see Drake approaching Baron and me, his teeth bared and his hackles raised.

Baron took a full step back.

I couldn't blame him.

Drake's power had increased again. Whatever he'd

done to himself, he was more threatening today than I'd ever felt from him before.

"Drake, get the hell off the field," I snapped.

My heart sped at the thought of fighting them both.

But Drake halted and shifted back to two legs, glaring at Baron. His human form looked no different than usual, which was another mystery. Shouldn't he be bigger in both forms?

"You're here to fight, old man. Not run your mouth," Drake said in a clear warning.

Kai appeared beside me, his hands fisted and looking ready to punch something. Specifically, Drake.

"Drake, get the hell off this field before I remove you," Kai warned.

"Your scent," Baron said to Drake, not backing down. In fact, now he looked suspicious more than anything. "It's not right. What have you done to yourself?"

"I accepted the alpha calling," Drake growled. "You're welcome to challenge me instead of this weakling and find out, old man."

His tone turned teasing, daring Baron to take the bait.

"You're unnatural," Baron said. "A beast contrived. You smell...like decay."

"Fight or leave," Drake spat.

"Same to you, asshole." Kai inched in closer to Drake, forcing him to back away from us.

I bit my lip, wondering if Kai was pushing him too far. But Drake backed away. He glared at Baron as he went.

Baron looked at me.

"I told you before I've challenged and fought many wolves in my life. None of them smelled like him—not while they still had a heartbeat. Something in him has been touched by an energy wolves do not possess."

"An energy," I repeated. "You mean magic?"

"A beasts' alpha power either exists or it doesn't. If you value the sacred laws of our kind, he cannot be allowed to compete."

"You say that as if it's up to me." I gave him a strange look. "But if you defeat me like you say, you'll be able to make that call."

"I..." He shot Drake a look. Then Kai. Then, finally, back to me. "I have spoken to my council, and we believe we can make an alliance with you. I would withdraw my challenge if you agree to the idea of working together." He gave me a pointed look. "From what I hear, you'll need the numbers when the witches come for you again."

Surprise had me blinking, searching for words.

A withdrawal hadn't even dawned on me. Was that a thing?

"Why would you withdraw?" I asked. "You sounded so convicted the other day when we spoke."

"Caleb was the closest thing to a friend I've ever had," Baron said. "I honor him by showing mercy to his daughter."

Mercy.

Something about the way he put it didn't sit well. Like pity.

Then again, it beat dying.

"I need to speak with my mate," I said.

"Of course. Take a few minutes. I'll await your decision."

With a parting glance at Drake, Baron returned to his pack mates. Drake stomped back to the sidelines in a huff, clearly fuming over the offer to withdraw, but I ignored him. Instead, I stared after Baron, stunned at his offer.

Finally, I looked at Kai.

"What do you think?" I asked.

"I don't know."

His reluctance dampened some of my excitement.

"You think it's a bad idea?" I asked.

"He called it mercy."

"Yeah, I heard it."

"Being shown mercy in an alpha challenge—that's not a legacy you want to leave. As alpha, you have to display your strength. Your dominance has to be absolute, or people will question you."

"If I let him withdraw, what does that mean for your fight with Drake?" I asked.

He shook his head. "It's still winner against winner."

I didn't answer.

Glancing up again, I saw movement along the tree line. Faces I didn't recognize. More Asheville pack come to watch, maybe? My eyes caught on their matching vests all decorated with the same symbol.

Recognition slammed into me just as Presley ran up.

A few members of the crowd murmured their disapproval at his interruption, but they went ignored.

"I see them," I said.

Kai pressed in closer to me, watching the newcomers warily.

"Let me guess," he said. "Those are your friends from yesterday?"

"I don't know about friends, but I just heard one of the Asheville pack members talking about them." Presley looked at me, eyes blazing with intensity. "They called them Hawley. Like from the story I told you."

My eyes widened.

Kai tore his gaze from the visitors who were moving steadily in behind Drake. He stared at Presley.

"Like from the story?" he asked.

Presley nodded. "I thought it was bullshit. But the symbol matches. And their name..." He leaned in, lowering his voice as he said, "What the hell do you think they're doing here?"

I looked back at them, noting the way they seemed to be glued to Drake. In fact, not a single one had glanced over at where the three of us stood in the center of things. If they were here to challenge for alpha, they clearly had their sights set on a different contender.

"They're here for Drake," I said.

As if he'd heard me, Drake looked up at me and then back at the strangers closing in on where he stood. His body stiffened, and he stilled, his scent changing to one of fear.

A feeling washed over me. A tugging on my chest. Absently, I reached for my necklace and wrapped my hand around the pendant. As soon as my palm closed over it, magic slammed into me.

Light poured in, eclipsing everything except for Drake himself. I focused on him, noting the rippling of his skin against whatever magical vision I'd suddenly called up. The image felt slippery, there one minute and gone the next, but I gasped when I caught sight of his body through the lens of the layers and layers of light.

Scars.

Everywhere.

They covered his entire body. Some were raised and pink as if fresh—or refusing to heal. Some were long faded but apparently deep enough to remain forever. Jagged gashes and clean, thin ribbons; each was a macabre piece of artwork all its own.

Even his hair had been hacked and slashed, some of the scars covering his scalp. His ear hung at an odd angle, sliced in half near the top.

I cringed at how painful it must have been, feeling all of those cuts.

Then I blinked, the magic shimmered, and the curtain lifted.

Drake's smooth, unblemished skin returned. And his expression was transfixed into utter fear as he watched the Hawley pack pick their way closer and closer to where he stood.

"Ash?" Kai asked, his voice low but urgent against my ear.

I let go of the necklace and shook myself to break free of the magic. And what I'd seen. But nothing I did would let me unsee that.

"Hold up." Presley pointed at the pendant. "Your shit's glowing."

I quickly tucked the pendant into my shirt.

"What did you see?" Kai asked.

I looked over at him, heart pounding as I tried to process it all. "Do you remember the boy from the story? The one who stole other wolves' power."

They both nodded.

"Remember how the oldest brother scarred the younger one so everyone would know?"

"Yeah," Presley said.

I looked back at Drake, dread crawling up through my spine as I thought back to everything that had happened. Drake sneaking off to be with the witches. His strange changes, especially when it came to the strength of his wolf. And the complete obsession he had with becoming alpha. Or better yet, keeping the pack from choosing an alpha at all. He didn't want the curse broken because it would reveal what he really was. A murderer and a soul-stealer. The worst kind of alpha this pack could possibly ever choose.

"The youngest brother from the story," I said. "It's Drake."

25

Kai snarled and started for Drake. Presley muttered a curse, but all I could hear was the roaring in my ears as I realized how much power Drake really had. If he was the boy in that story, that meant he'd stolen the souls of wolf shifters to get here. If he could do that and change his appearance to hide those scars, what else could he do?

"Kai, get away from him," I called sharply as my thoughts crashed on top of one another.

Drake whirled at that. The fear transformed to fury when he saw Kai coming his way.

"Stone, back the hell off," Drake yelled.

We had to stop him. But first, we needed to clear this field of possible victims for him to use. If he got any stronger, I wasn't sure if I could take him.

My wolf snarled at that, but I couldn't deny the truth.

"Not happening," Kai roared back. "I know what you are. Hawley."

Drake's eyes narrowed.

Behind him, the Hawley pack snarled loud enough to draw everyone's attention.

"We've come to collect our vengeance," one of them declared as they all pressed in closer.

Nearby, some of our pack noticed the visitors—and the tension they'd brought with them.

"This is a private event," I heard one of them say.

A female.

I looked over and spotted Tiffany striding over to head off the Hawley pack.

"You're not welcome here," she told them coldly.

Behind her were a few others I recognized, including Teddy, the bartender from Bo's.

"Shit, this is not going to end well," Presley muttered.

I looked over at him. "Keep the rest of the pack clear of this," I said, urgent now that I was beginning to recognize the danger everyone was in. If Baron was right, Drake didn't need to fight me or even Kai. He could pick any one of the pack members who were here to watch. He'd done it with Devon, I realized. Killed Devon and stole his power, adding it to his own. "We can't let him near the rest of the pack."

"I'm on it," Presley said and then took off running.

I hurried to Kai's side, careful not to touch him. Even now, I could sense his wolf already rising. It wouldn't take much to set him off, and I had to do what I could to avoid a fight.

"You can watch the challenge," I called to the Hawley pack. "But if you intervene at all, you will be removed."

"We're not here for your challenge."

It was the same man who'd spoken before. My wolf sniffed, sensing him as a leader of some kind.

"What do you want?" I asked.

His gaze flicked to something over my shoulder, but I

didn't turn. Not when I could feel his animosity growing stronger.

"We're here for what's ours," he said. "Drago Gatti tortured and killed seven of our pack. He nearly did the same to our alpha. We've come to serve justice for his crimes."

"Justice." Drake laughed.

Someone stepped up beside me.

I looked over to see Oscar, Warren, and Mitch had joined us.

"What's this interruption all about?" Warren asked.

"This is the Hawley pack," Kai said, never taking his eyes off Drake as he spoke.

"Hawley?" Warren frowned.

"They've come for Drake. Or Drago as he's apparently known to them. He's wanted for murder of their pack members. And dark magic soul stealing."

The elders were quiet.

"I thought that was a damned children's story," Mitch muttered.

"It's our story," the Hawley leader said. "Drago will answer for what he did to us."

"Be that as it may," Warren said. "You are interrupting an official alpha challenge. Once we're finished here, we can discuss these accusations."

"This is completely inappropriate."

I looked over to see Baron glaring from Drake to Warren and back again.

"This interruption is a violation of our sacred traditions," he added.

"We will wait," the Hawley man said.

The fury in his eyes had not diminished, but he took a step back. Then another. His pack mates followed his lead.

Finally, near the trees, they stopped and waited.

"This is a strange turn of events," Warren said. "We'll need to discuss. In the meantime," his gaze flicked to me, "I believe the Asheville alpha awaits your answer."

"I..."

"The Hawley pack," Baron said abruptly. He frowned, and I watched as he seemed to be fitting pieces together for himself. Finally, he rounded on Drake. "They lost wolves. And nearly an alpha. Because of a boy who used black magic to gain power."

Oscar's hands fisted.

"You're the boy," Baron declared, a snarl lacing his tone. "I knew there was something wrong. Something dark in you."

Drake's gaze landed on mine. His eyes narrowed as if he blamed me for all of this. Then he swung to Baron. His expression transformed into one of pure violence. "I told you to stop running your mouth, old man. Now, it's too late."

Drake leaped, shifting in mid-air as he flew past the elders and straight for Baron. The older alpha shifted too, his claws raking down Drake's front leg as they slammed into one another. The impact sent them tumbling away from us. Their snarls rang out, echoing across the field until screams from the crowd drowned them out.

The Asheville pack roared, and the Hawley pack shifted then sprinted back toward the field.

Asheville and Hawley collided in an all-out brawl.

Kai yanked me back, and Oscar pressed in against my other side.

My pulse sped.

Adrenaline poured through me.

This wasn't how it was supposed to be.

On the sidelines, Presley was still trying to convince

people to move out of the way. So far, he was having minimal luck. A couple of ours joined in the fight, attacking Hawley and Asheville at random.

"Where's Idrissa?" I yelled. "Idrissa," I screamed.

Kai shielded me with his body as the fight between Baron and Drake raged on not far from where we stood. Idrissa and Isaac appeared from the direction of the barn.

"We need to get the others out of here," I told Idrissa, breathless.

"What the hell just happened?" she demanded.

"There's no time to explain," I said. "Just make them leave. It's not safe."

"I'm on it." She tore off into the crowd, calling for Silas and Presley to help her and shouting orders to the rest of the pack.

"We need to get you out of here," Oscar said.

"We need to make sure our people don't get hurt," I told him, the force of my voice enough to keep him from arguing.

He looked at Kai. "Protect her," he said.

"With my life," Kai told him.

He nodded once and then turned, calling for Warren and Mitch to go with him.

"Come on," Kai said, tugging me toward the barn, but I planted my feet.

"We have to stop Drake," I told him. "If he gets close enough to anyone and kills them, he'll steal their essence and add it to his power. That's how he's getting so strong. We have to stop him from hurting Baron—"

Alpha power surged, knocking the breath from my lungs. I looked over in time to see Drake's wolf rip into Baron's throat. The older wolf grunted and then fell as the wound began to run with blood.

"No!" I sprinted for Baron, but strong arms grabbed me and held me back.

"You can't fight him," Kai insisted. "Not like this."

Right.

Two legs versus four.

Not a fair fight.

Rage boiled beneath my skin as I watched the light fade from Baron's eyes. He looked over, whimpering with the movement that only seemed to cause him to bleed faster. Our eyes met.

Drake was too busy reveling in his kill to notice, howling at anyone who booed him in a clear challenge to come try and stop him. No one did.

I looked back at Baron again, inching closer despite Kai's struggle to restrain me.

Baron's wolf disappeared as he shifted back to his human form.

With each breath he struggled to take, more blood gushed from his wound.

My eyes widened. "No," I called, finally rushing forward as Kai let me go.

Drake had wandered toward the crowd that Idrissa was trying to make leave. Not everyone wanted to listen, apparently. And I had no doubt the Asheville pack wasn't going to let Drake walk away from what he'd just done. But I couldn't think about that now. Instead, I dropped to my knees before a wheezing Baron.

"You can't heal like this," I told him. "You have to shift back."

"Take care..." he rasped.

He lifted his hand, reaching toward mine. I wrapped my palm around his and held tight. My eyes watered, and the image of my father flashed before me. He'd died like this. Bloodied and on his back, on the ground at my feet. And all I'd been able to do was watch it happen.

"You can heal," I said, my voice breaking. "You have to."

"Defeat him," Baron rasped, ignoring my words. "Take ... my pack. Protect them."

He ended the request in a fit of coughs that had blood bubbling from his mouth.

I bit my lip, nodding through my tears.

"Swear it," he said, clearly straining with the effort of speaking anymore.

"I swear," I said.

He sighed, relieved.

"Now, kill me."

"What? No, I—"

"You have to," Kai said grimly.

I looked up at him, horrified.

"If you don't, the kill goes to Drake, and he gets Baron's soul or whatever. If you do it—"

"I'm the winner of the challenge," I said, tears leaking from my eyes as I realized what must be done.

"Do it," Baron rasped then coughed up blood.

I fumbled at the back of my boot then slid my knife free. My hand shook, but Baron's eyes met mine. Through the glassy look of pain, he nodded.

A tear fell. Just one. Sliding down my cheek and landing on Baron's bloodied arm. I stared down at it, the noise of the crowd fading for a moment. I thought of my dad. The way he'd bled out just like this. And everything that had followed. Coming here. Finding out what I was. Who I was meant to be. I'd had to fight for it every step. But these people, they'd been fighting a lot longer than I had. My dad had fought his whole life. For me. Baron had fought for his pack.

And the only way none of that fighting went to waste

was to make them all safe now. What mattered were the ones left behind. The wolves desperate for an alpha. Not just any alpha. One who would give them back what they'd lost.

That damn sure wasn't Drake.

I drew my hand back, and with a cry of anguish, brought the blade down and buried it in Baron's chest.

26

I released Baron's hand and got to my feet, wiping the tears as I looked up at where Kai stood over me, a silent sentinel.

"We have to end this," I said.

"I know." His eyes searched mine as if looking for the answer to a question neither of us wanted to ask.

"We do it together," I said. "Fuck sacred law."

Kai's eyes glittered. He nodded. "I'm right beside you, Ashes. Let's go kick some darkness-coated ass."

Across the field, Drake finally realized he'd been relieved of his reward. His wolf zeroed in on us, and I felt the alpha power begin to grow and gather around him.

Presley, Silas, and the twins appeared, all four of them in human form but bruised and disheveled.

"We got as many of them to leave as we could," Presley said, breathless. "The rest are either already fighting or refusing to abandon you guys."

"Okay, see if you can get the Hawley pack to back off," I said.

"The Hawley pack is dead," Idrissa said quietly.

I rounded on her. "All of them?"

"Look."

I followed the direction she pointed and saw the Asheville pack standing over half a dozen dead wolves.

"Dammit," I said, hating how it had ended for them. They'd only wanted justice for losing what they'd lost.

But we didn't have time to mourn or regret. Not while the Asheville pack was still reeling from their own loss.

"They're untethered," Kai said, and I realized he'd felt it too.

The chaos coming from them all.

"No," I said, determined to keep this from getting worse. "They're not."

I stepped away from the others and strode toward the Asheville wolves. Some of them bared their teeth, and I could feel how vulnerable and exposed I was out here. Not just to them but to Drake whose eyes still tracked my every move.

"I won the challenge," I called in a clear voice that sounded way calmer than I felt about all of this. "I am your new alpha. You will submit."

Growls followed.

A couple of the wolves lowered their heads, but most remained standing.

Drake howled, and I whirled, prepared for a full-on attack as he finally realized I'd stolen his kill. Behind me, the Asheville pack howled too, and I called up as much alpha power as I could muster, sending it out toward Baron's pack.

One by one, their howls fell silent.

Drake's large yellow eyes narrowed on mine. But when he lurched toward me, he stopped short again, suddenly snapping his head toward the trees.

A second later, he growled and took off for the woods, vanishing into the trees.

I didn't have time to question what had made him run off.

Turning back to the Asheville pack, I doubled down on the alpha power. My wolf rose to the surface, demanding to be recognized. This was bigger than anything I'd done before. Not with Vinny and not with Kai. This was more than I knew I possessed, and I used it all to remind them they still had a leader.

Me.

One by one, the Asheville pack wolves lowered their heads and bared their necks in submission.

I let out a long breath, relief making my knees wobbly.

An arm slid around my waist, and Kai caught me, holding me upright.

"Just breathe," he said at my ear.

"I did it," I said, breathless and shocked.

"Damn right you did," Idrissa said as the others joined us.

"Now, maybe release them?" Isaac suggested.

Idrissa hit him.

"What?" he demanded.

"Stand up," I called.

The Asheville wolves rose to their feet and looked at me expectantly.

I gestured to Baron's body still lying on the field. "Prepare his body. Tonight, we'll honor Baron and give him a send-off fit for an alpha."

The wolves howled, and some shifted as they prepared to collect Baron's body.

I felt some of my alpha energy wane. Exhaustion was close on its heels.

"I could sleep for a week," I murmured.

"Uh, sorry to ruin your plans, but Drake's back," Isaac said.

At the sight of Drake's wolf re-emerging from the trees, alarm shot through me, replacing my exhaustion with adrenaline all over again.

"Uh, actually, that can't be Drake," Presley said uncertainly. He'd turned away to face the opposite side of the field.

"What? Why?" I demanded.

"Because that's Drake right there." He pointed, and beyond the pack who'd begun moving out of the way, I spotted him.

Sure enough, it was Drake's wolf stalking this way.

"The fuck…?" Isaac trailed off, fear and horror twisting his features.

I did a double-take, glancing back and forth between both versions of the same wolf. My confusion turned to dread as I realized what I was seeing.

"Impossible," Kai breathed.

"The story," I said. "Remember? They're twins."

"Right, but these two have the exact same energy signature," Idrissa said. "Can't you feel it?"

"It's not exactly the same," I said, shaking my head as everything clicked into place. The reason we'd never caught Drake doing anything incriminating despite always having someone watching him. "It's close, though. And that's been our downfall."

"We were following the wrong brother," Presley realized, anger overtaking his shock. "That's why we could never catch him slipping away."

At his words, one of the Drakes pulled back his lips to reveal rows of sharpened teeth. It reminded me of a smug sort of smile that sent ripples of anxiety up my spine. They both continued to stalk toward us from opposite directions.

"Uh, what exactly is the plan for double the murdery fun?" Idrissa asked.

Kai and I looked up. Our eyes met.

We didn't have time for mercy. Or diplomacy. Not when the largest two sets of teeth I'd ever seen were coming straight for me and my mate.

Heart thudding wildly, I gave the only answer there could be.

"Kill them both," I said.

Kai nodded grimly. "One for you, one for me."

"What about us?" Idrissa demanded.

"Guard the perimeter," I said, quickly now with the Drakes getting closer.

"Bullshit, we're fighting him too," Presley declared.

Dammit. They'd be on us in a moment.

Idrissa started to agree with Presley.

But I stopped them.

"They're coming for me and Kai," I said urgently now. "I know you can feel that. Whatever's making you want to challenge them is a trap. Drake wants to take your wolf essence. Don't let him close enough. Protect the others."

"We'll take care of it," Silas said firmly.

He grabbed Idrissa, steering her away. Isaac did the same with Presley, who was already cussing me out, but at least he was going.

"Do what you have to do, Ashes," Kai said. "No mercy."

"Drake can't be alpha," I agreed.

Kai wore a murderous look as he turned to face the Drake behind me. "He won't."

The Drake before me rushed at me then.

I shifted and threw my entire being into the fight. Snapping teeth grazed my fur, but I didn't stop. I didn't even pause to breathe. One wrong move, and this monster would take me down. He was stronger than before. That was unmistakable.

Or maybe this one had never been Drake at all.

One of them was an imposter. A brother who had supposedly banished his sibling as punishment. Apparently, he'd forgiven him. Or maybe the story had gotten it wrong. Maybe they'd never been enemies, to begin with.

As our teeth and paws clashed, I felt the alpha power in me rise. Strong and commanding and absolutely dominant.

Drake met my power with his as he came at me again.

I felt it immediately, the hard reality of what I was facing: we were evenly matched. Power for power. Bite for bite. Claw for claw.

There'd be no winning against this beast.

It would come down to sheer stamina, and even then, I wasn't sure I could hold him off. We'd kill each other before it was over. My wolf responded to that thought immediately.

At least, we'll take him with us.

Wow, okay.

My wolf was a grim bitch.

Still fighting for my life, I threw my body sideways to avoid an incoming attack and used the two-second window to search frantically for Kai.

Sensing another attack from behind, I whirled and deflected just in time. Out of the corner of my eye, I spotted Kai just as he turned and saw me too.

Our eyes locked, and he nodded, sending a clear message. Through the bond, I felt the push he was giving me. The encouragement.

I knew what he wanted even before he pushed the words right into my mind.

Use the magic.

For a split second, I thought about resisting. But then Drake-the-second came at me again, and his razor-sharp teeth grazed my hip, breaking the skin beneath my fur just enough to draw blood.

I snarled, both in pain and rage.

Desperation crashed over me.

I knew what I had to do.

The door I'd shut on the magic in my mind swung open with a bang. My wolf howled as the magic joined with my wolf's natural power. My blood sang with it. The bond filled with it. And then Kai added his own alpha power, and I felt the surge of our joined influence spring to life like a lion loosed from its cage.

The potency of it slammed into me a second before it did the same to Drake, causing him to falter in his next attack. The beast before me lowered his head, too helpless against the sheer power Kai and I were emanating now.

I exhaled, watching as Drake-two-point-oh finally stopped trying to eat my throat for dinner.

Glancing over, I saw Kai's Drake doing the same slow bow toward the ground.

My wolf exhaled.

Finally.

I'd just begun to turn and search out the others when a snarl rang out. The Drake in front of me bucked against the alpha power shoving at him. Straining forward, he lunged at me, his teeth aimed straight for my throat.

Magic surged, stronger than before. A pink glow flashed, temporarily blinding me. I shut my eyes at the same time my wolf leaped in defense.

My teeth sank into a furry throat.

For two beats, I felt his heartbeat pulsing against my mouth.

Then, I bit down. And ripped.

Blood filled my mouth. I gagged, my human side taking over as the reality of what I'd just done hit me fully. Drake fell at my feet, his body convulsing as blood poured from the wound I'd just ripped. With paws coated in blood, I backed away, spitting and coughing and gagging against the coppery taste.

Drake didn't get up.

He made a choking sound as he struggled to draw a breath, and then, finally, he was quiet.

Large yellow eyes stared frozen up to the sky.

I looked over, terrified for Kai now that the magic had slid away again. But he was standing over his own Drake just like I was. His mouth and face were covered in blood, and the Drake at his feet was just as still as mine.

Holy shit.

We'd done it.

We'd won our alpha challenge.

Together.

Except that now, we were down to just two. Kai and me.

As if he'd read my thoughts, Kai looked up, and we locked eyes. Between us, the bond hummed with tension. He started toward me, and I felt his relief mix with my own as we both realized the other was safe and unharmed.

By the time I reached him, he'd shifted back to human form. Uncaring of our audience or decorum or anything else besides feeling my mate's arms around me, I said screw it and shifted too.

Kai caught me in his arms, pulling me close and burying his face against my hair. "I was so worried—"

He didn't finish the sentence.

I didn't need him to.

We felt the same.

"It's over," I said on a long exhale. "He can't hurt us anymore."

Kai drew back and looked down at me, his eyes swirling with another storm. I tensed, my nerves feeling nearly as exposed as my physical body.

"What is it?" I asked.

"Don't look now, but Warren's headed this way," Kai said grimly.

"I'm sure he's relieved," I said, confusion coloring my words.

"He has the rest of the council with him. They look very serious."

I bit my lip. "Kai," I began. "The alpha challenges…"

He looked down at me again, smoothing my hair.

"They can't make us do anything we don't want to," he said. "Don't let them tell you differently."

"Okay," I said, but inside, my stomach twisted with uncertainty. Warren had made it clear that the pack's sacred laws dictated one winner of these challenges. Kai and I had defeated Drake. Or the Drakes. Whatever. That left only him and me. Two potential alphas. But there could only be one.

27

A blanket landed around my shoulders. I glanced behind me to see Amberly pushing the fabric into place, covering my backside. She shot me a smile and then offered Kai a towel. He took it, tugging my blanket closed around my middle before covering himself.

"Sorry," Amberly said as I turned to face her. "I'm working with what I've got."

"This is fine, thanks," I told her.

"You both did great," she said, squeezing my arm.

I looked past her to where the two wolves lay bloodied and lifeless in the stained grass. Some of the pack members had come forward to collect the two bodies. But apart from them, sure enough, Warren, Mitch, and Oscar were all headed this way. Behind them, Hector and Clem marched with inflated purpose.

I swallowed hard and braced myself for the ultimatum I knew was coming.

"Well done, the two of you," Warren said. The words were delivered warmly, but they were dismissed too quickly to be enjoyed. As usual, Warren was moving on to the next line item. "The two of you showed real alpha strength today. I think I can speak for the entire pack when I tell you we all felt your power. And were called to it."

Kai slipped his hand into mine.

I held tight.

"You are both free to recover over the next few days. We have much to process and clean up, of course." He glanced over to where the closest Drake was being loaded up. "Who knew he was a twin?"

"You might have if you'd taken the time to look into his past when he arrived," I said.

Warren shrugged, clueless. "Anyway, please let us know when you're both ready to face the next challenge," he went on. "As I said before, take all the recovery time you need. It's been a hell of a day."

"There won't be another challenge," Kai said.

"Excuse me?" Warren looked between us, clearly confused.

"We choose not to challenge one another," Kai said.

"I'm afraid that's not an option," Hector said.

Oscar growled at him.

"Kai, our laws are clear," Clem said as if explaining something to a child. "Alphas are chosen based on a showing of strength and power."

"Something we've clearly done," Kai said.

"Yes, but there can only be one."

"Says who?" I asked.

"Says history," Clem sputtered.

"Historically, is it normal for an alpha to take a mate?" I asked.

Clem frowned. "Yes, of course."

"And is that mate recognized as part of the pack's leadership?"

"They are, but there's—"

"Kai and I have chosen one another as mates," I said. "And we've defeated all challengers. Together."

"Yes, but therein lies the problem. You cannot be alpha *together*. There is only one alpha in a pack."

"Actually, the alpha is the one to decide that." Amberly spoke with a gleam in her eye that clearly irritated Warren.

"Amberly, this isn't—"

"Warren Jeremiah Close, the longer this curse goes on, the more you become like your father. I really hope that goes away when this thing is finally broken."

I bit back a smile as Warren's face flushed red.

"Alphas are chosen by winning against anyone who challenges them," Amberly went on. "These two both won a challenge. Now, it's up to them to challenge each other. If they don't, and especially considering they're mates, they rule together. That's the hierarchy; it's just never been done quite like this before."

Warren said nothing. I wasn't sure if that was good or bad at this point.

"Need I remind you, it's highly possible Ash needs to be alpha in order for this curse to break," Kai pointed out.

"Kai," I warned. "Probably not helping your case."

But he ignored me. "We're a team. A package deal." He shrugged. "I guess if someone has a problem with it, you can challenge us for the position."

My jaw dropped at that. Not just the implication but that he'd just casually said it to the council.

The council.

"If not," Kai said when no one spoke up, "Ash and I have just become alpha, and that means we make the rules."

"First rule," I added. "Kai and I are both alpha."

"This is complete disrespect," Clem said. "Our ancestors would never have tossed aside tradition so callously."

"Our ancestors were the ones who cursed us," I said, "and the ones responsible for the war with the hexerei in the first place. Without the bad blood between us, the curse would never have been cast."

Clem muttered, but I didn't back down.

"If there was ever a time for change, this is it. You can either change with us, or you can find a new pack."

Hector's eyes narrowed. "What are you saying, girl?"

"I'm not a girl. I'm your alpha." My wolf unleashed her alpha power just enough to make his knees knock a bit.

Hector hunched, his shoulders folding in as he was forced to bow.

"You'll recognize us as your alpha now," I said.

"Pledge your loyalty or go," Kai added.

"I have a choice?" he asked, his voice strained.

"Of course," I said. "You'll always have a choice."

A beat of silence passed and then, "I pledge my loyalty."

I eased up on the power surge, and Hector straightened. He looked at me, smoothing his rumpled jacket. I recognized the tightness behind his eyes, but he'd spoken the words. And his wolf had felt them, genuinely. If it hadn't, I would know.

"There's going to be a new council," I said. "One of our choosing. And one of the people's choosing. From now on, you're a member of the pack just like everyone else until a vote can be cast."

He nodded, disappointment flashing, but he didn't argue. Warren started to, but Amberly shushed him.

Kai turned to him. "Ash is right. We're starting over. That means the council will be rebuilt just like everything else. It's time for change."

"You don't know anything about running an entire town full of wolves," Clem said. His mouth curled in disdain as he eyed us both. "I give you a week at best."

"Challenge accepted," Kai said. "Is there anything else you want to challenge us for?"

Clem stared back at him. "I'm going to take the second option," he said at last. "This is no longer the pack for me."

"You have twenty-four hours to leave town," Kai told him. "If you return, you will first ask our permission to step foot on our lands or we'll see it as a threat."

Clem turned and walked away, shoulders stiff.

"You two go," Amberly said into the silence that followed. "I'll see that everything gets cleaned up. But you two should take some time to do the same."

"Thanks," Kai said, but I hesitated.

"Are you sure?" I asked. "Does it feel wrong to run off when everyone needs us?"

"Babe," Kai said, tugging on the blanket I still wore as a dress. He leaned in close and dropped his voice to a whisper. "I need you."

The look in his eyes wasn't about victory or relief or any of the things defeating Drake and becoming alpha implied. It was pure molten lust. And the blood in my veins heated in response. Suddenly, my wolf was hungry for her mate. Her fellow alpha. And the human in me wasn't in the mood to talk her out of it either.

"Well, when you put it like that," I said, and his mouth curved as his hands landed on my hips and gripped hard.

"Take me home, Ashes."

..*

Home, it turned out, was still a long way off. Kai and I made it as far as the retrieval team loading the Drakes onto a trailer to be carted off when we were stopped.

"Leaving so soon?" boomed a male voice.

I faltered at the familiarity of the voice. Unfortunately, the particular sound and familiarity of it were permanently embedded into my brain.

Cohen.

Scanning, my eyes landed on him as he emerged from the trees. Flanking him were his armed guards, and beside him was Kel.

"Shit," I said.

"Is that…?" Kai trailed off.

"Hexerei," I whispered.

When I hesitated, Kai took my hand. "Come on. Let's take care of this so I can take you home."

"I like the last part, at least," I said, letting him pull me along.

Out of the crowd, Idrissa and Isaac appeared, falling into step beside us. I shot them both a grateful smile that vanished all too soon as we stopped in front of Cohen and his gun gang.

The air between us felt charged.

Around the field, wolves began to realize the true identity of the visitors. The Asheville pack growled but kept clear. The remaining lone wolves, however, swarmed to our sides.

"We have to get in front of this," I said.

Kai hesitated, and I could see it in his eyes; he couldn't quite bring himself to care about the safety of his enemies.

"They have guns," I reminded him.

That seemed to focus him.

"Stop," we both shouted to the wolves stalking toward the hexerei.

The growls and snarls fell silent.

"You're not welcome here," Kai said darkly. He was eyeing Cohen specifically, and I could feel the rage rising in him, not that I blamed him.

"We've come to collect what was promised us," Cohen told him in a hard voice.

Damn. This wasn't going to end well.

I looked at Kel, silently pleading.

"There is nothing for you here," Kai spat. "We've chosen our next alpha. It's pack business."

"Choosing an alpha seems very much my business," Cohen said. "Especially considering the stake I have in all this."

Cohen looked pointedly at me.

Kai held my hand more tightly as if daring Cohen to try to take me by force, which was fine since, nope. I was absolutely *not* here for that idea.

"Ash isn't your business," Kai snarled.

"That's where you're mistaken." Cohen nodded at Kel. "Show them."

Kel shot me what looked like an apologetic grimace before holding her hand out, palm up. The scar she bore, the one matching my own thanks to the blood oath we'd taken together, glowed.

"What the..."

Isaac's voice startled me.

I turned sharply to see him and Idrissa standing directly behind me. Neither one wore clothes, and neither one looked like they gave two shits about it either.

Idrissa gave me an encouraging nod. "We got you," she whispered. "And you got this."

"What is the meaning of all this?"

I groaned inwardly as Warren came rushing up.

He glared at Cohen, the sharpness of his expression enough to make even me wince. If political death staring were an Olympic event, Warren would have won gold.

"Warren, you're no longer in charge here," Kai reminded him.

Warren ignored Cohen, who looked deeply intrigued by Kai's comment.

"Your kind are not permitted on pack lands," Warren told Cohen. "Or have you forgotten the only part of our treaty that still holds?"

He spat the word treaty so hard spittle flew from his mouth.

Cohen's lip curled as he stared at Warren.

"I haven't forgotten a thing," Cohen said, his voice way too calm. "In fact, I've remembered that your curse breaker owes me, and now I've come to collect."

"Owes you?" Warren snorted. "We don't owe you a damned thing. Especially after what your kind did to ours. Get off our land."

Cohen's eyes flashed with temper. "This marks a blood vow," he snapped, nodding at Kel's hand.

"We wouldn't make a blood vow with a spook," Warren scoffed.

Well, shit. This was awkward.

"Ash," Cohen said expectantly, all calm smugness. Bastard.

I sighed as Warren's accusatory gaze landed on me. In fact, every pair of eyes who'd gathered around this debacle was now watching me. Basically, the entire freaking pack.

Slowly, I lifted my hand, and sure as shit, my scar was glowing too.

"Does it hurt?" Isaac peered over my shoulder, sounding awed.

"No," I said. With my other hand, I touched a finger to the raised scar. Not even warm. So weird.

"Ash vowed to return what was taken from us," Cohen said. "When she's fulfilled her promise, we'll go." His eyes glittered, and behind the mask of diplomacy he wore, I saw the truth. He wasn't going to leave. The moment he had magic again, he'd use it to destroy us all. And now that meant he'd take out what was essentially two packs instead of one.

The Asheville wolves remained mostly curious from what I could tell. But Cohen's threat put us all in danger. And it was all on me now.

"What does the glow have to do with it?" Idrissa piped up. "Why now?"

"You'd have to ask your chosen one that question," Cohen said.

"Ash has been upfront with us about everything," Warren said stiffly. "We're aware of her status."

Status. Wow. Okay.

"She can't be a witch and be alpha," Cohen said. "It's against our sacred laws and, if I'm not mistaken, yours."

"Actually, the laws state you can't be involved in dark magic and be the alpha of a pack."

I looked up at Kel in surprise. She smiled, a slow, diabolical kind of smile that had me smiling back in kind. She was a friend, after all.

"What did you just say?" Cohen's voice dropped low. Dangerously so.

"You have no right to speak to me in that tone. And in front of our enemies, no less. Careful, or I'll make sure your soul is the next one stolen."

Kel stilled, and I realized Cohen had just admitted to the exact thing I'd suspected all along.

"You helped Drake," I said. "Gave him the power he needed to steal those souls."

"He assured me the heads of the elders who broke our trust once before." Cohen glared at Warren. "In exchange, I provided him the means for gaining his abilities."

"How did you do it?" I demanded. "You don't have magic."

Cohen didn't answer.

Kel turned to me. "He gave them hemlock. Once a month on the full moon during an earth ritual performed by one of ours. It gave him the power to kill and steal the essence of his victims."

"Monster," Idrissa snarled.

"This is all very riveting," Cohen said dryly. "But I'm done waiting." He lifted a brow pointedly. "You've discovered your magic, yes?" Cohen's gaze was shrewd. Calculating.

I hesitated, but Kai squeezed my hand.

"Yes," I said.

Warren's eyes narrowed.

"You used it to defeat Drake and his twin just now, did you not?" Cohen pressed.

I didn't answer. The dude was just being a prick, outing me so I had no choice but to share with the class.

"You used magic?" Warren asked. "In the fight?"

"We both did," Kai said.

"You have magic too?" Warren asked incredulously.

"Ash has magic," Kai clarified. "But we both have access to it through the mate bond. It's what allowed us to defeat two wolves with the power of twenty." His eyes narrowed as he stared Warren down. "Or did you want

Drake to become alpha so he could steal the soul of every wolf in this pack?"

Warren sputtered, but it was Cohen who spoke.

"Excuse me?" Cohen's eyes narrowed at me, and I realized immediately this wasn't going to be good. He glared at me. "You've managed to share your magic with your mate, yet you claim not to know how to give it back to me?"

"Give it back?" Warren frowned. "What is this all about?"

"I want what was promised, girl," Cohen said.

"I can't give it to you," I told him.

"Lies."

At that, Kai took a step forward, and the men behind Cohen drew their guns. Shit.

"I won't ask again," Cohen warned.

"Are you saying you don't have magic...at all?" Warren's tone had taken on a new note. Smoother. Silkier. And way more confident.

Shit.

I didn't even have to look over to know there'd be a gleam in his eye. He thought this was his chance. To end them.

"Warren, if you move a muscle, I'll be the one to stop you," I snapped.

He looked over at me, startled. "They're vulnerable."

"Count the guns, Dad," Idrissa said. "Do they look vulnerable to you?"

"But—"

"Warren," Amberly hissed.

"Cohen, listen to me. I don't know how to do what you're asking," I said. "The moment I do—"

"Give it to me or your mate dies." Cohen snapped his fingers, and the men all pointed their guns at Kai.

My eyes widened.

Panic slammed into me.

"Stop," I said.

"Give me the magic," Cohen shot back.

"Ash, just do what he says," Kel said quietly, almost pleading. "And we'll leave you in peace."

Cohen smiled, his eyes lighting up with pure evil. "Yes, we'll leave you in peace. After all, there is peace in death, is there not?"

"Spooks be gone," Warren roared.

Some of the pack members nearby shifted, and their wolves advanced closer. Cohen shouted at his men, and they adjusted their position, re-aiming their weapons at each of the wolves now threatening to attack.

Cohen lunged, his hand snaking out and snatching the moon pendant hanging around my neck. He pulled, and I felt the chain give as the necklace slid off me, now in Cohen's grip.

Kai slammed his fist into Cohen's jaw.

A gun went off.

The necklace went flying.

A loud crack split the air, and I looked up in time to see the pendant explode. Tiny shards of moonstone rained down around me as the bullet tore right through the stone.

One of the particles fell, and I caught it in my open palm.

Staring down at the remains, I felt the last hope of escaping Cohen drain away. The necklace was gone now; nothing but dust. And I had a feeling he intended to do the same to us.

"No," Cohen roared, but then light exploded.

I stumbled back, only remaining on my feet thanks to Kai's grip around my waist.

"Ash." Kai gestured to my hand, and I unfurled my fist to see the shard of moonstone glowing against my palm. Smoke curled from its surface, and then magic itself began leaking from within.

I stared as the strange-feeling liquid soaked my palm and then slowly receded.

Not receded.

Soaked in.

The sensation underneath my skin was unmistakable.

One second, I was holding the source of the magic in my palm. The next, the source of the magic *was* my palm. A white light, brilliant and blinding, tore from the broken stone. It sent a ray of glowing moonlight straight up to the sky and, then it slammed into me.

I gasped, nearly losing my balance as I stumbled against the force of it.

Just as quickly as it had come, the light winked out again.

The piece of the stone in my hand shriveled and then turned to dust, which was carried off by the breeze. My skin looked completely normal again. No glowing light. No strange tingling sensations. But I felt it. Inside me.

The magic.

Everything that had been contained in that stone was part of me now.

All of the magic I'd promised to Cohen, mine.

Someone gasped, but not a single person in our gathering spoke a word.

Then it was Cohen breaking the silence.

"You bitch," he breathed, either too shocked or too angry to yell. "Give it back."

"I…I don't know how," I stammered, still reeling over what had just happened. I stared down at my fists, but they were normal again. Completely unassuming. Deep inside me, the magic lay coiled like a sleeping snake. Nothing I did or thought seemed to wake it.

Cohen's eyes bulged with pure, raw fury. "Give it back now," he roared.

"I don't know how," I screamed back at him.

"Ash," Kai whispered my name like it was a question.

I looked at him, only for a second, and found all of my own questions mirrored back at me in his dark, stormy gaze. Instead of being able to answer a single one, I shook my head, at a loss.

Something built in the air between us all.

A sort of desperate anticipation. And I knew—knew in a way I couldn't explain—that something terrible was about to happen.

The magic inside me woke as if prodded by its own awareness.

"Then you'll pay," Cohen seethed, his voice silky with the promise of pain.

When I looked up again, Cohen wasn't even looking at me. Instead, he was looking down at Kai with pure rage written across his twisted expression.

"Kill him," Cohen snarled, and then it all went to hell.

Want to know what happens next? Read Wolf Chosen, book 3, available now!

THE
LONE WOLF
SERIES
WOLF
CHOSEN
HEATHER HILDENBRAND

ABOUT THE AUTHOR

Heather Hildenbrand was born and raised in a small town in northern Virginia where she was homeschooled through high school. She's only slightly socially awkward as a result. She writes paranormal and fantasy romance with plenty of abs and angst. Her most frequent hobbies are truck camping with her doodle, talking to her plants, and avoiding killer slugs.

Heathe also writes contemporary romance as Violet Stafford. You can find out more about Heather and her books at www.heatherhildenbrand.com.

OTHER TITLES BY HEATHER HILDENBRAND

Dragon Unleashed
Dragon Compelled

To Hunt A Wolf
To Kiss A Wolf
To Keep A Wolf

Midnight Cursed
Midnight Hunted
Midnight Bound

A Witch's Call
A Witch's Destiny
A Witch's Fate
A Witch's Soul
A Witch's Prophecy
A Witch's Hope
Twisted Tides

The Girl Who Cried Werewolf

OTHER TITLES BY HEATHER HILDENBRAND

The Girl Who Cried Captive
The Girl Who Cried War

The Winter Witch
The Spring Witch

A Witch's Heart

Midnight Mate

Goddess Ascending
Goddess Claiming
Goddess Forging

Kiss of Death
Knock Em Dead
Death's Door
Dead to Rights
Dead End

The Girl Who Called The Stars
The Girl Who Ruled The Stars

Alpha Games
Alpha Trials
Alpha Chosen

Dirty Blood
Cold Blood
Blood Bond
Blood Rule
Broken Blood
One Hour: bonus novella

OTHER TITLES BY HEATHER HILDENBRAND

Imitation
Deviation
Generation

Guarded by the Alpha

Alpha Undercover

Mated to the Wilde Bear
The Bear's Fated Mate

Protected By the Bear
The Badge and the Bear

Tragic Ink: A Havenwood Falls story

For a complete list of titles, visit www.heatherhildenbrand.com

www.ingramcontent.com/pod-product-compliance
Lightning Source LLC
Chambersburg PA
CBHW020340310726
48979CB00015B/2443/J

* 9 7 8 1 9 6 1 4 5 5 0 3 0 *